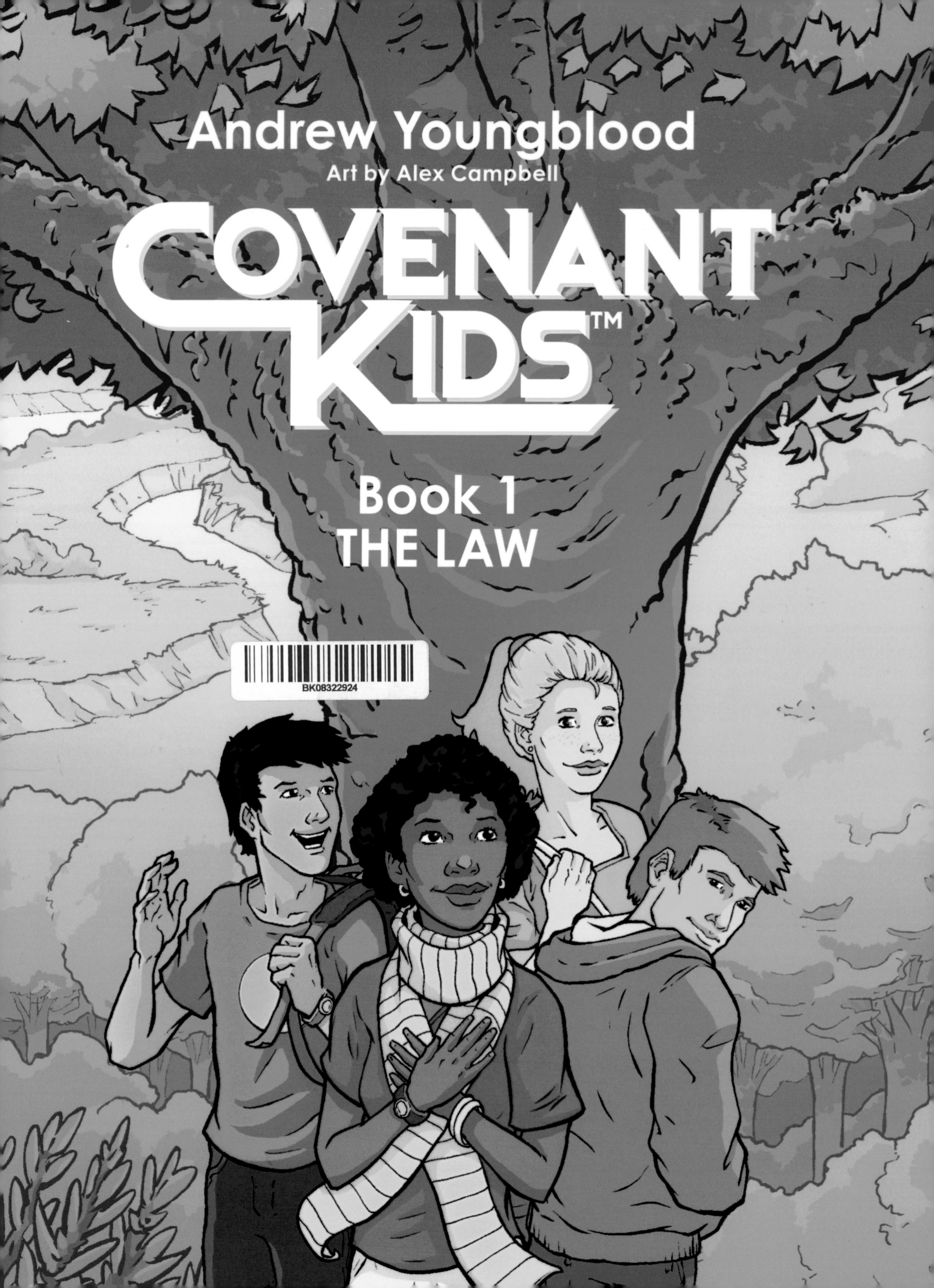
Andrew Youngblood
Art by Alex Campbell
COVENANT KIDS™
Book 1
THE LAW

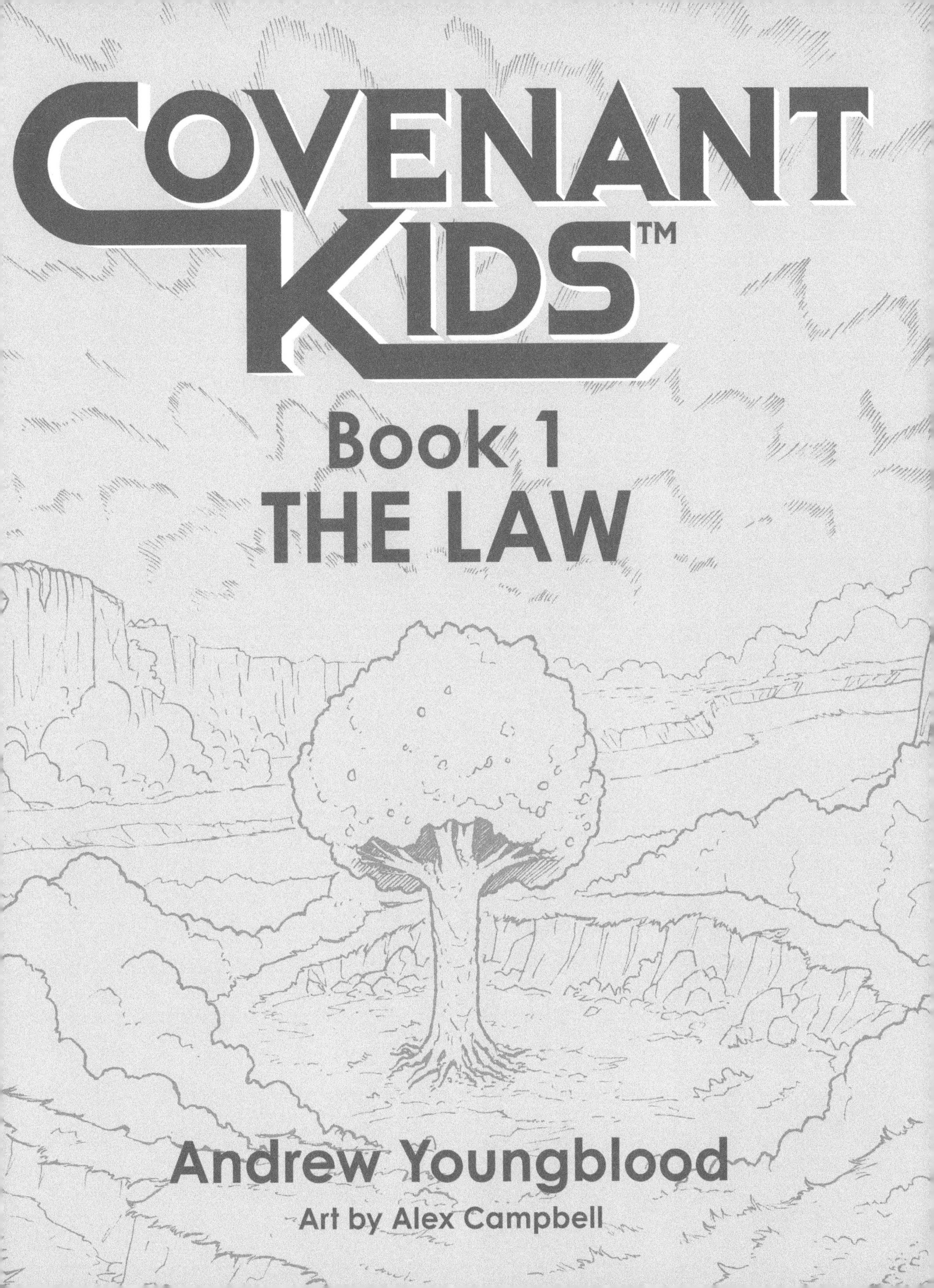

COVENANT KIDS™

Book 1
THE LAW

Andrew Youngblood

Art by Alex Campbell

To my children
whose imagination led to the birth of this project.

Chapters

DAY ONE

In the Beginnings . . .

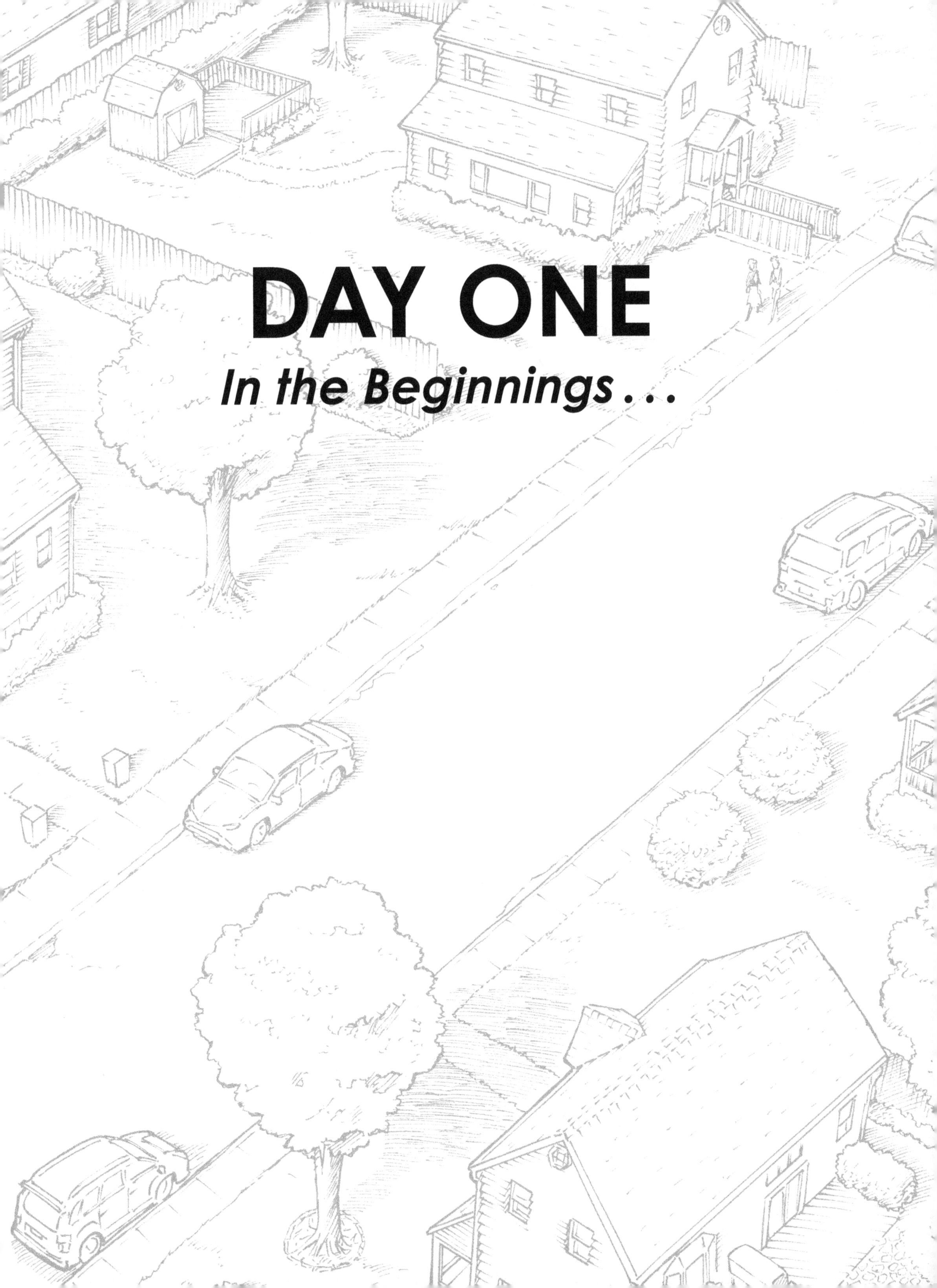

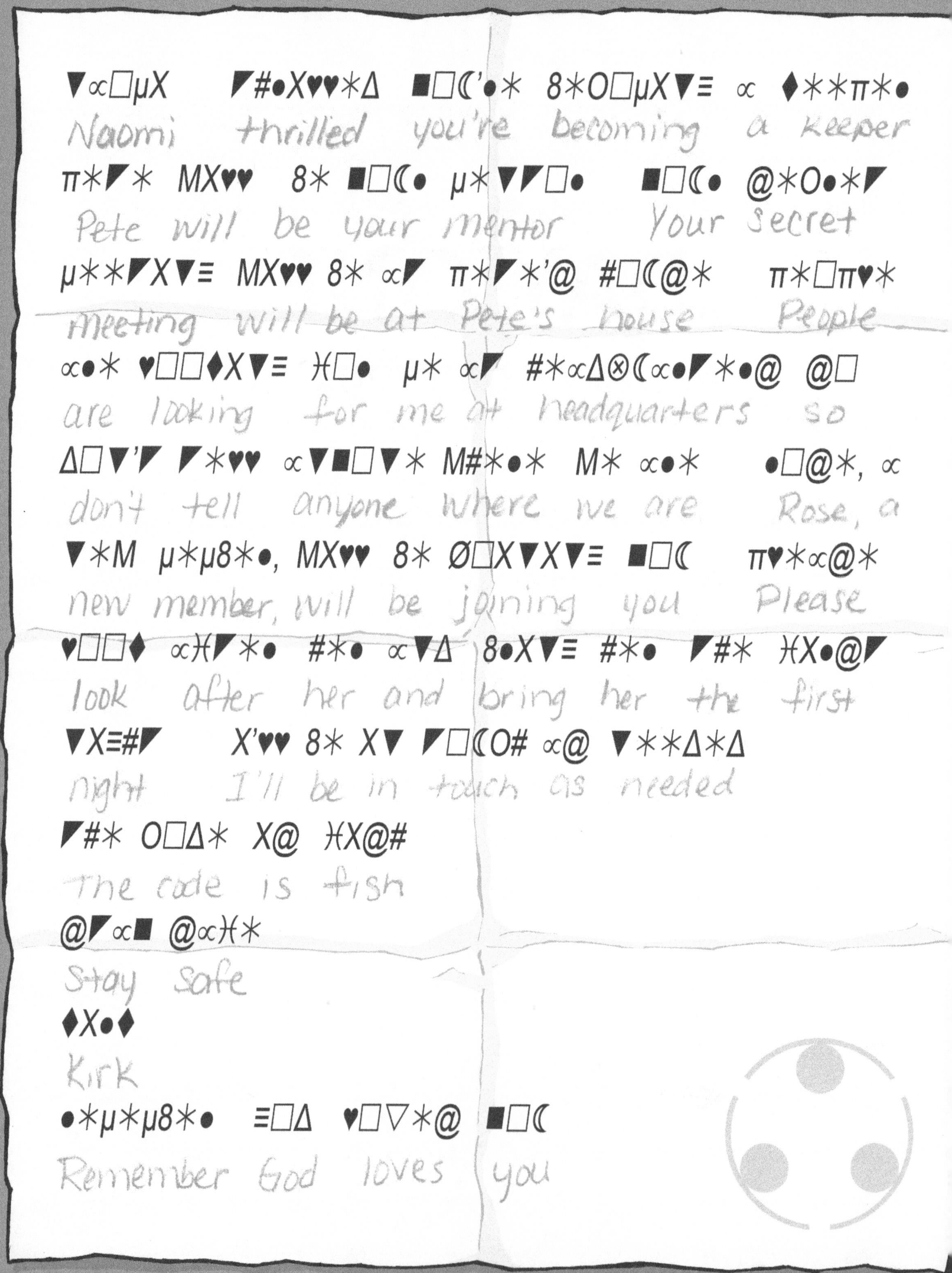

▼∝□µX   ▼#•X♥♥*∆   ■□(('•*   8*O□µX▼≡   ∝   ♦**π*•

Naomi   thrilled   you're   becoming   a   keeper

π*▼*   MX♥♥   8*   ■□((•   µ*▼▼□•   ■□((•   @*O•*▼

Pete   will   be   your   mentor   Your   secret

µ**▼X▼≡   MX♥♥   8*   ∝▼   π*▼*'@   #□((@*   π*□π♥*

meeting   will   be   at   Pete's   house   People

∝•*   ♥□□♦X▼≡   )(□•   µ*   ∝▼   #*∝∆⊗((∝•▼*•@   @□

are   looking   for   me   at   headquarters   so

∆□▼'▼   ▼*♥♥   ∝▼■□▼*   M#*•*   M*   ∝•*   •□@*,   ∝

don't   tell   anyone   where   we   are   Rose,   a

▼*M   µ*µ8*•,   MX♥♥   8*   Ø□X▼X▼≡   ■□(π♥*∝@*

new   member,   will   be   joining   you   Please

♥□□♦   ∝)(▼*•   #*•   ∝▼∆   8•X▼≡   #*•   ▼#*   )(X•@▼

look   after   her   and   bring   her   the   first

▼X≡#▼   X'♥♥   8*   X▼   ▼□(O#   ∝@   ▼**∆*∆

night   I'll   be   in   touch   as   needed

▼#*   O□∆*   X@   )(X@#

The   code   is   fish

@▼∝■   @∝)(*

Stay   safe

♦X•♦

Kirk

•*µ*µ8*•   ≡□∆   ♥□▼*@   ■□(

Remember   God   loves   you

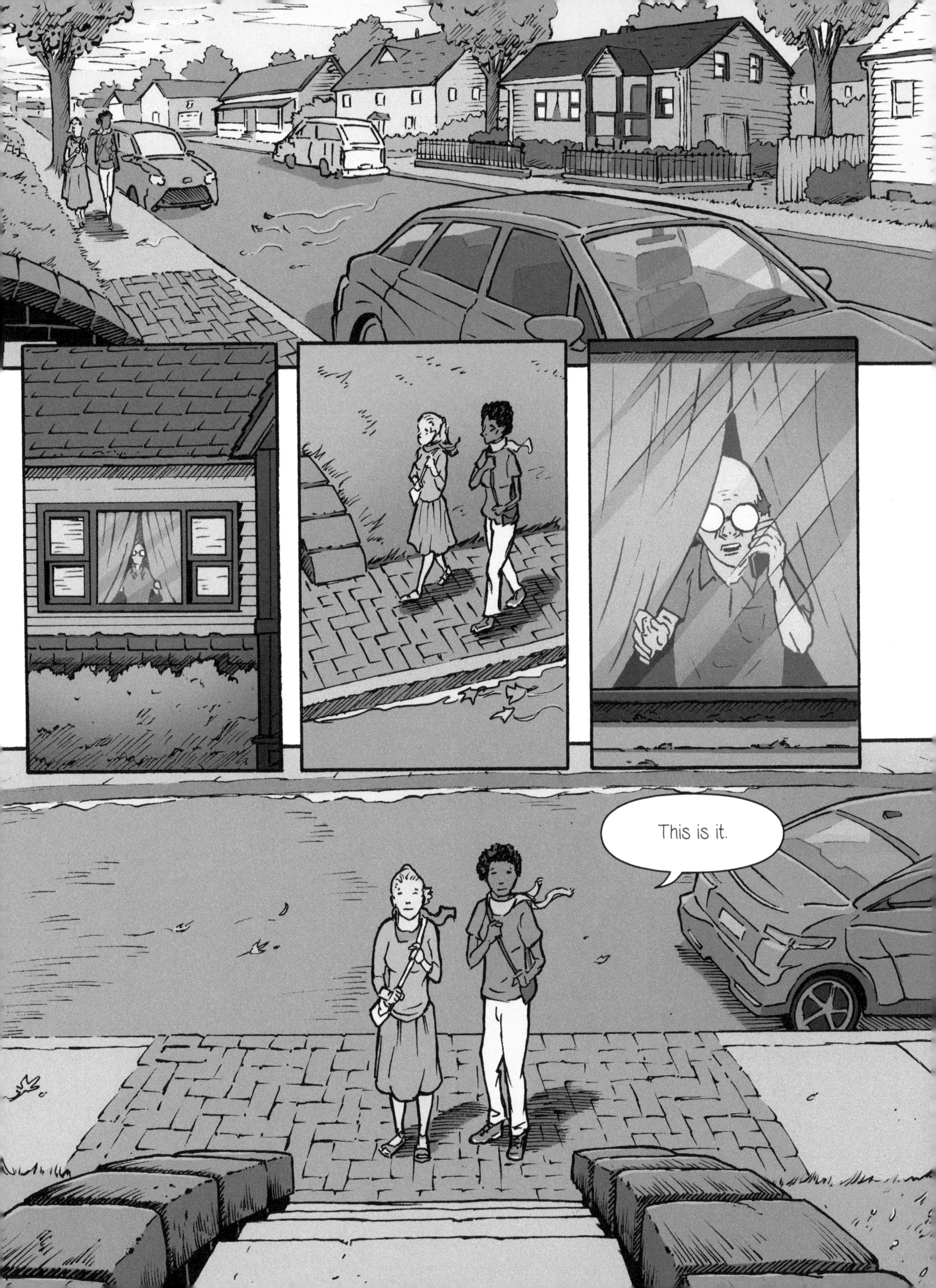
This is it.

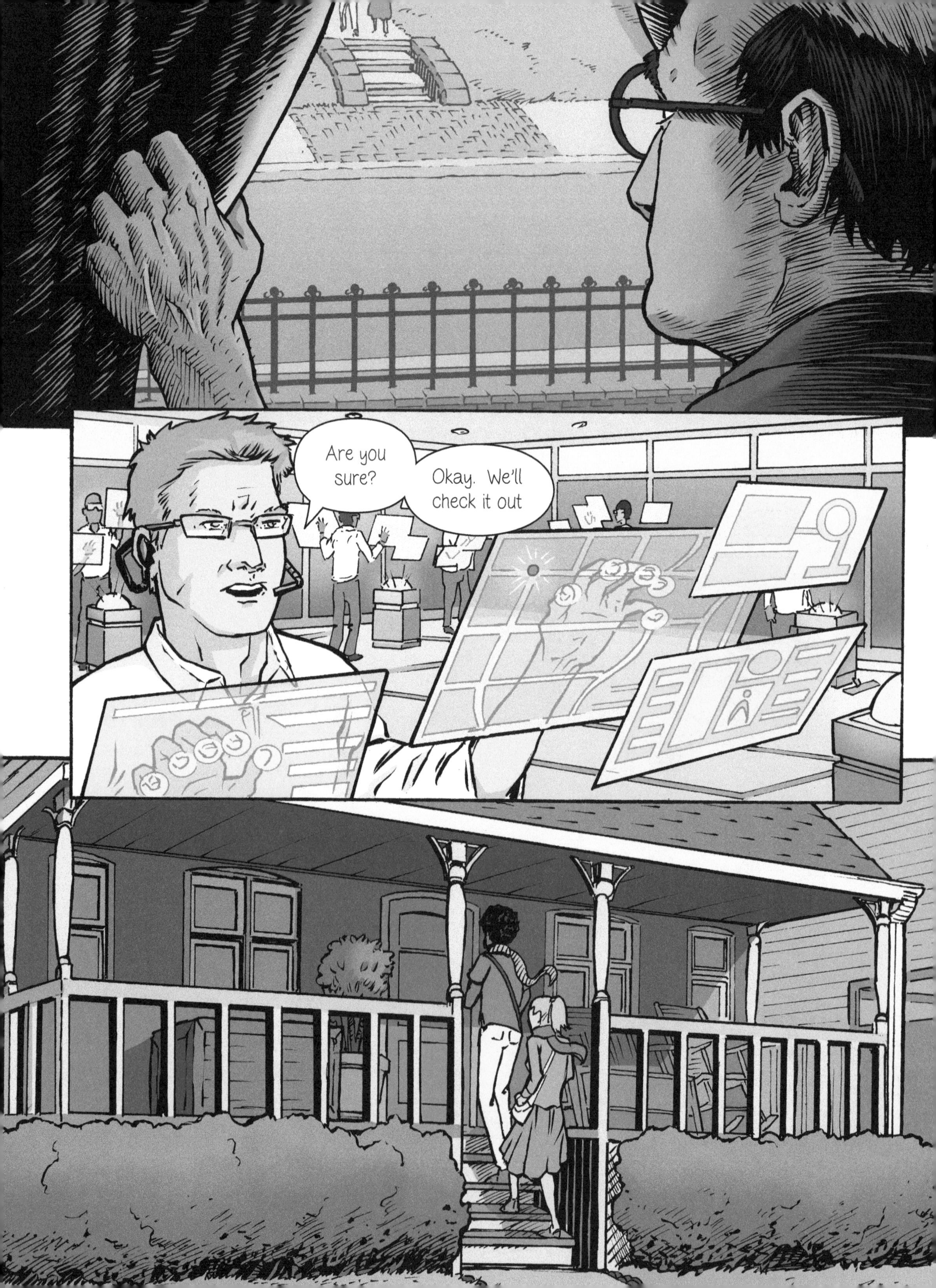
Are you sure?
Okay. We'll check it out

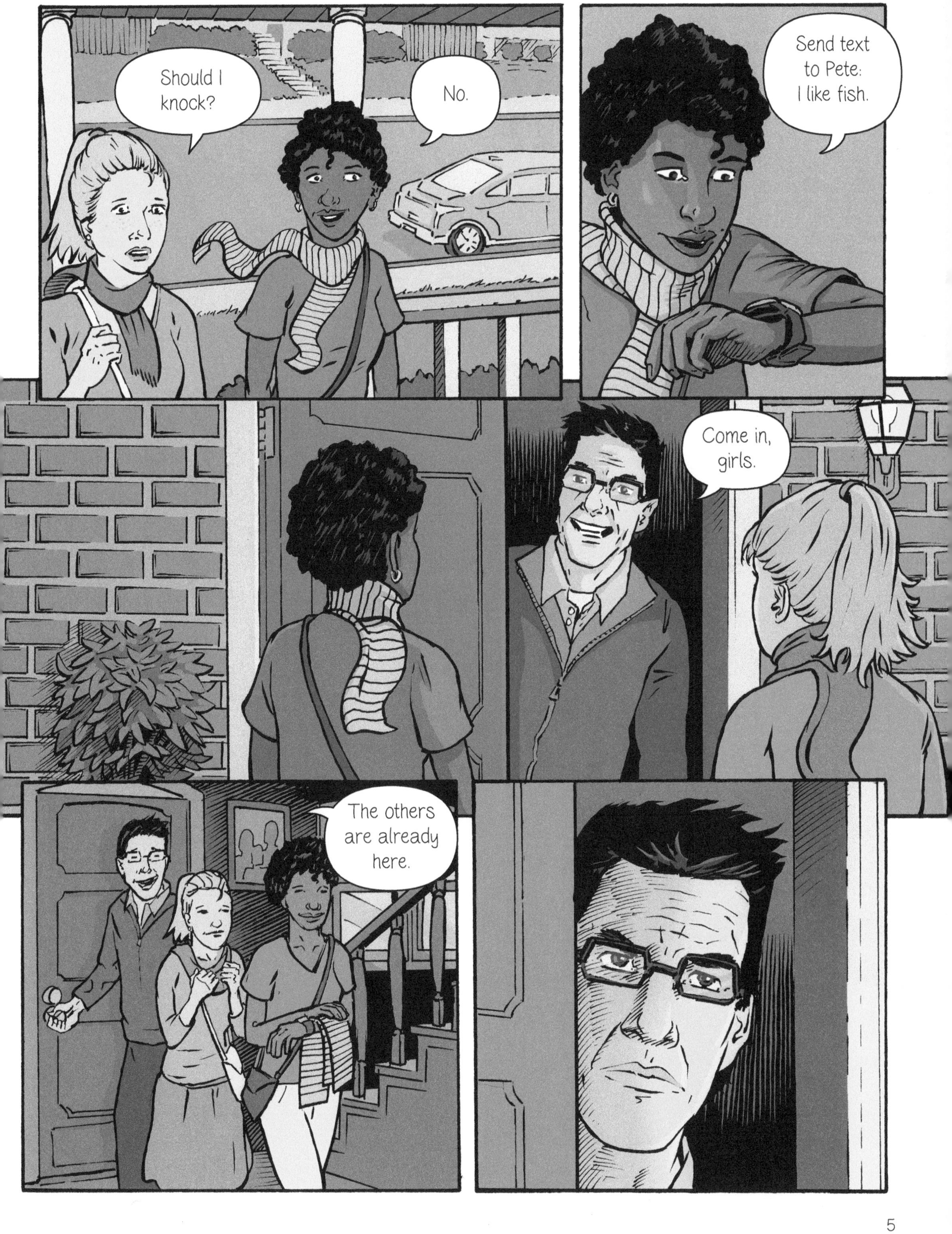

Should I knock?
No.
Send text to Pete: I like fish.
Come in, girls.
The others are already here.

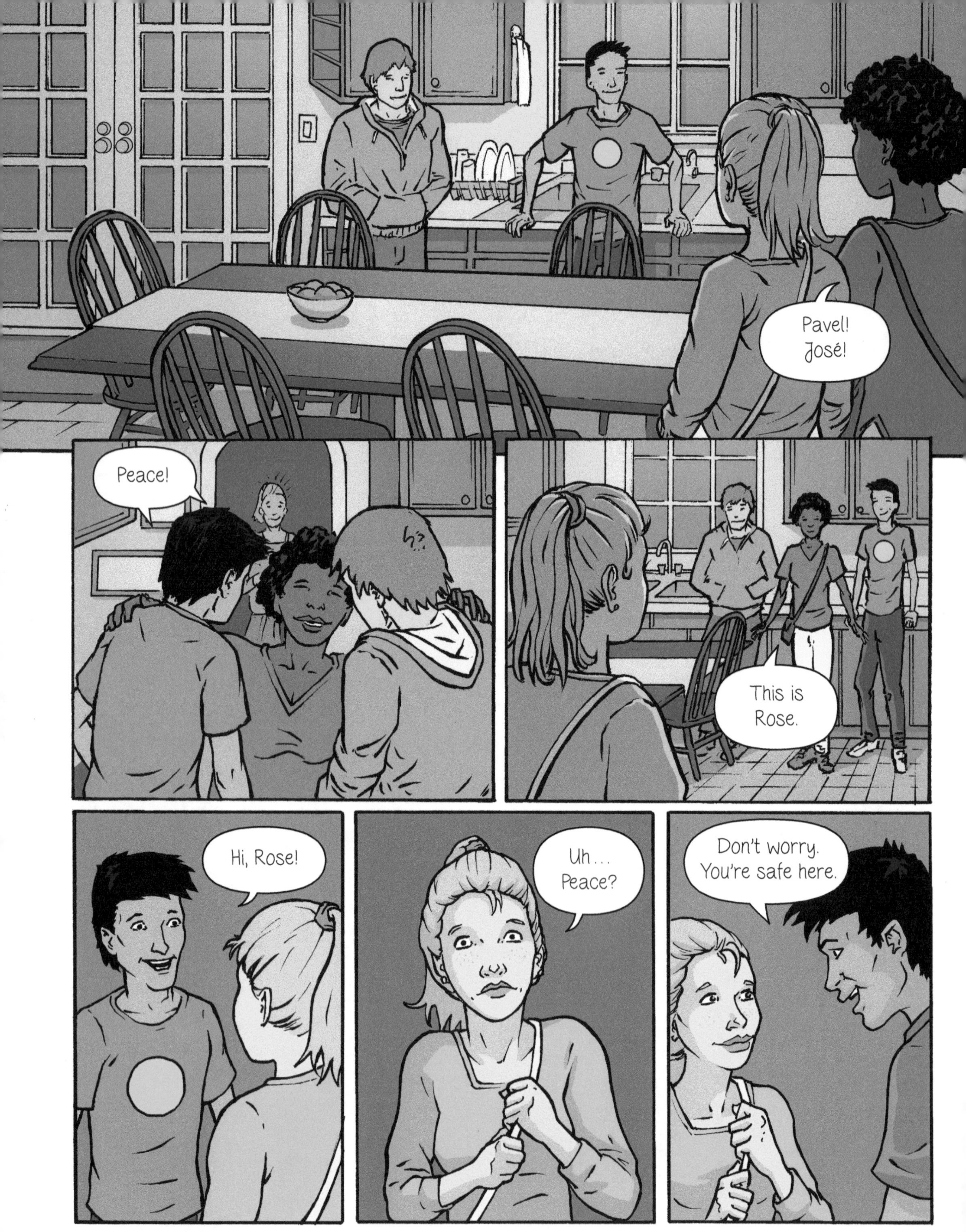
Pavel! José!
Peace!
This is Rose.
Hi, Rose!
Uh... Peace?
Don't worry. You're safe here.

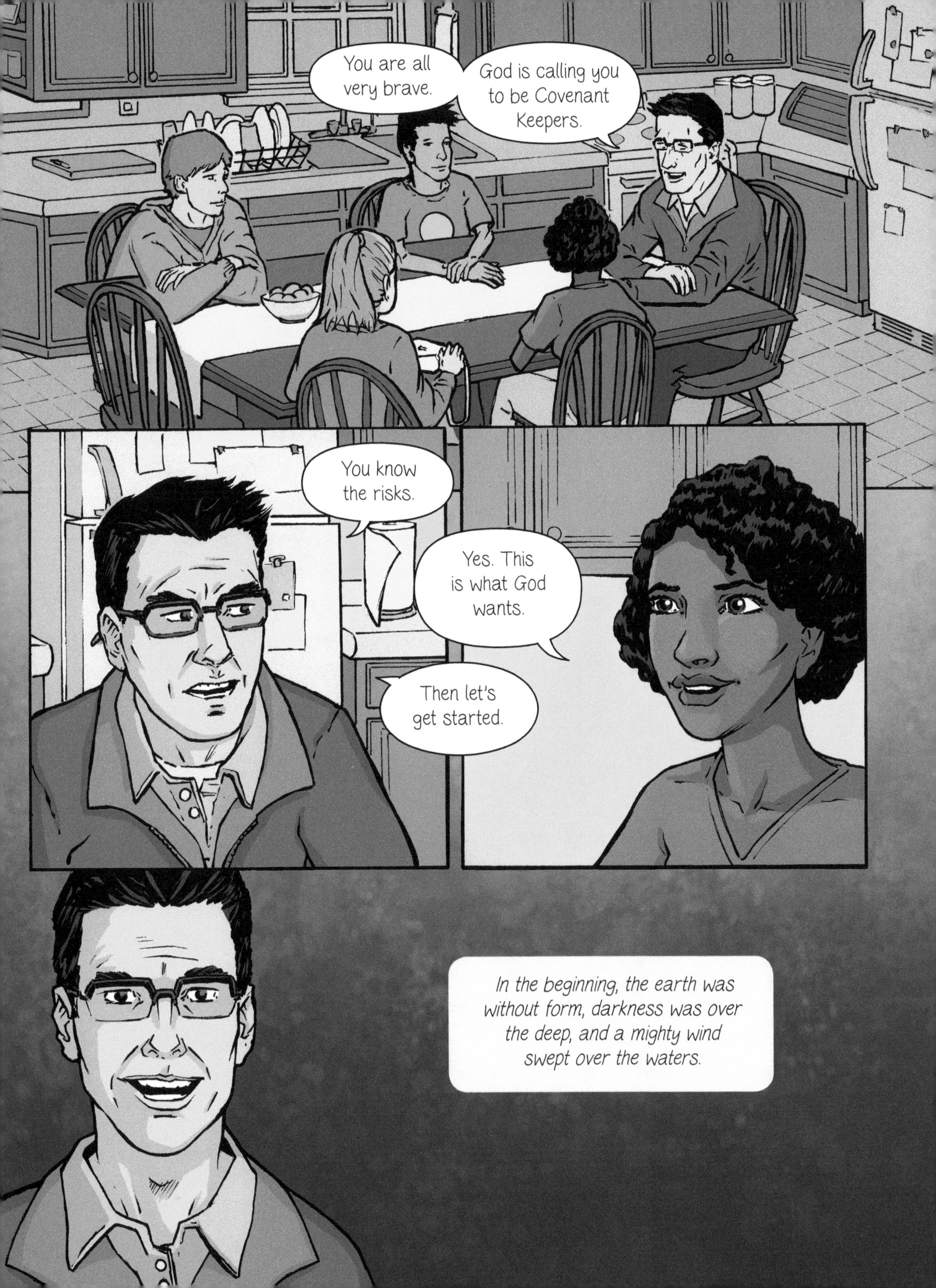
You are all very brave.
God is calling you to be Covenant Keepers.
You know the risks.
Yes. This is what God wants.
Then let's get started.
In the beginning, the earth was without form, darkness was over the deep, and a mighty wind swept over the waters.

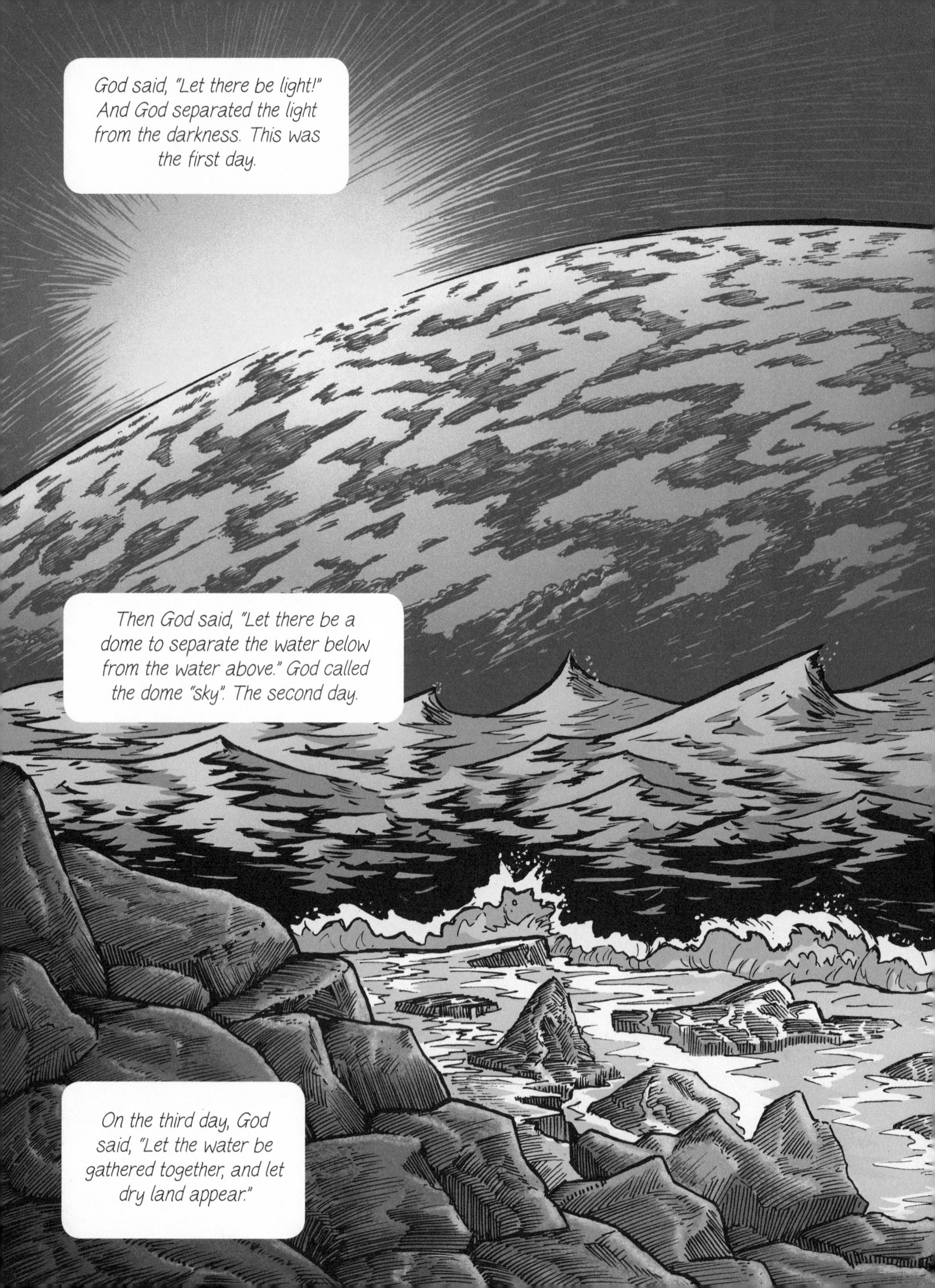
God said, "Let there be light!" And God separated the light from the darkness. This was the first day.
Then God said, "Let there be a dome to separate the water below from the water above." God called the dome "sky". The second day.
On the third day, God said, "Let the water be gathered together, and let dry land appear."

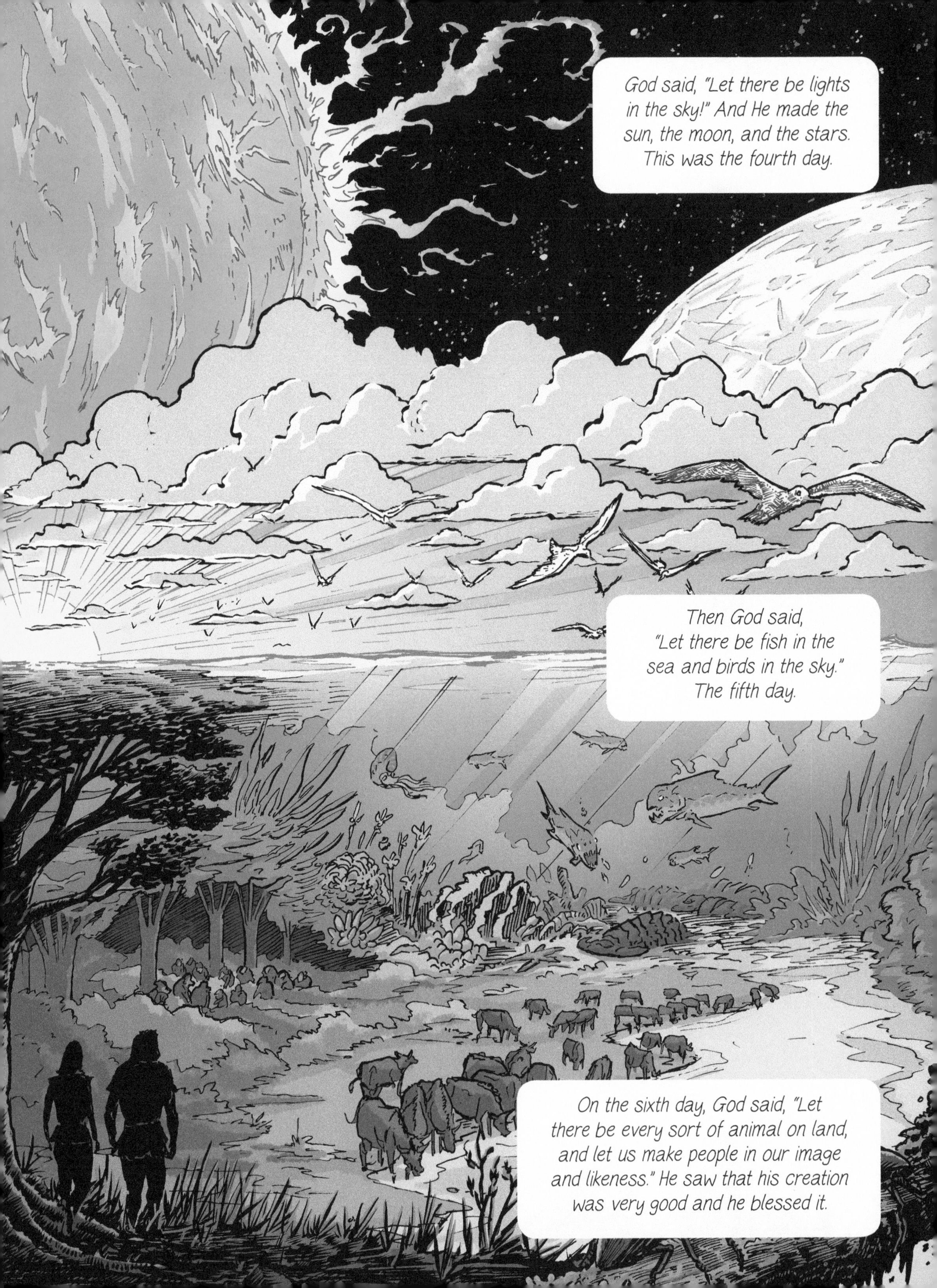
God said, "Let there be lights in the sky!" And He made the sun, the moon, and the stars. This was the fourth day.
Then God said, "Let there be fish in the sea and birds in the sky." The fifth day.
On the sixth day, God said, "Let there be every sort of animal on land, and let us make people in our image and likeness." He saw that his creation was very good and he blessed it.

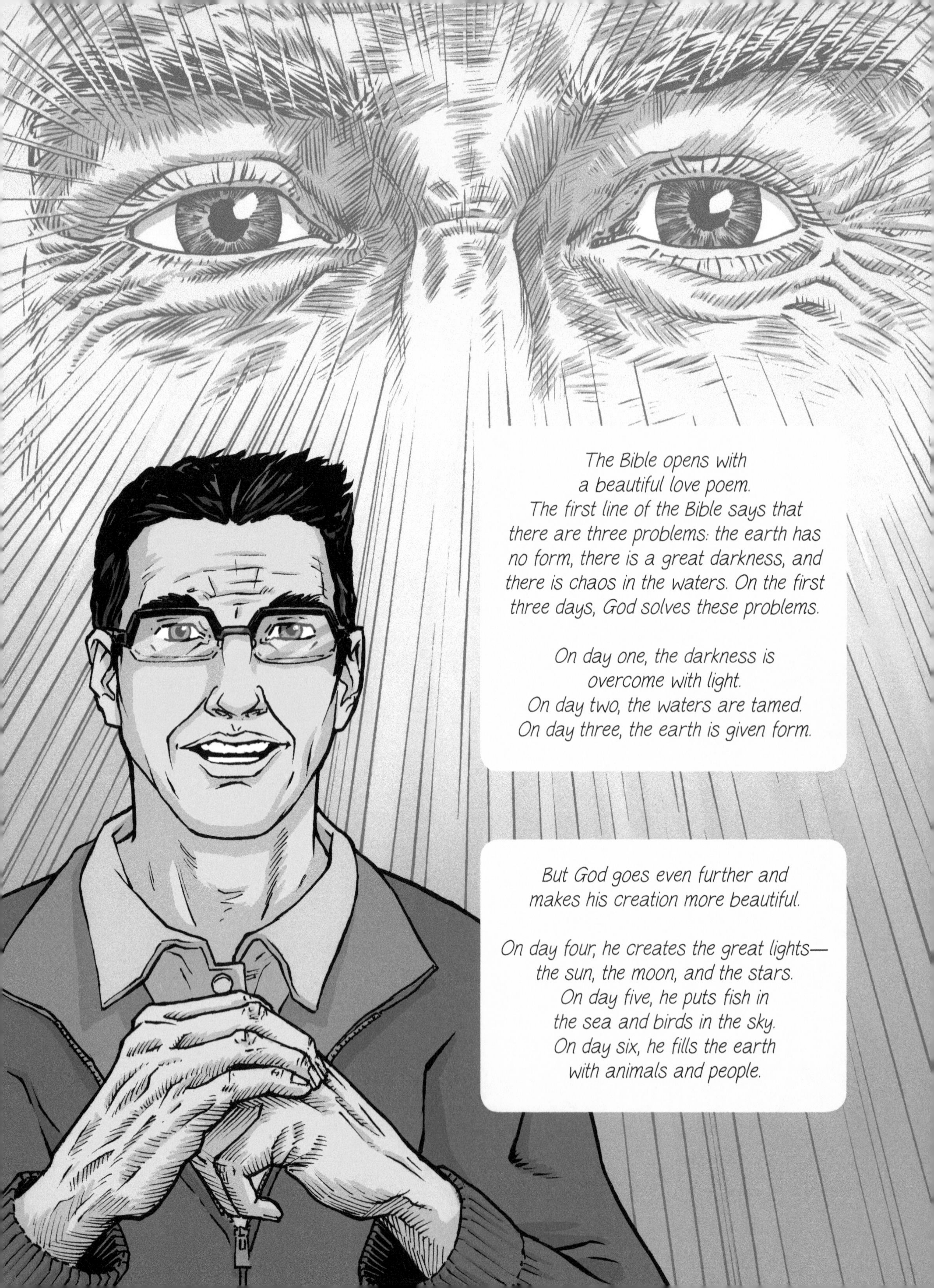
The Bible opens with a beautiful love poem. The first line of the Bible says that there are three problems: the earth has no form, there is a great darkness, and there is chaos in the waters. On the first three days, God solves these problems.
On day one, the darkness is overcome with light. On day two, the waters are tamed. On day three, the earth is given form.
But God goes even further and makes his creation more beautiful.
On day four, he creates the great lights—the sun, the moon, and the stars. On day five, he puts fish in the sea and birds in the sky. On day six, he fills the earth with animals and people.

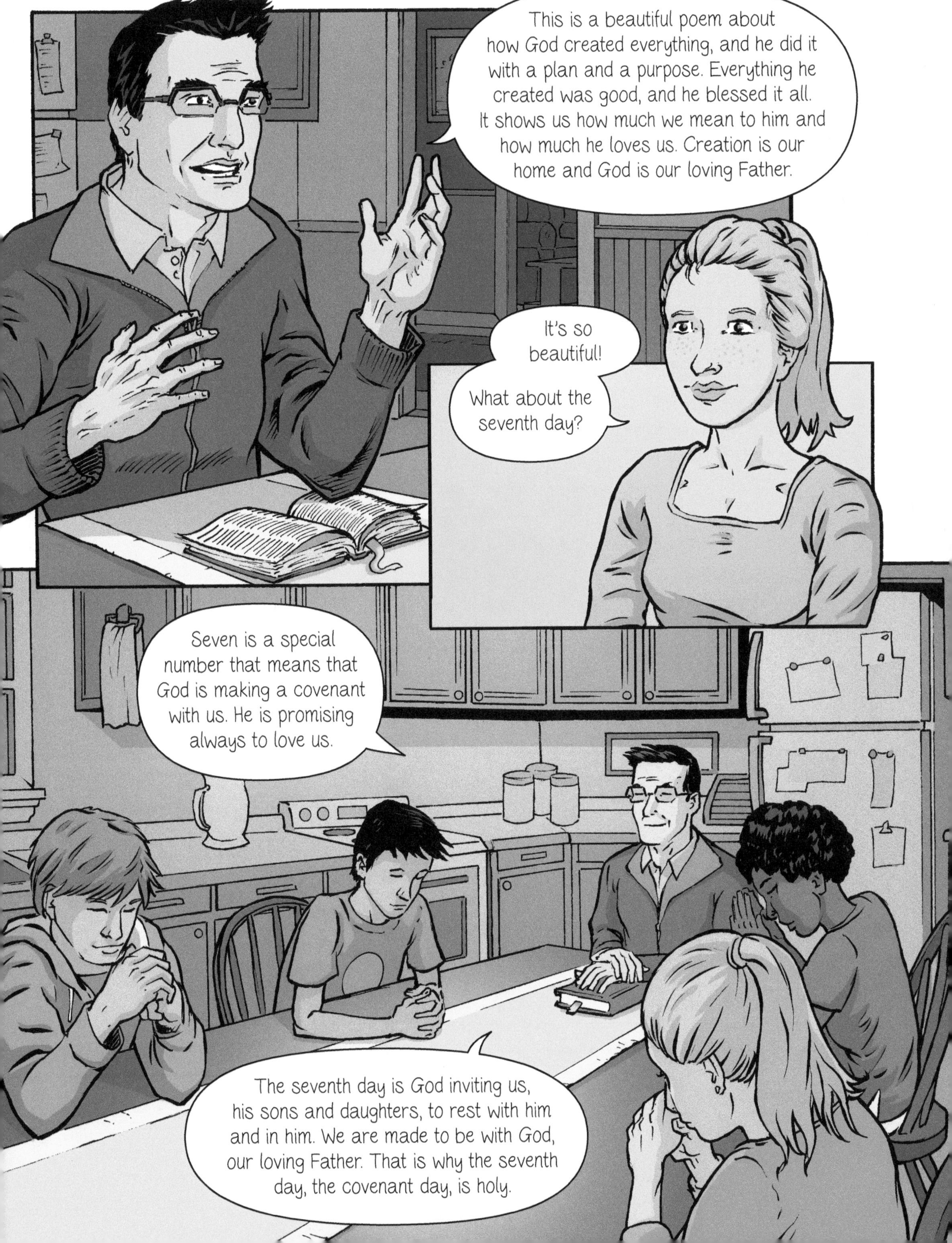
This is a beautiful poem about how God created everything, and he did it with a plan and a purpose. Everything he created was good, and he blessed it all. It shows us how much we mean to him and how much he loves us. Creation is our home and God is our loving Father.
It's so beautiful!
What about the seventh day?
Seven is a special number that means that God is making a covenant with us. He is promising always to love us.
The seventh day is God inviting us, his sons and daughters, to rest with him and in him. We are made to be with God, our loving Father. That is why the seventh day, the covenant day, is holy.

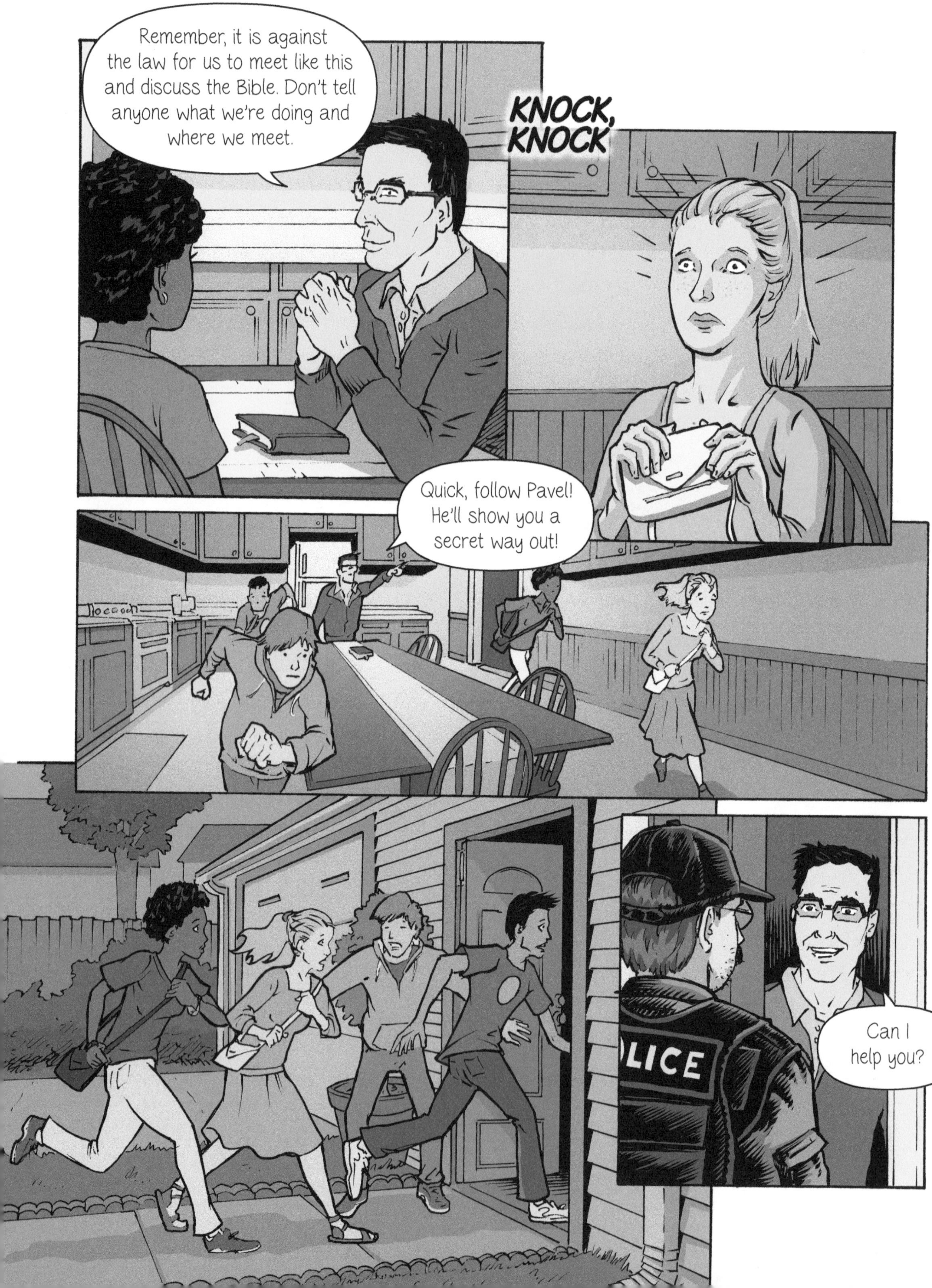
Remember, it is against the law for us to meet like this and discuss the Bible. Don't tell anyone what we're doing and where we meet.
KNOCK, KNOCK
Quick, follow Pavel! He'll show you a secret way out!
LICE
Can I help you?

DAY TWO

Tricks and Lies

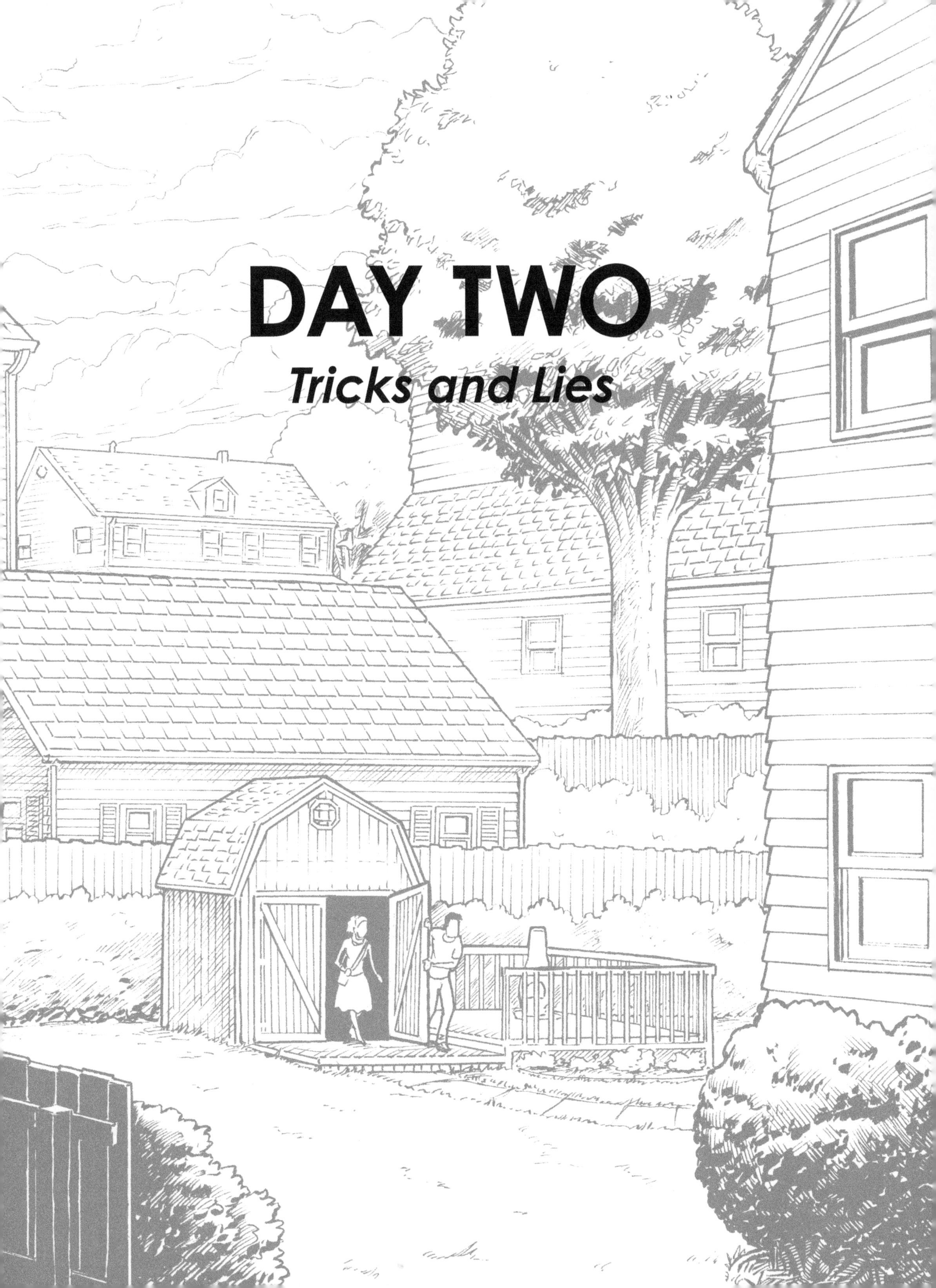

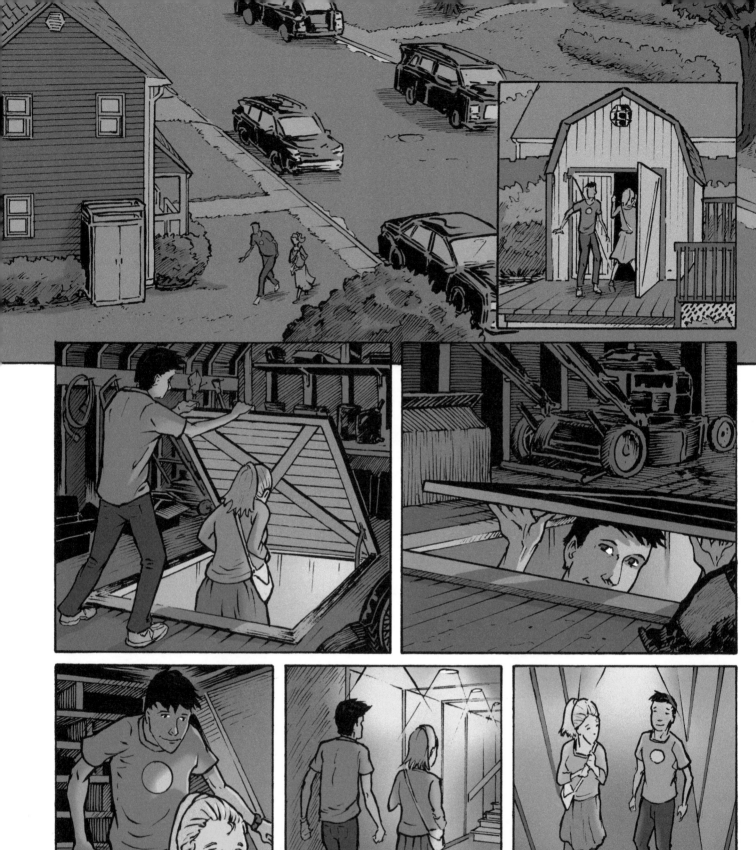

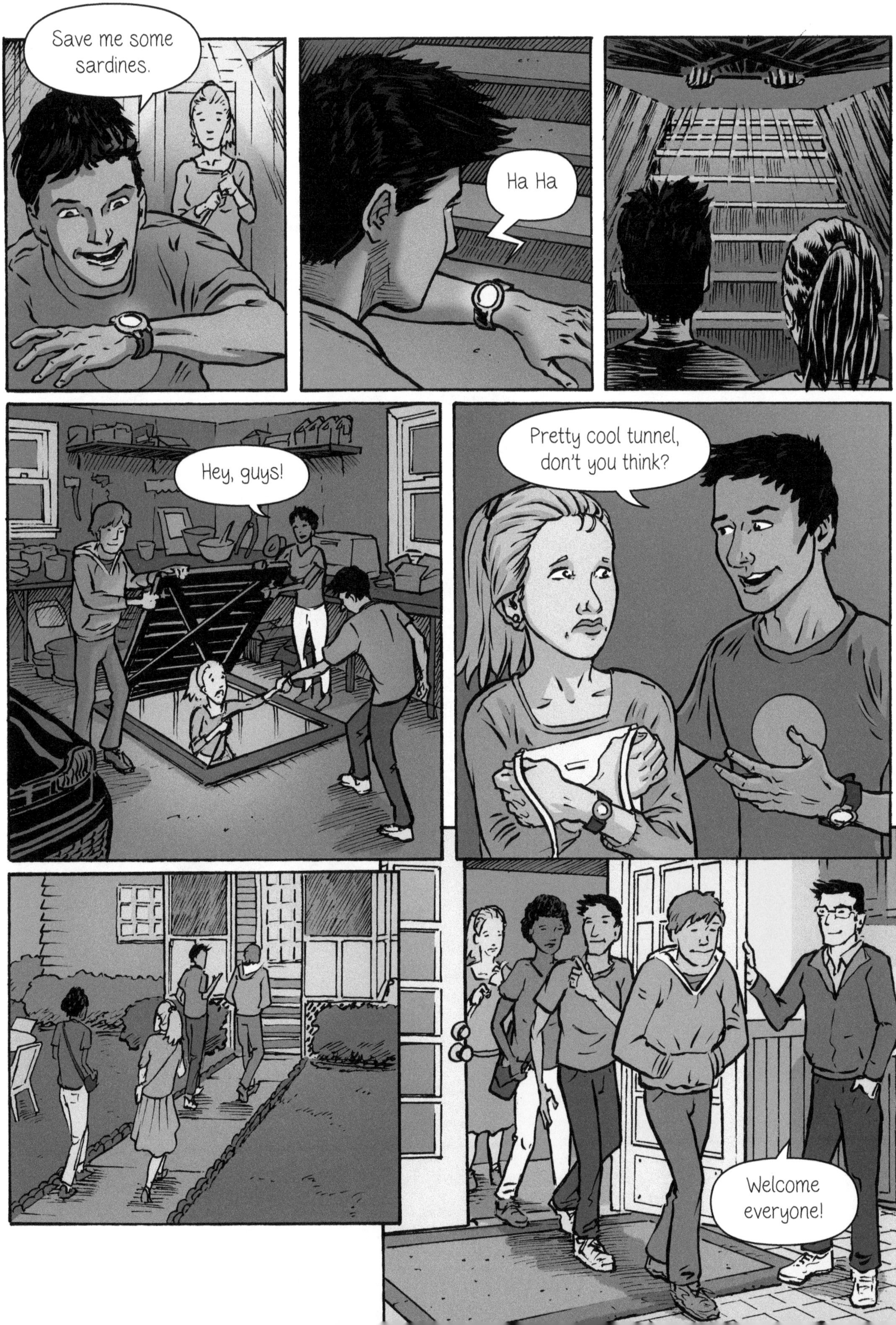
Save me some sardines.
Ha Ha
Hey, guys!
Pretty cool tunnel, don't you think?
Welcome everyone!

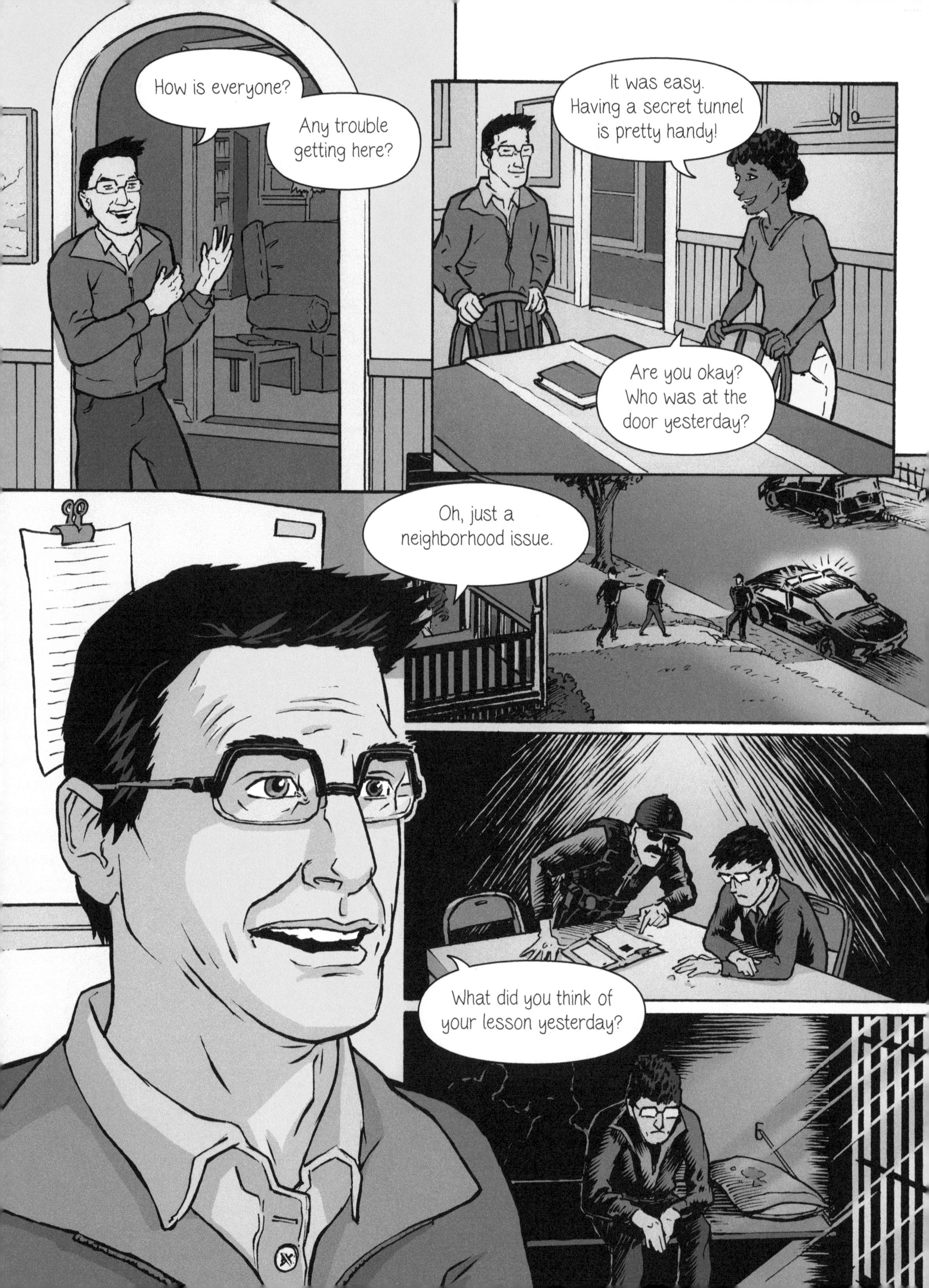
How is everyone?
Any trouble getting here?
It was easy. Having a secret tunnel is pretty handy!
Are you okay? Who was at the door yesterday?
Oh, just a neighborhood issue.
What did you think of your lesson yesterday?

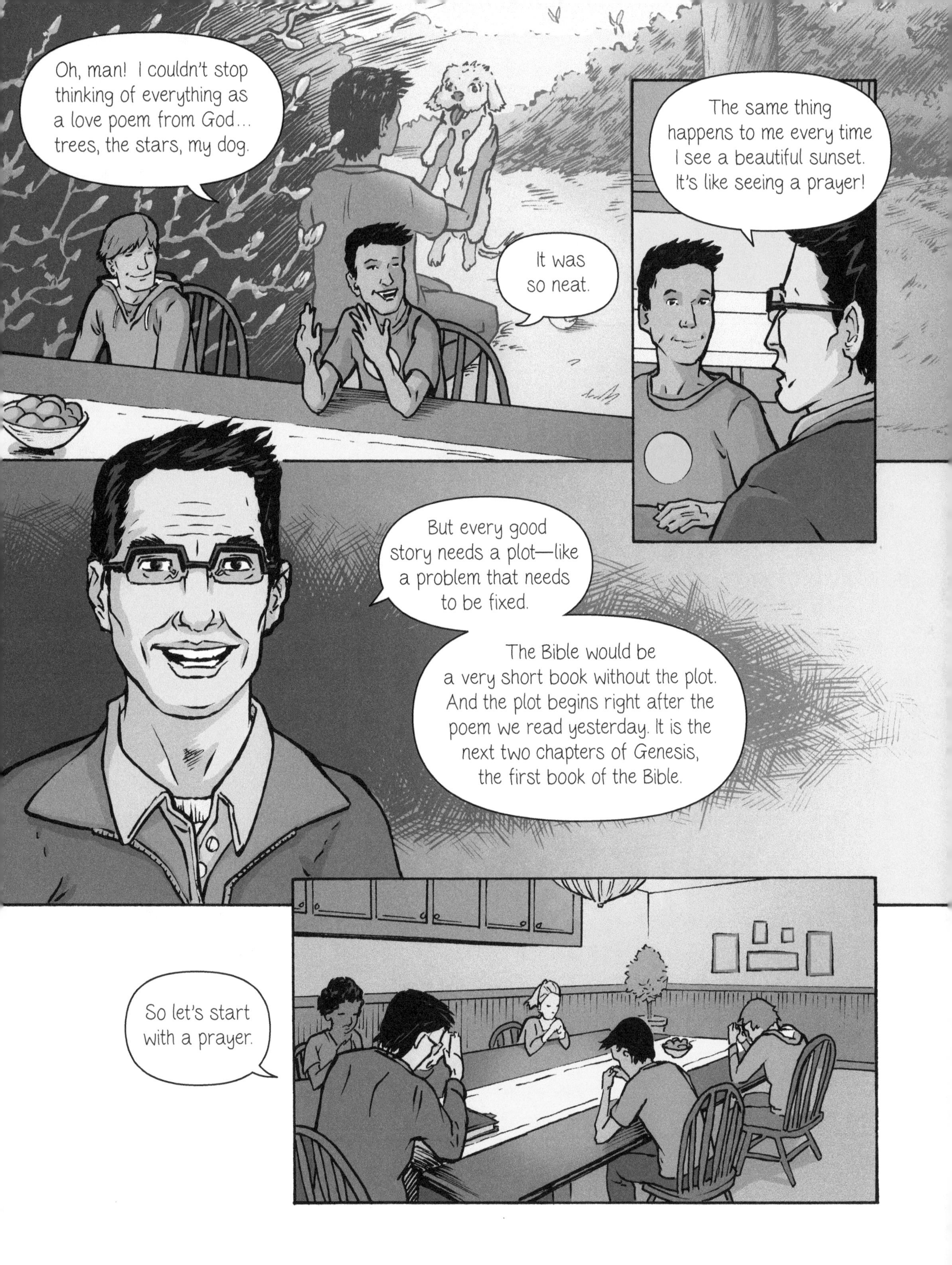

Oh, man! I couldn't stop thinking of everything as a love poem from God... trees, the stars, my dog.
It was so neat.
The same thing happens to me every time I see a beautiful sunset. It's like seeing a prayer!
But every good story needs a plot—like a problem that needs to be fixed.
The Bible would be a very short book without the plot. And the plot begins right after the poem we read yesterday. It is the next two chapters of Genesis, the first book of the Bible.
So let's start with a prayer.

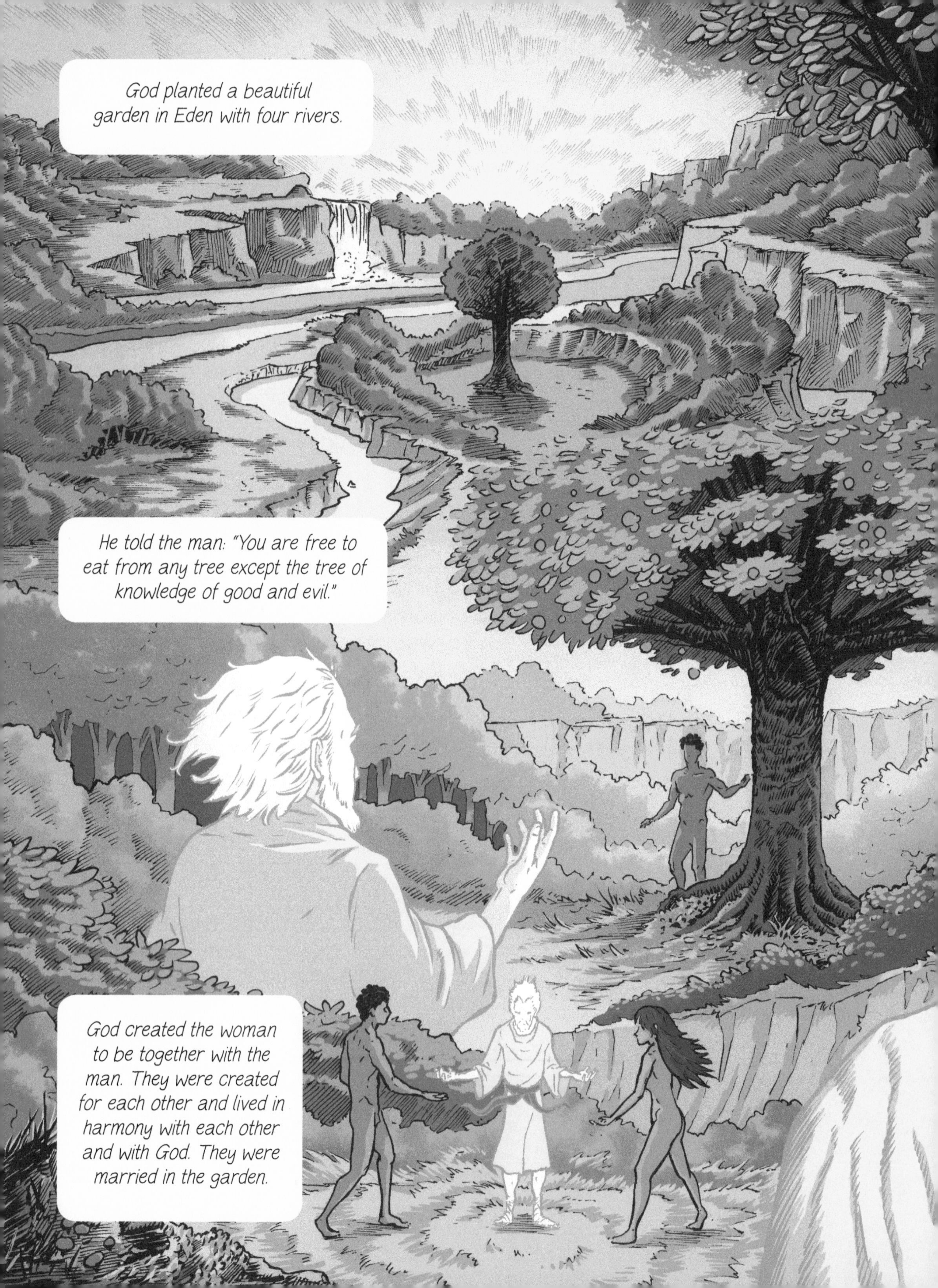
God planted a beautiful garden in Eden with four rivers.
He told the man: "You are free to eat from any tree except the tree of knowledge of good and evil."
God created the woman to be together with the man. They were created for each other and lived in harmony with each other and with God. They were married in the garden.

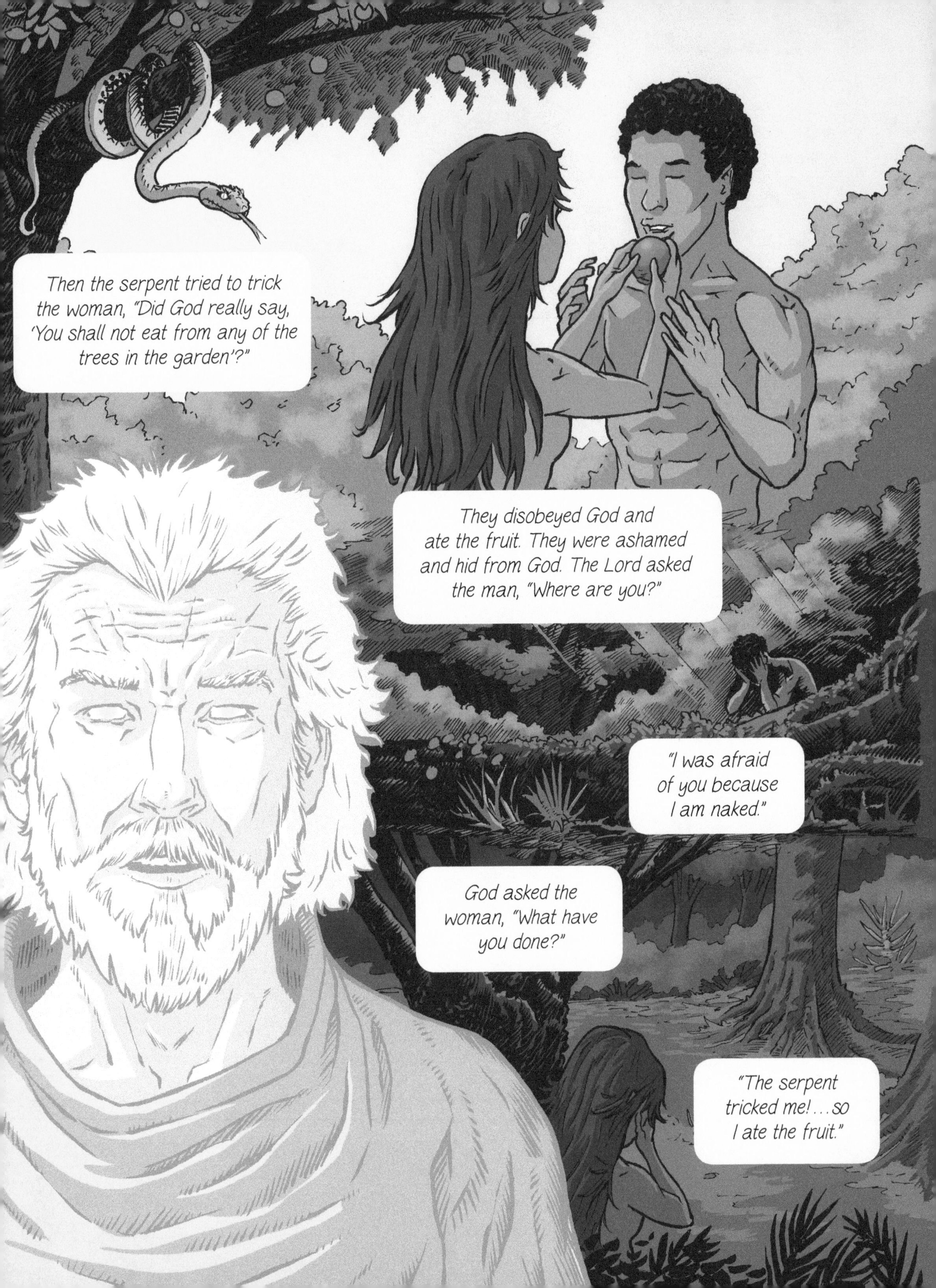
Then the serpent tried to trick the woman, "Did God really say, 'You shall not eat from any of the trees in the garden'?"
They disobeyed God and ate the fruit. They were ashamed and hid from God. The Lord asked the man, "Where are you?"
"I was afraid of you because I am naked."
God asked the woman, "What have you done?"
"The serpent tricked me!...so I ate the fruit."

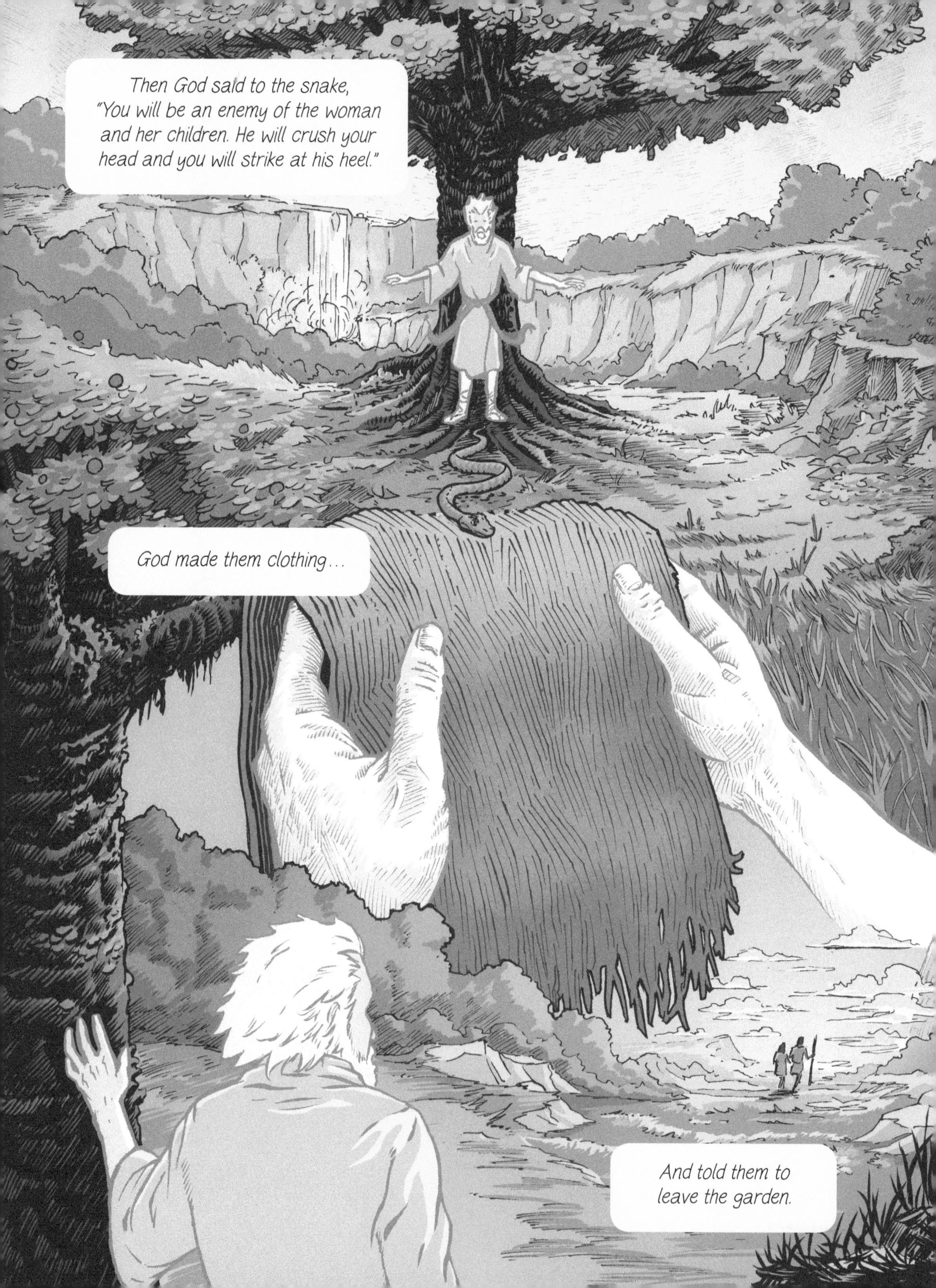
Then God said to the snake, "You will be an enemy of the woman and her children. He will crush your head and you will strike at his heel."
God made them clothing...
And told them to leave the garden.

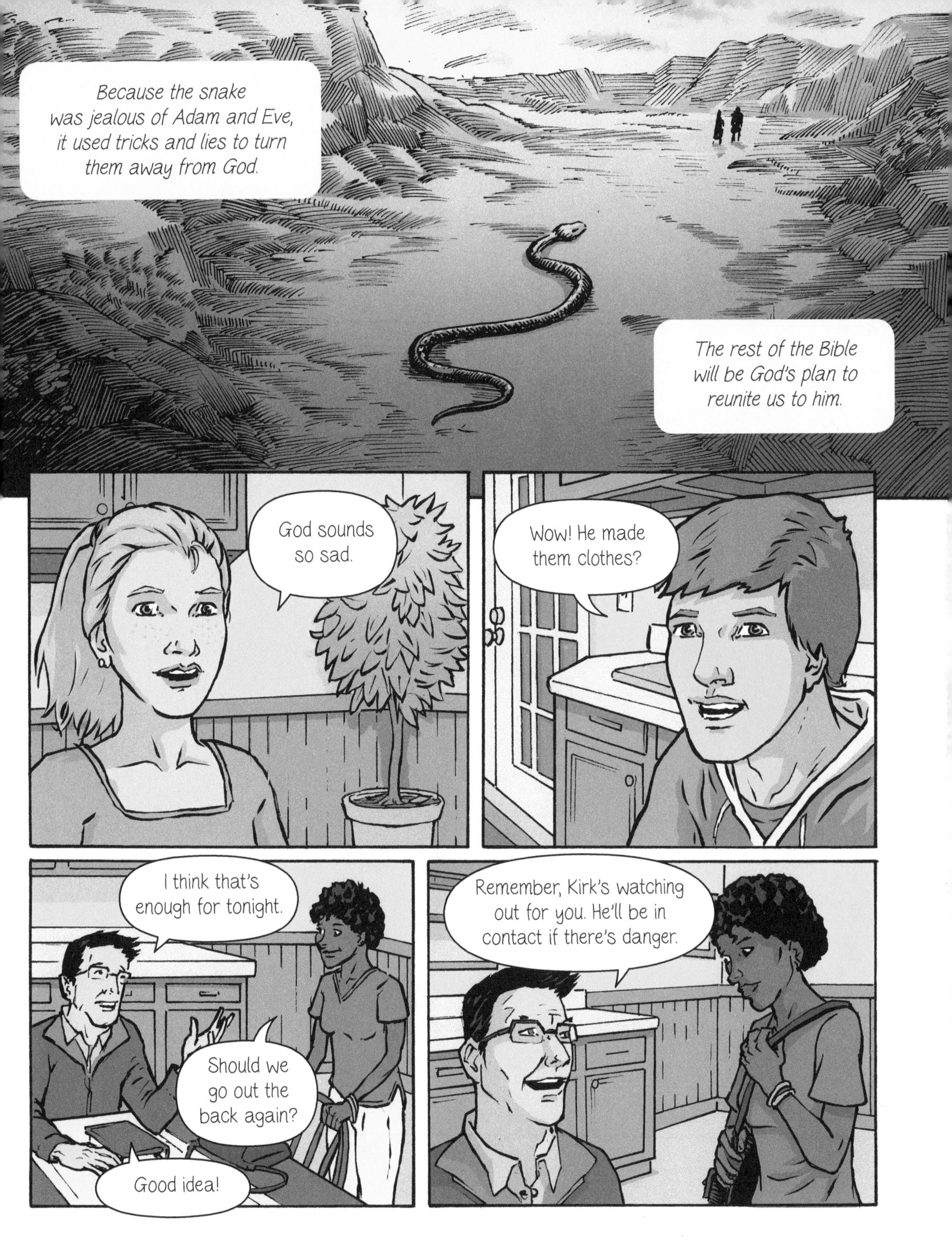
Because the snake was jealous of Adam and Eve, it used tricks and lies to turn them away from God.
The rest of the Bible will be God's plan to reunite us to him.
God sounds so sad.
Wow! He made them clothes?
I think that's enough for tonight.
Should we go out the back again?
Good idea!
Remember, Kirk's watching out for you. He'll be in contact if there's danger.

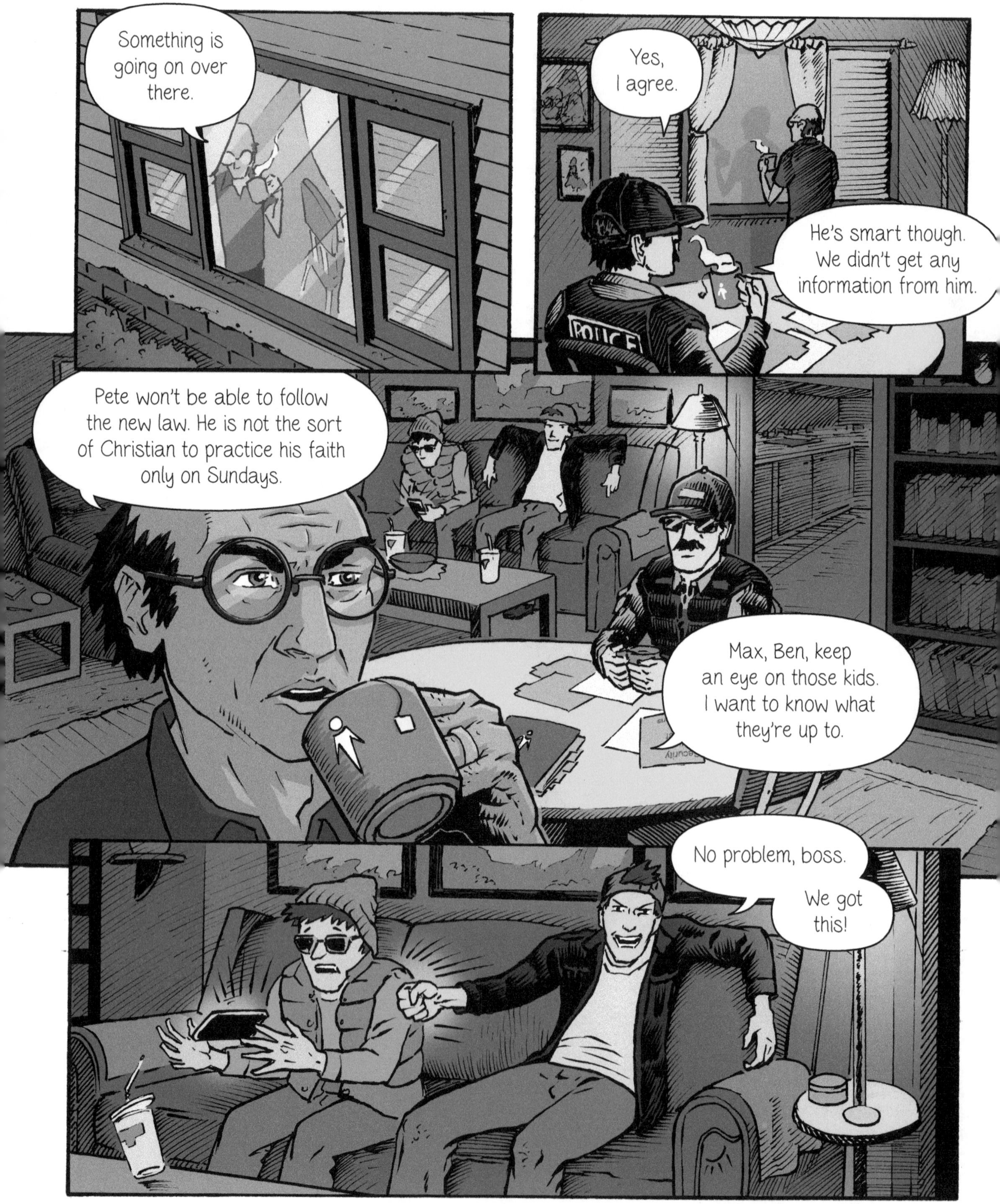
Something is going on over there.
Yes, I agree.
He's smart though. We didn't get any information from him.
POLICE
Pete won't be able to follow the new law. He is not the sort of Christian to practice his faith only on Sundays.
Max, Ben, keep an eye on those kids. I want to know what they're up to.
No problem, boss.
We got this!

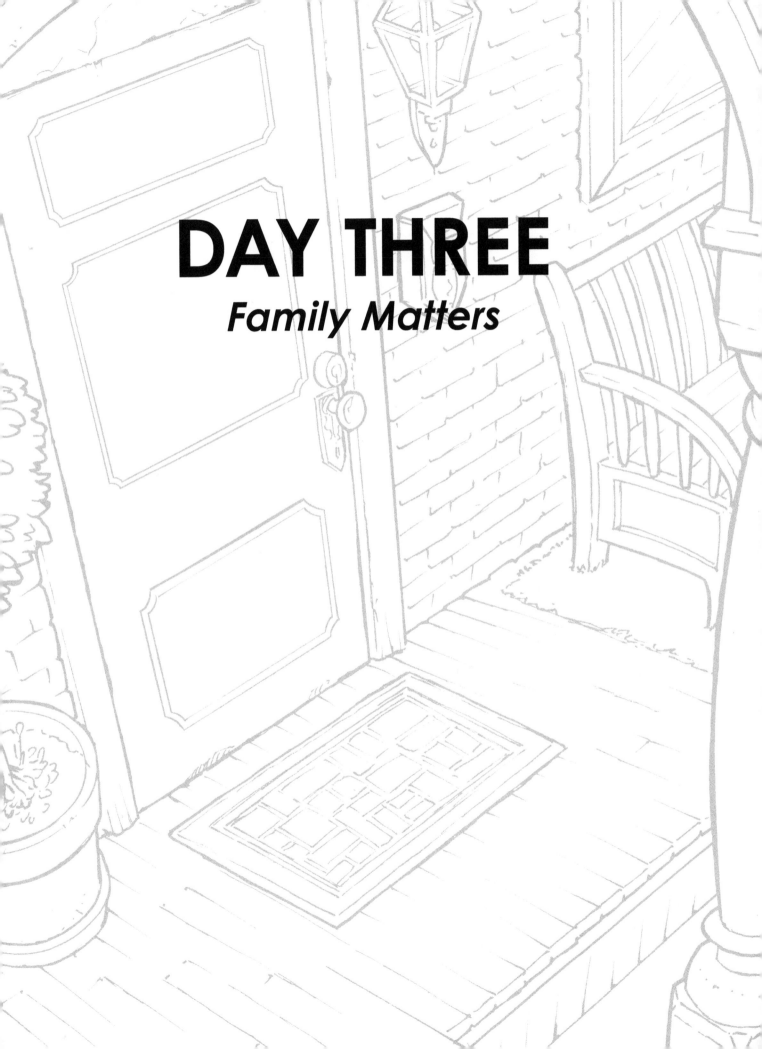

DAY THREE
Family Matters

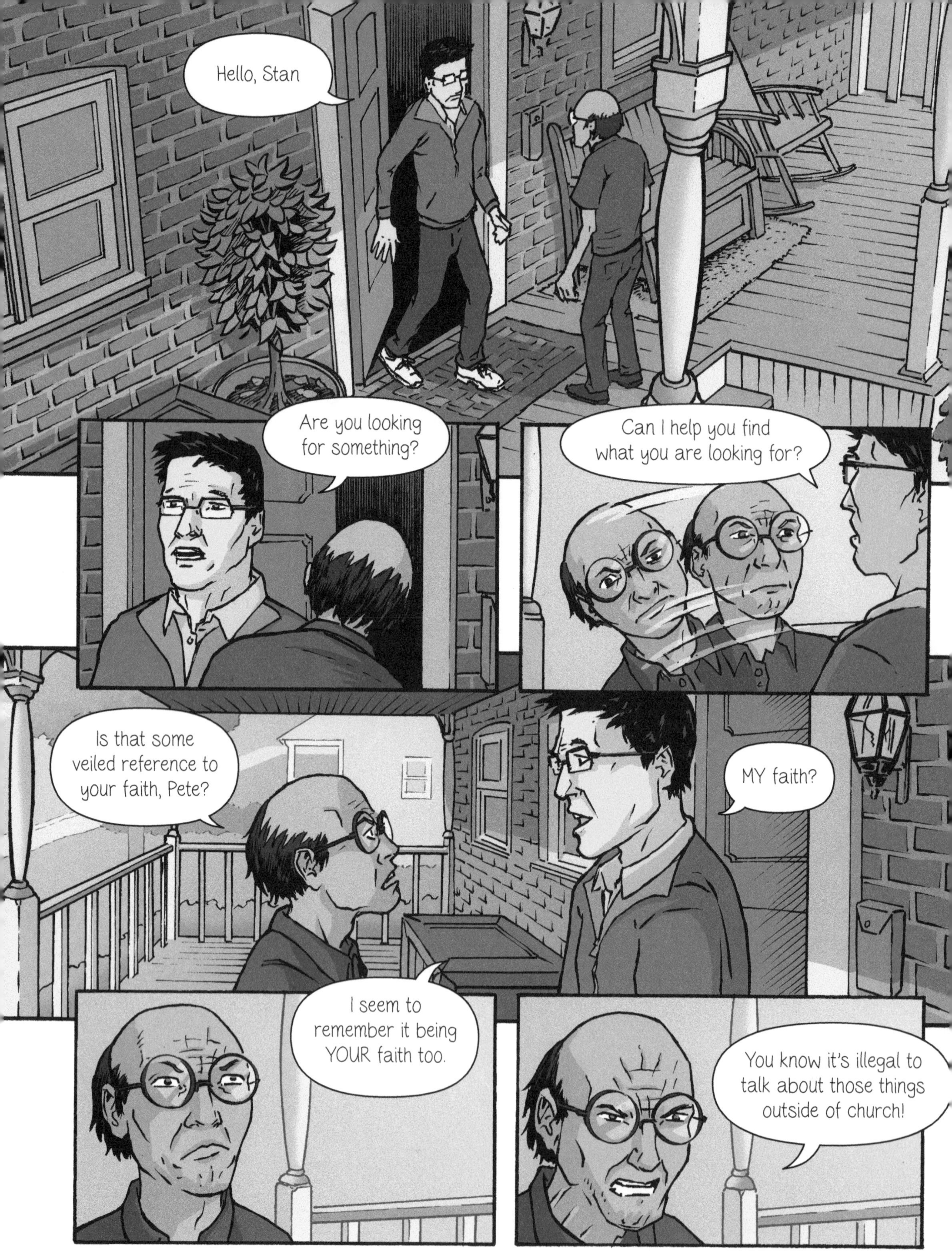
Hello, Stan
Are you looking for something?
Can I help you find what you are looking for?
Is that some veiled reference to your faith, Pete?
MY faith?
I seem to remember it being YOUR faith too.
You know it's illegal to talk about those things outside of church!

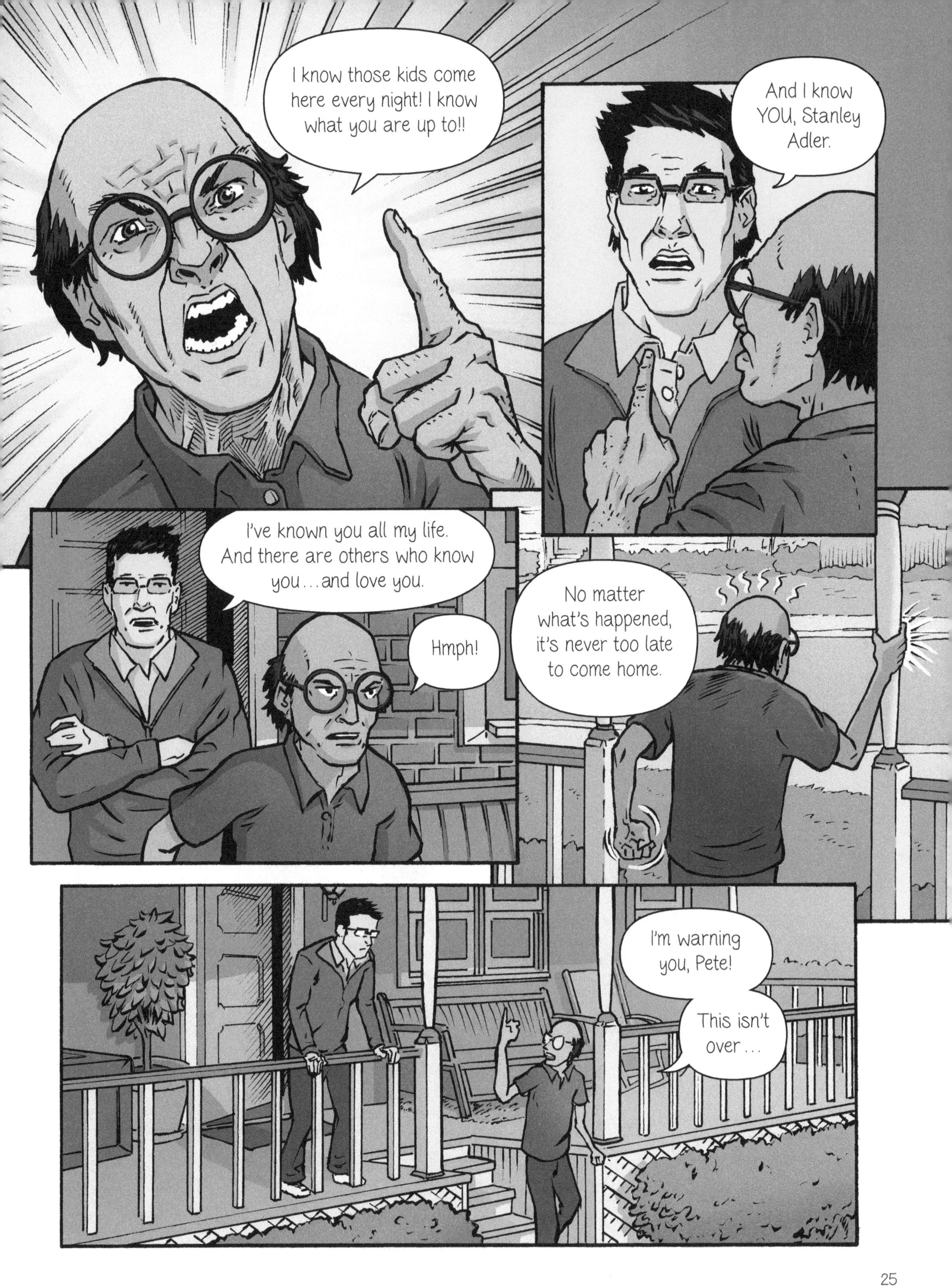
I know those kids come here every night! I know what you are up to!!
And I know YOU, Stanley Adler.
I've known you all my life. And there are others who know you...and love you.
Hmph!
No matter what's happened, it's never too late to come home.
I'm warning you, Pete!
This isn't over...

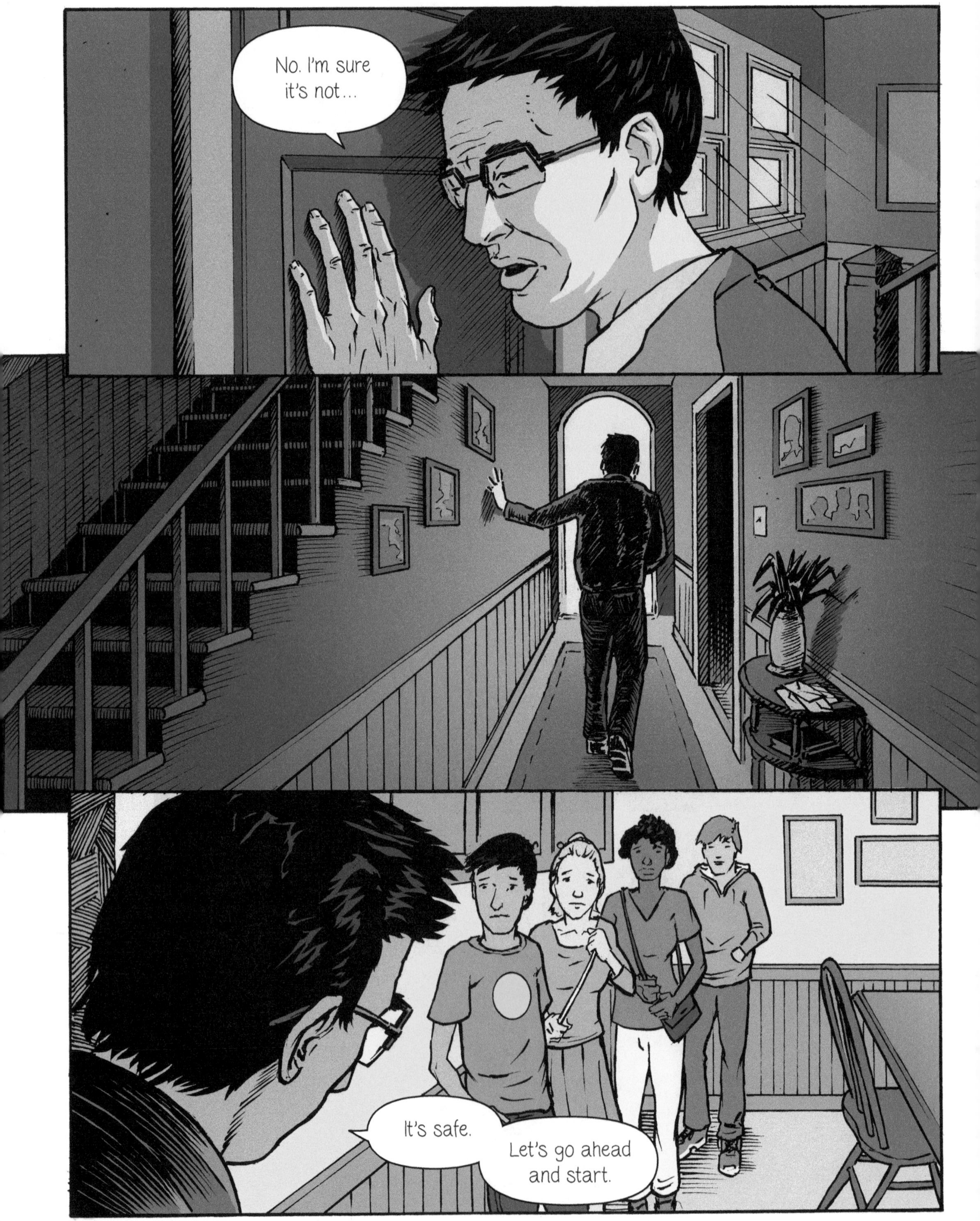
No. I'm sure it's not...
It's safe.
Let's go ahead and start.

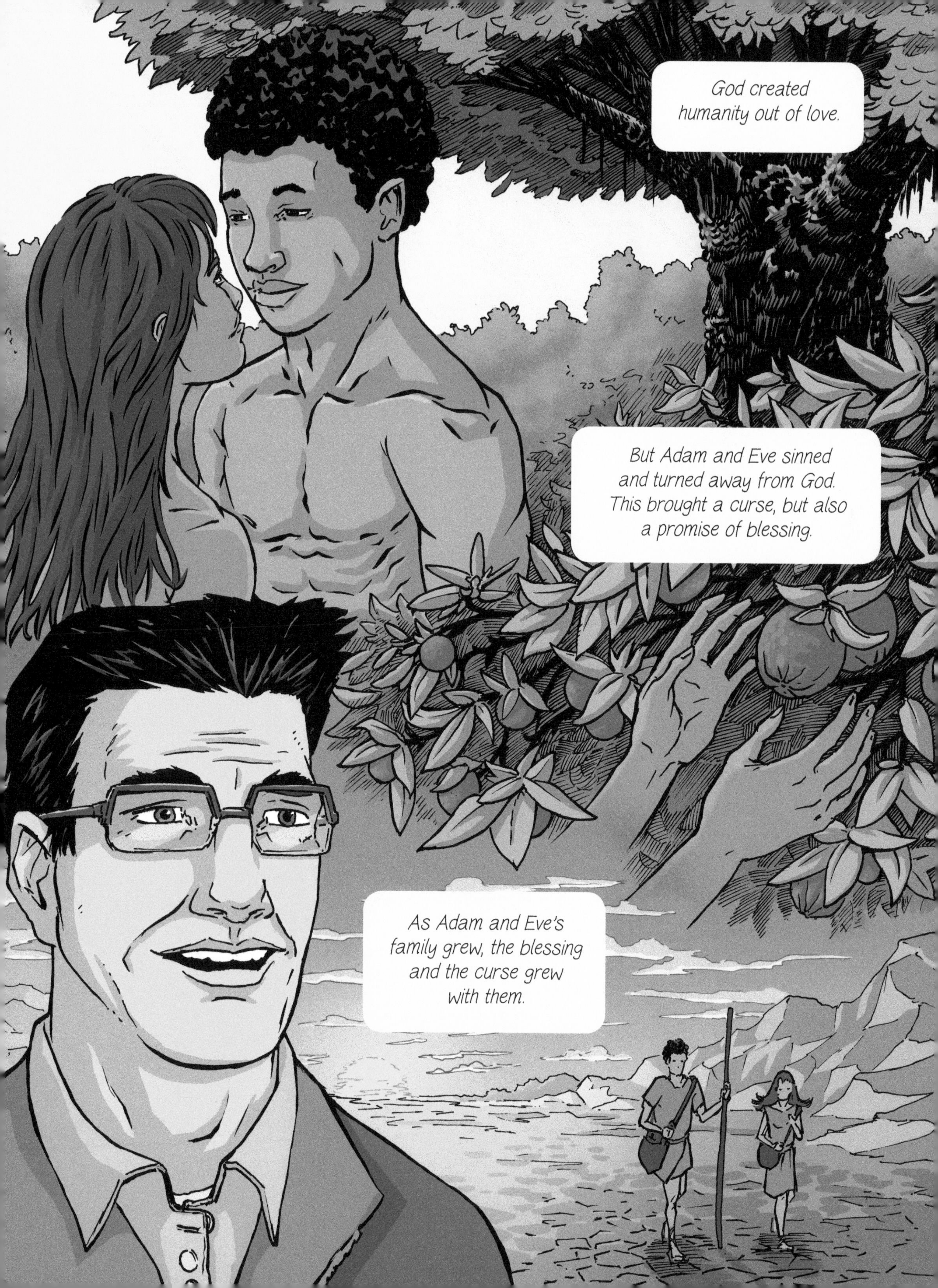
God created humanity out of love.
But Adam and Eve sinned and turned away from God. This brought a curse, but also a promise of blessing.
As Adam and Eve's family grew, the blessing and the curse grew with them.

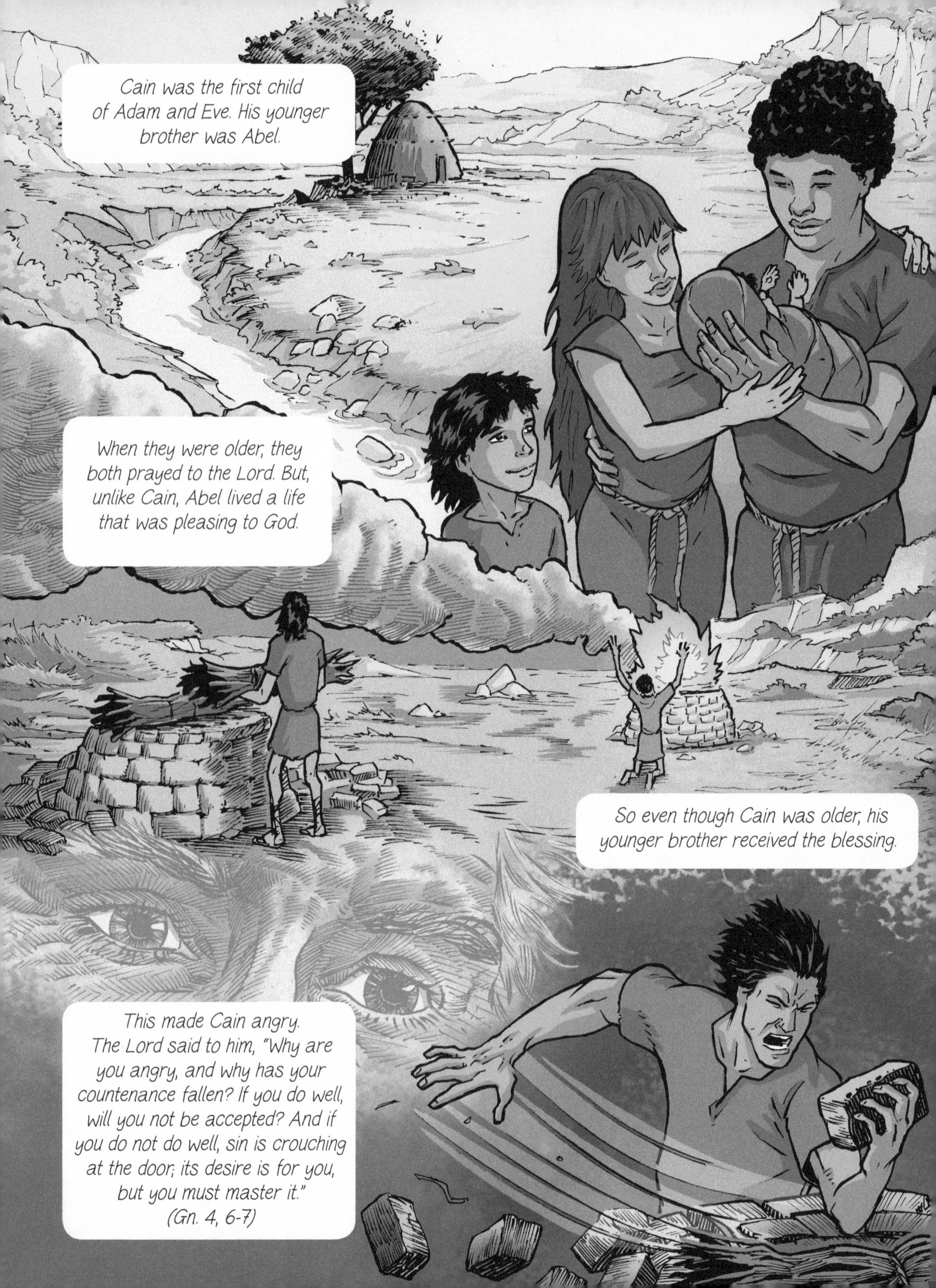
Cain was the first child of Adam and Eve. His younger brother was Abel.
When they were older, they both prayed to the Lord. But, unlike Cain, Abel lived a life that was pleasing to God.
So even though Cain was older, his younger brother received the blessing.
This made Cain angry. The Lord said to him, "Why are you angry, and why has your countenance fallen? If you do well, will you not be accepted? And if you do not do well, sin is crouching at the door; its desire is for you, but you must master it." (Gn. 4, 6-7)

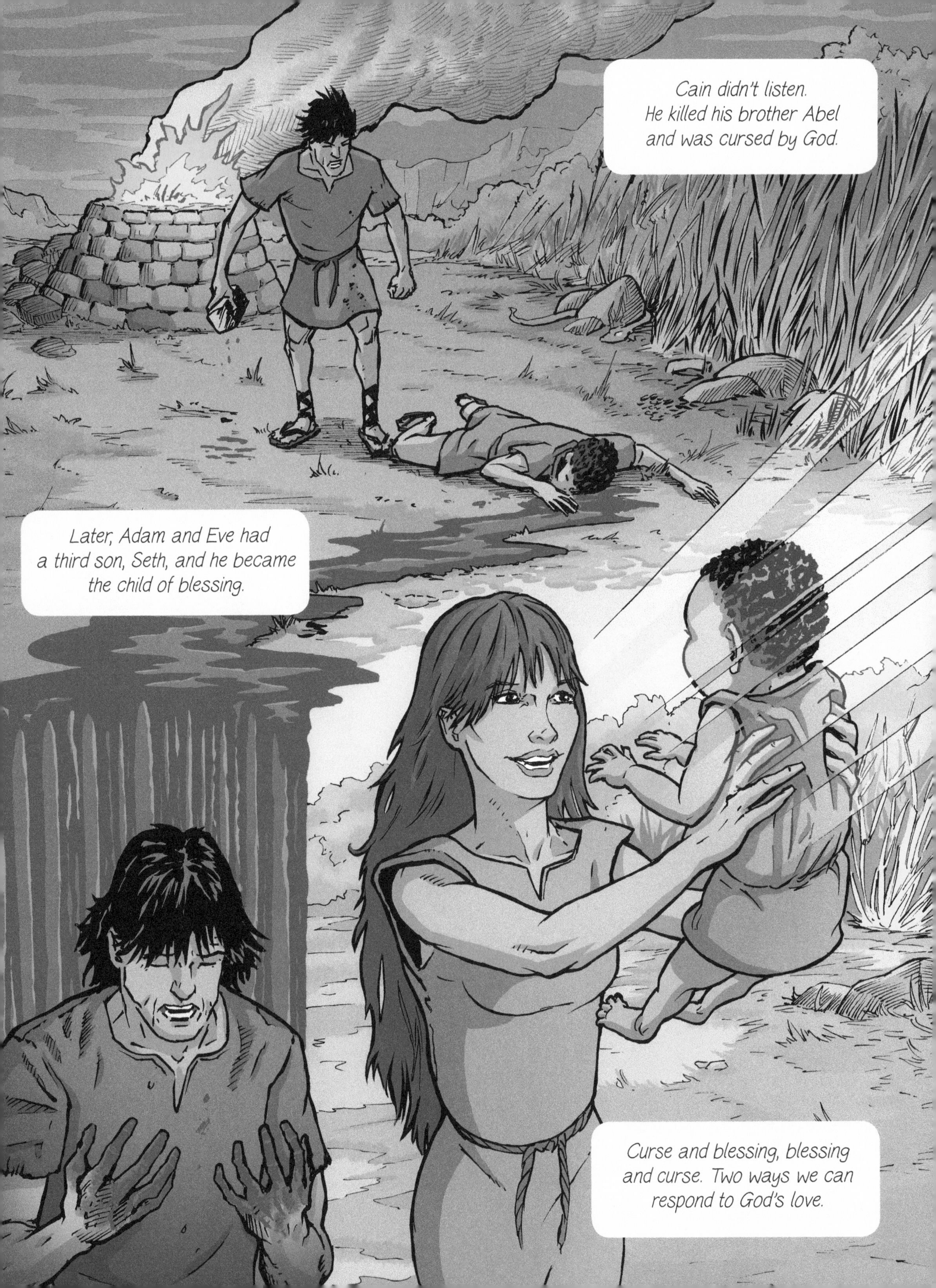
Cain didn't listen. He killed his brother Abel and was cursed by God.
Later, Adam and Eve had a third son, Seth, and he became the child of blessing.
Curse and blessing, blessing and curse. Two ways we can respond to God's love.

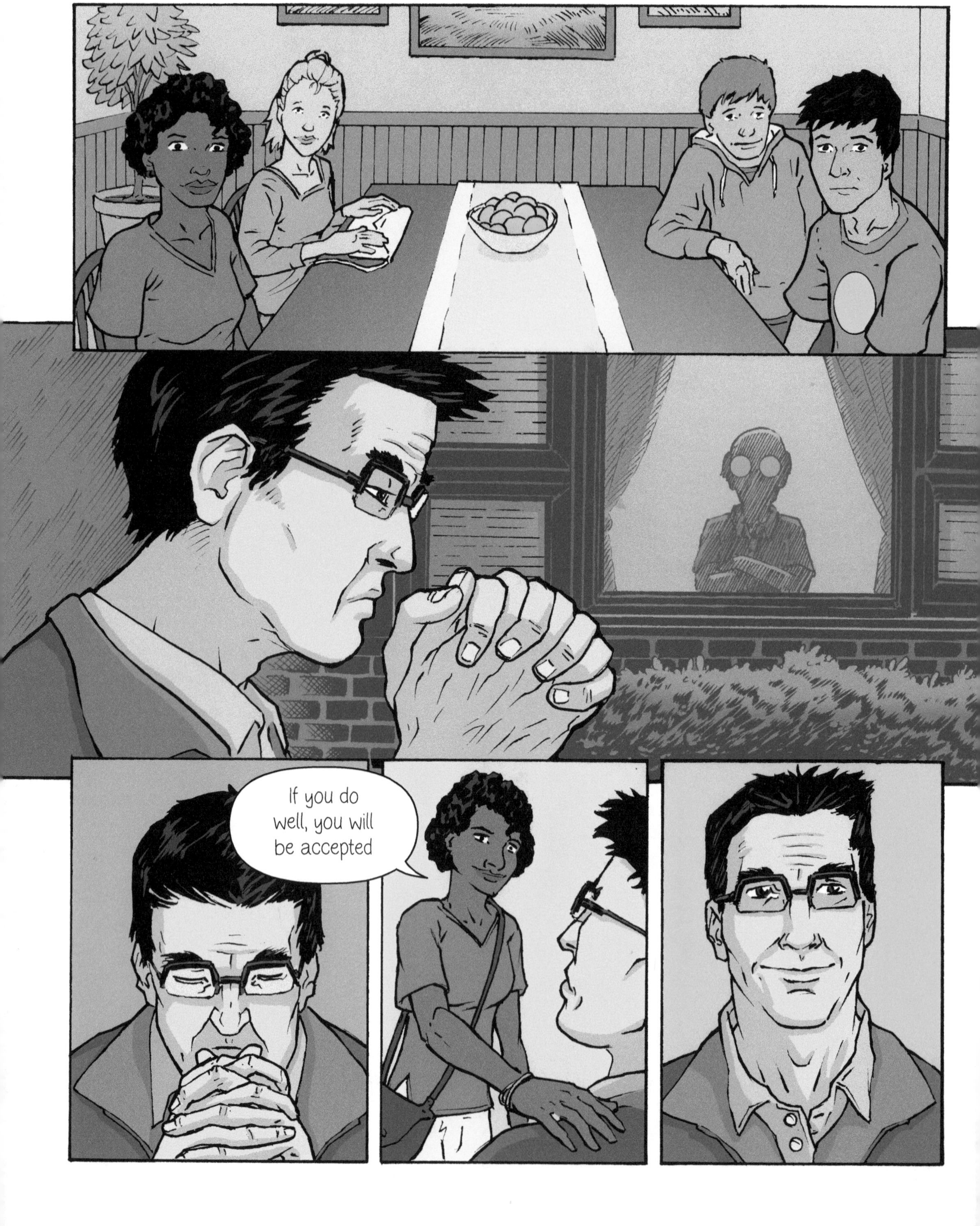
If you do well, you will be accepted

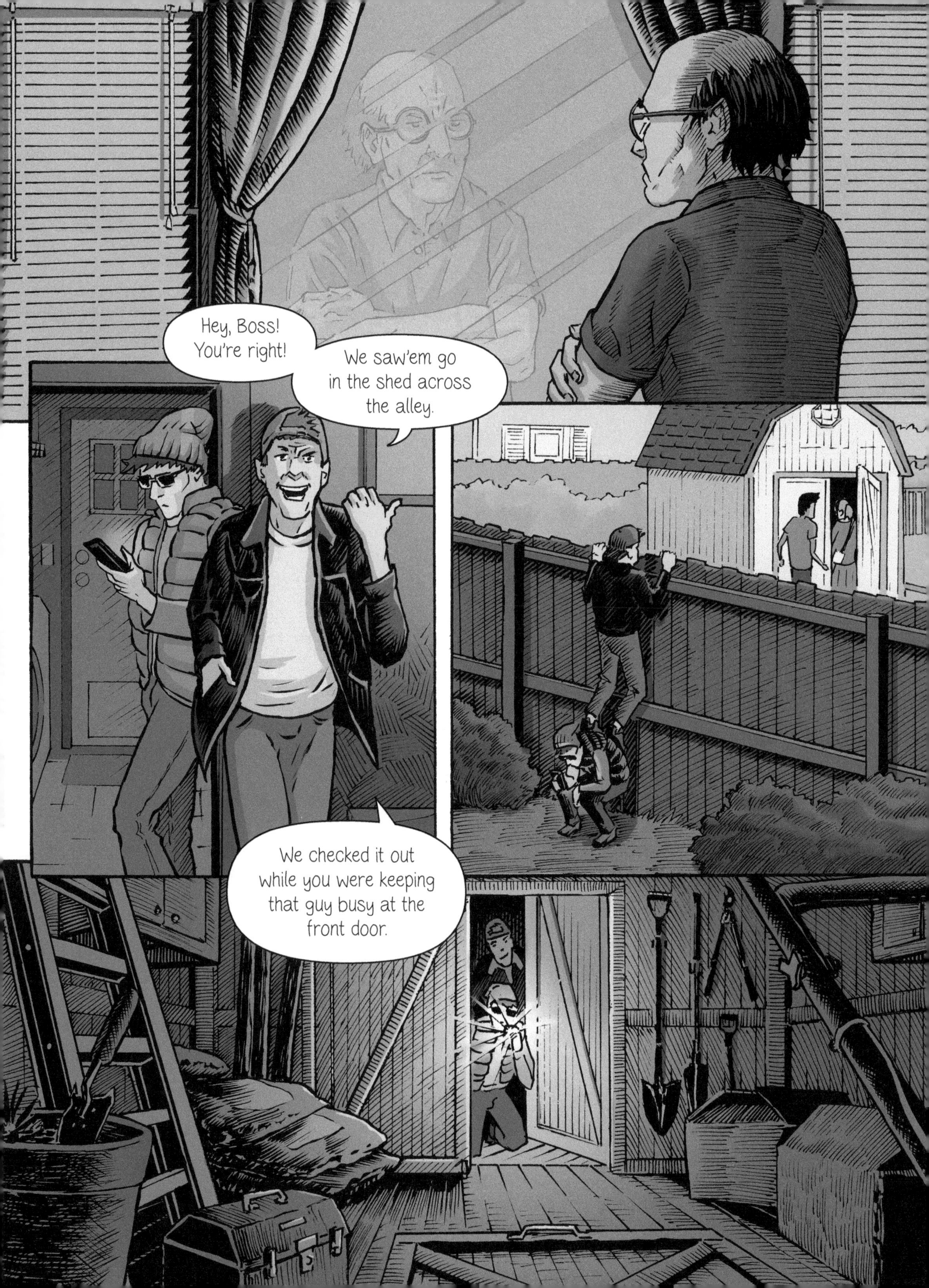
Hey, Boss! You're right!
We saw'em go in the shed across the alley.
We checked it out while you were keeping that guy busy at the front door.

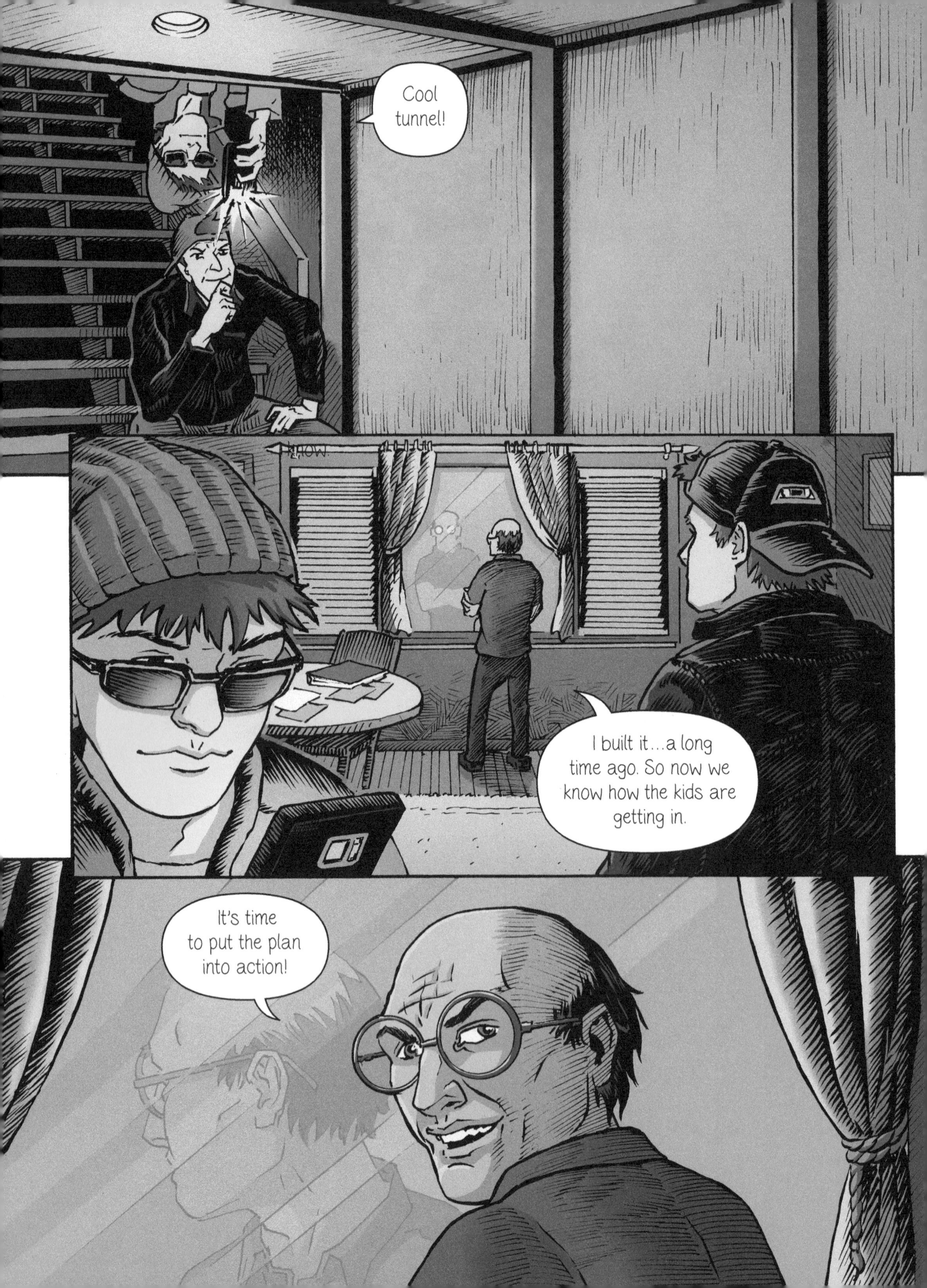
Cool tunnel!
I built it…a long time ago. So now we know how the kids are getting in.
It's time to put the plan into action!

DAY FOUR

Signs of the Covenant

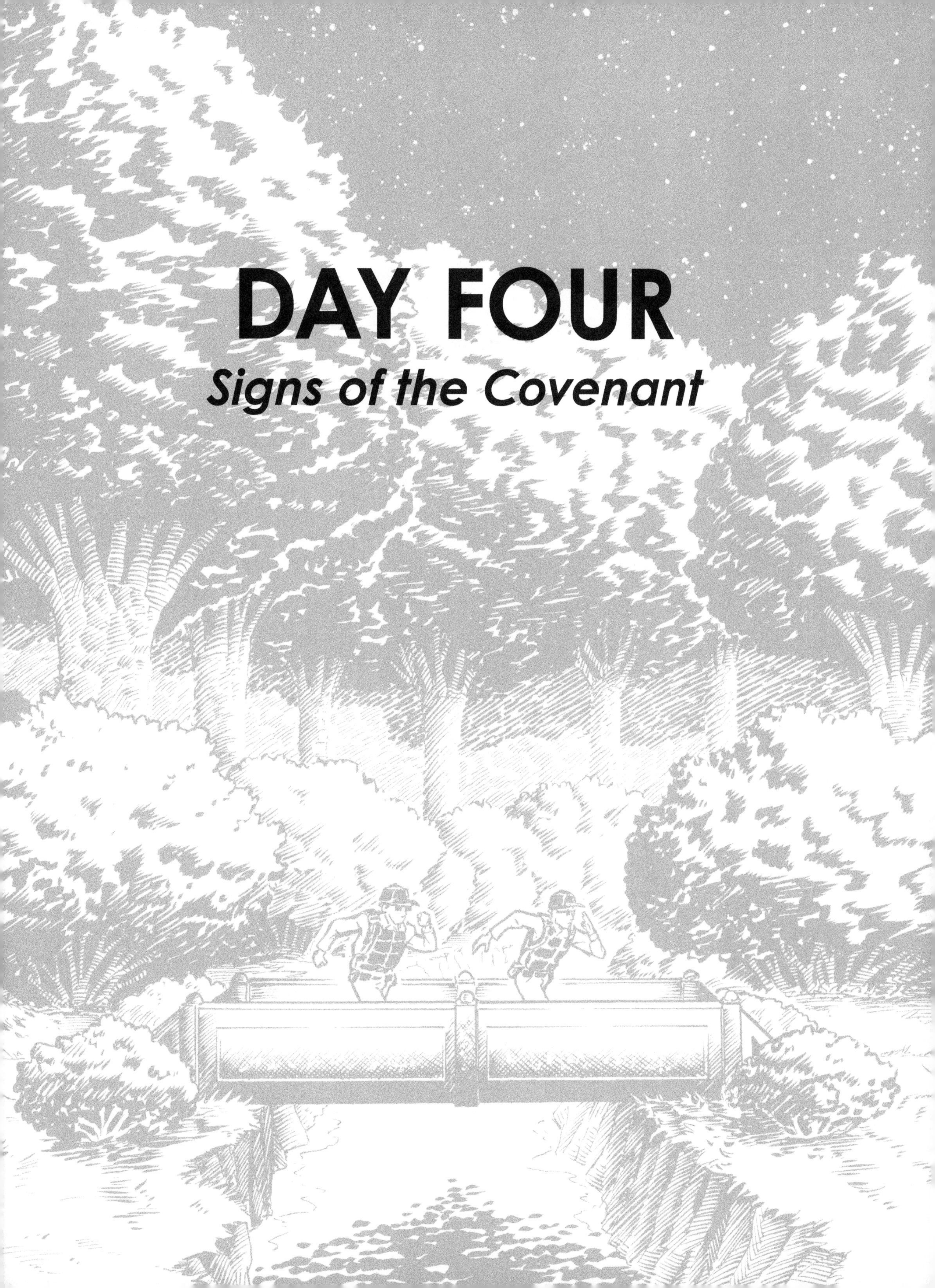

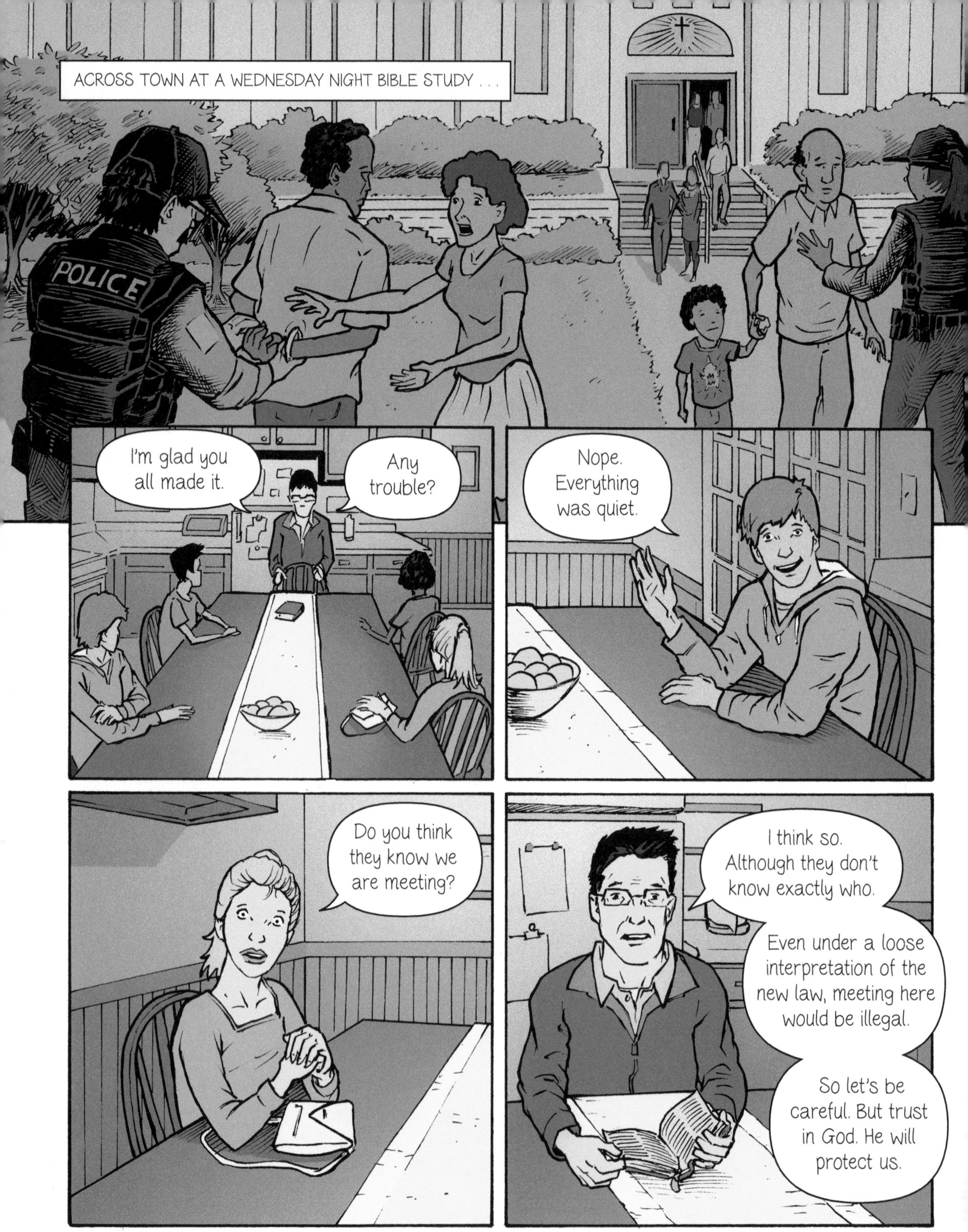
ACROSS TOWN AT A WEDNESDAY NIGHT BIBLE STUDY . . .
POLICE
I'm glad you all made it.
Any trouble?
Nope. Everything was quiet.
Do you think they know we are meeting?
I think so. Although they don't know exactly who.
Even under a loose interpretation of the new law, meeting here would be illegal.
So let's be careful. But trust in God. He will protect us.

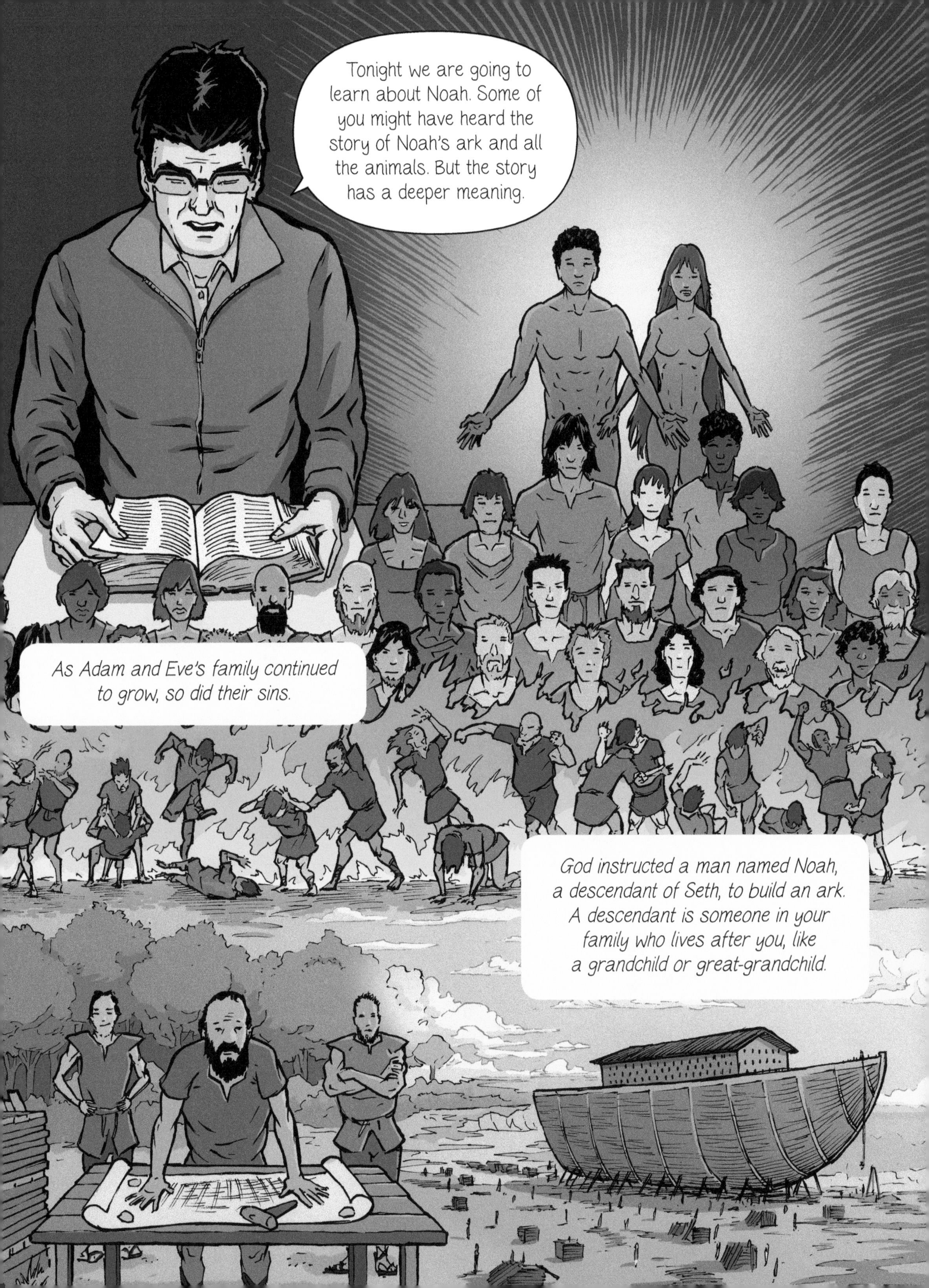
Tonight we are going to learn about Noah. Some of you might have heard the story of Noah's ark and all the animals. But the story has a deeper meaning.
As Adam and Eve's family continued to grow, so did their sins.
God instructed a man named Noah, a descendant of Seth, to build an ark. A descendant is someone in your family who lives after you, like a grandchild or great-grandchild.

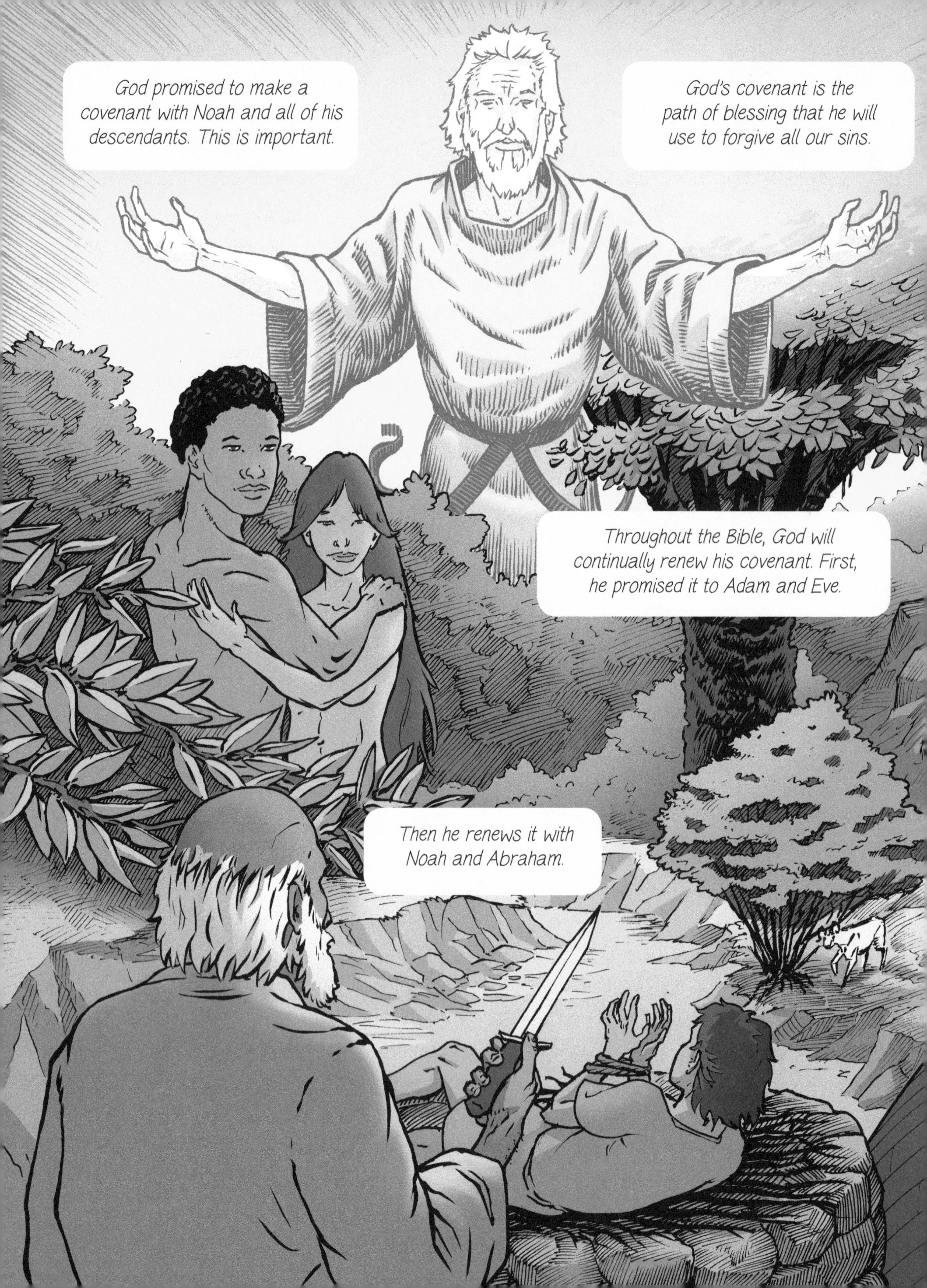
God promised to make a covenant with Noah and all of his descendants. This is important.
God's covenant is the path of blessing that he will use to forgive all our sins.
Throughout the Bible, God will continually renew his covenant. First, he promised it to Adam and Eve.
Then he renews it with Noah and Abraham.

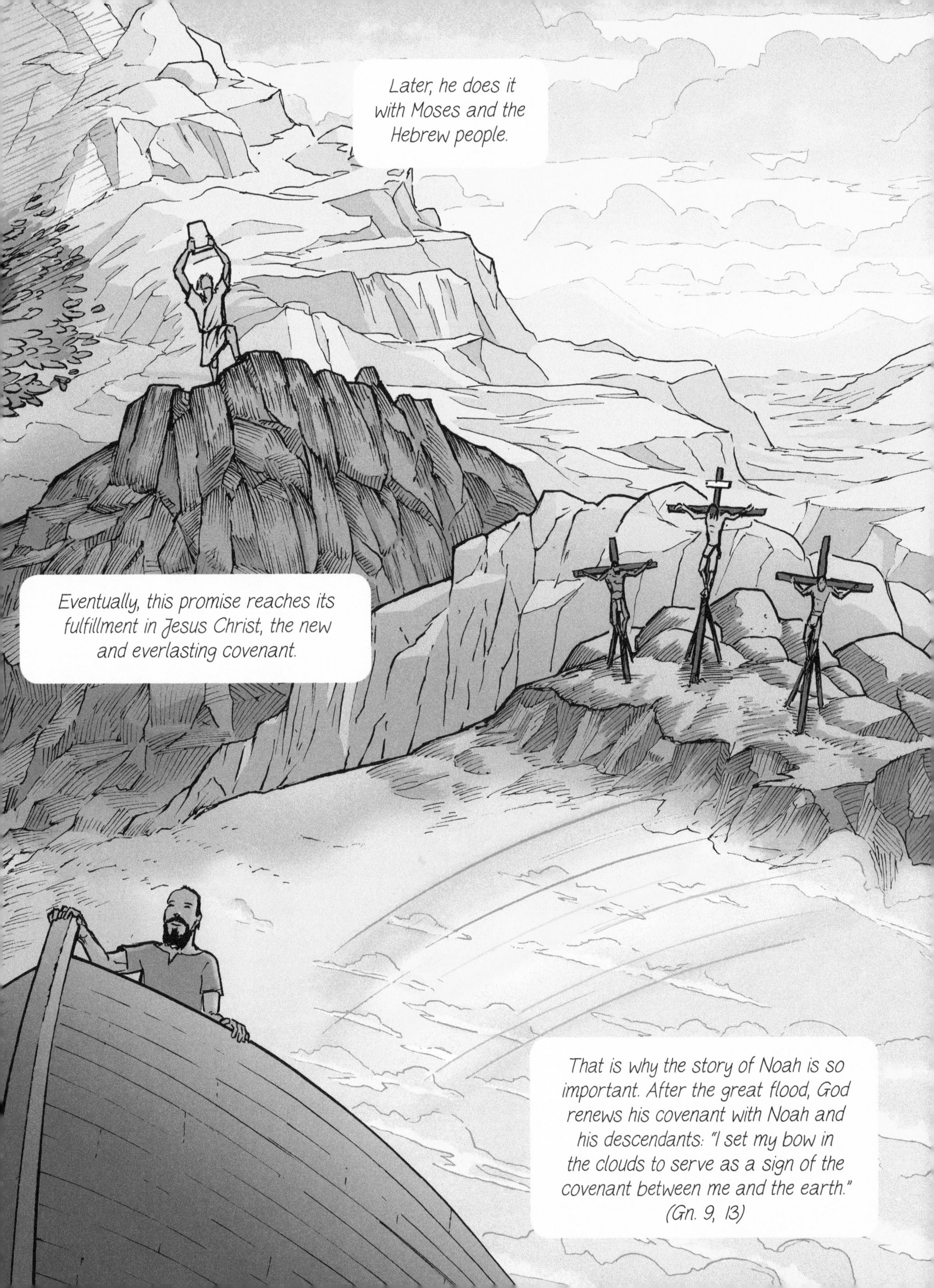
Later, he does it with Moses and the Hebrew people.
Eventually, this promise reaches its fulfillment in Jesus Christ, the new and everlasting covenant.
That is why the story of Noah is so important. After the great flood, God renews his covenant with Noah and his descendants: "I set my bow in the clouds to serve as a sign of the covenant between me and the earth." (Gn. 9, 13)

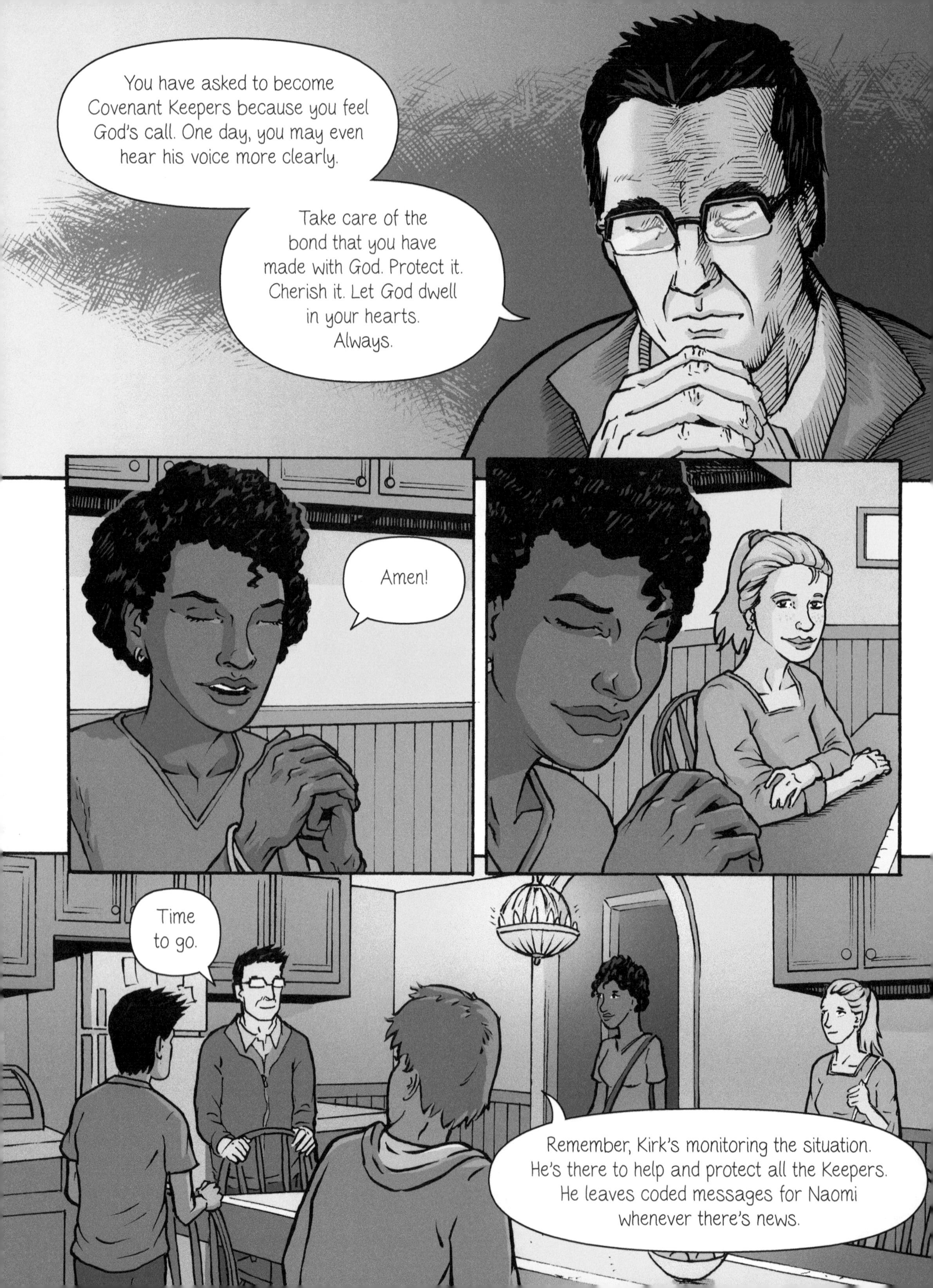
You have asked to become Covenant Keepers because you feel God's call. One day, you may even hear his voice more clearly.
Take care of the bond that you have made with God. Protect it. Cherish it. Let God dwell in your hearts. Always.
Amen!
Time to go.
Remember, Kirk's monitoring the situation. He's there to help and protect all the Keepers. He leaves coded messages for Naomi whenever there's news.

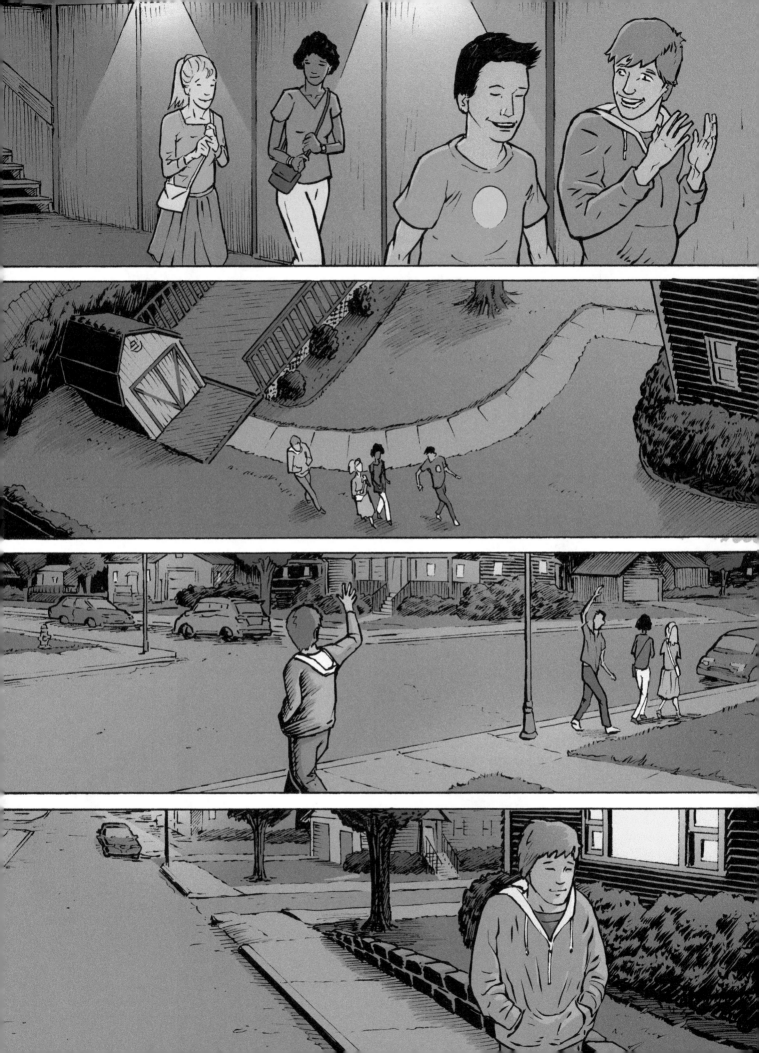

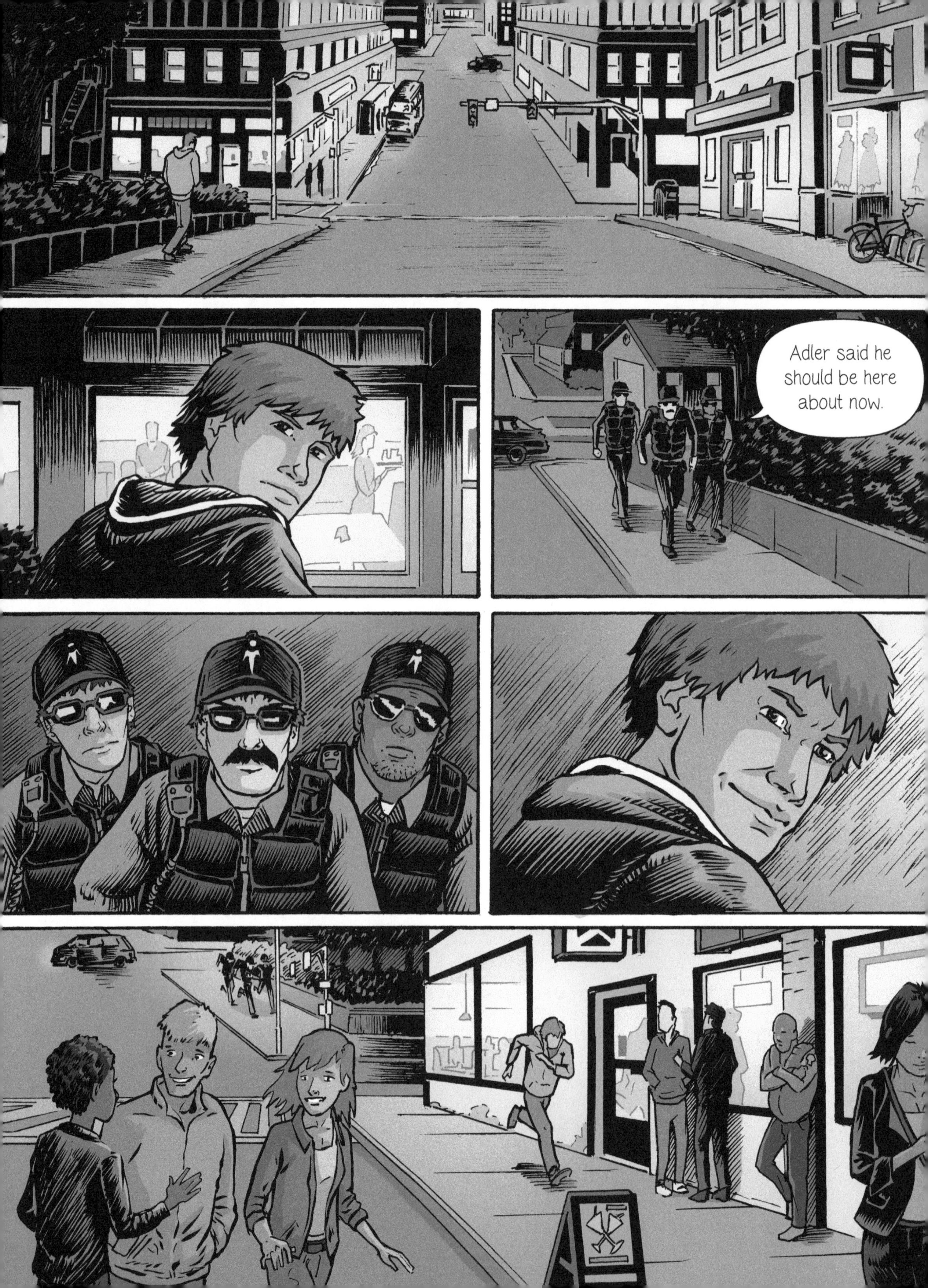
Adler said he should be here about now.

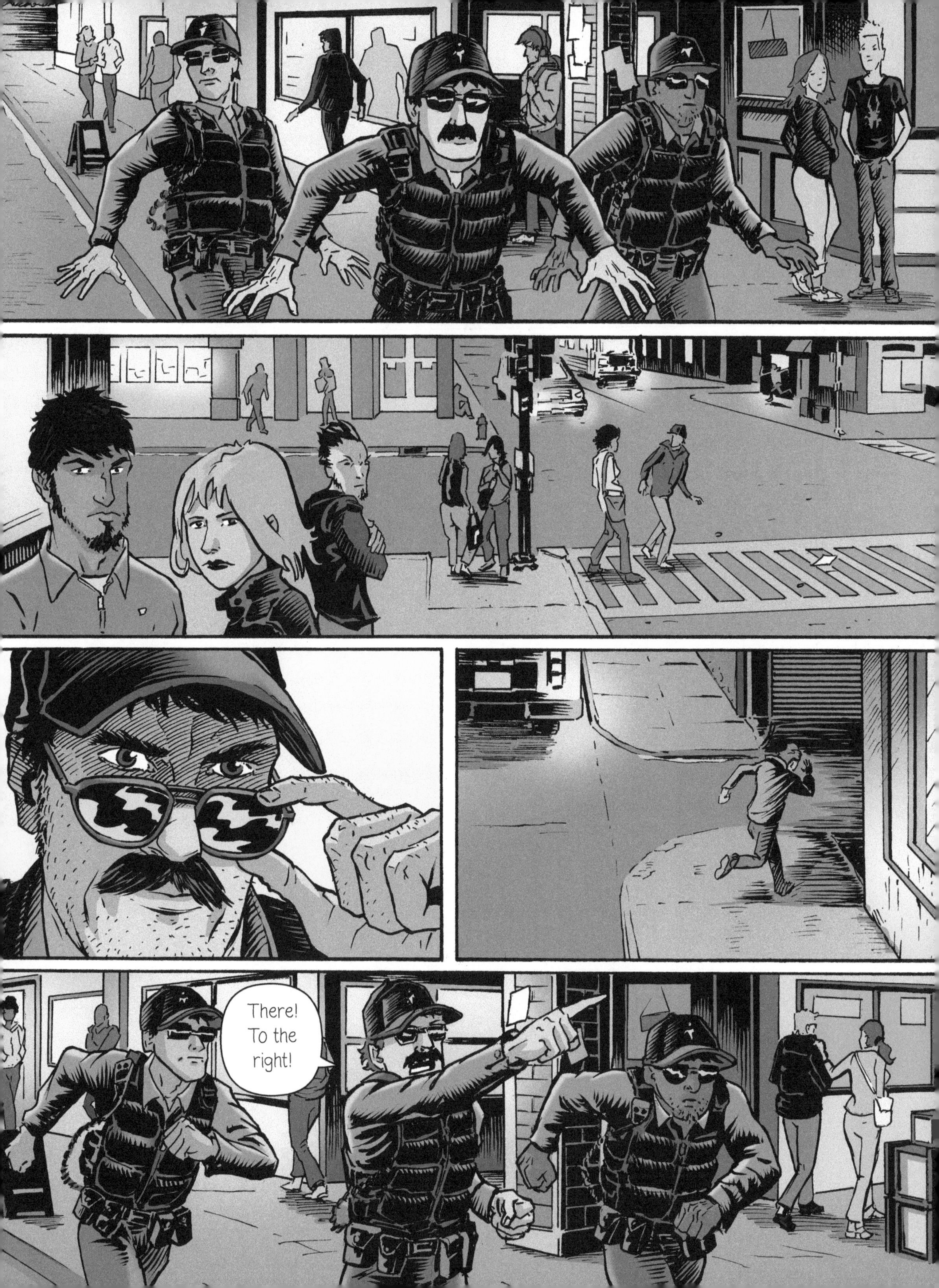
There!
To the
right!

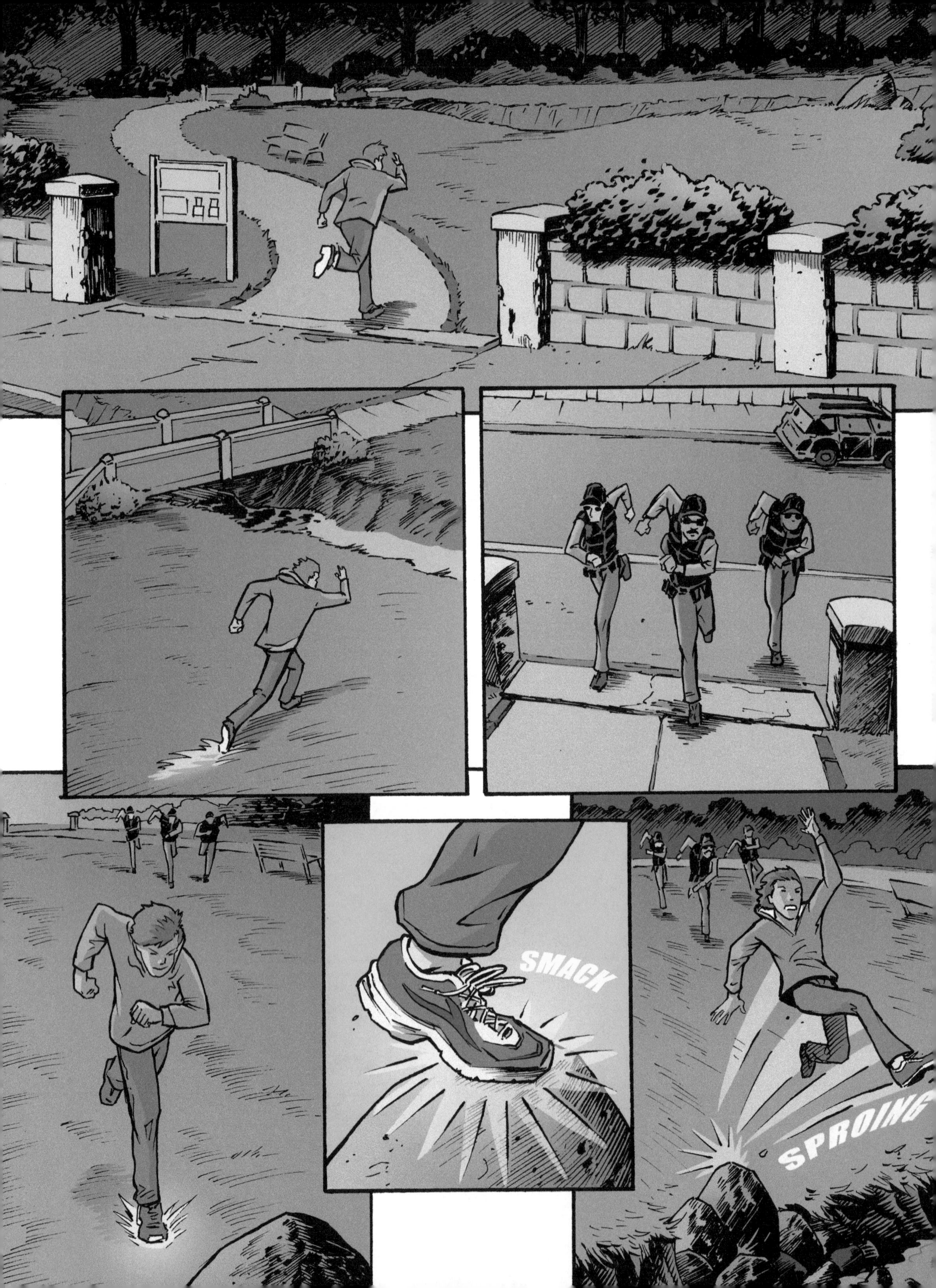
SMACK
SPROING

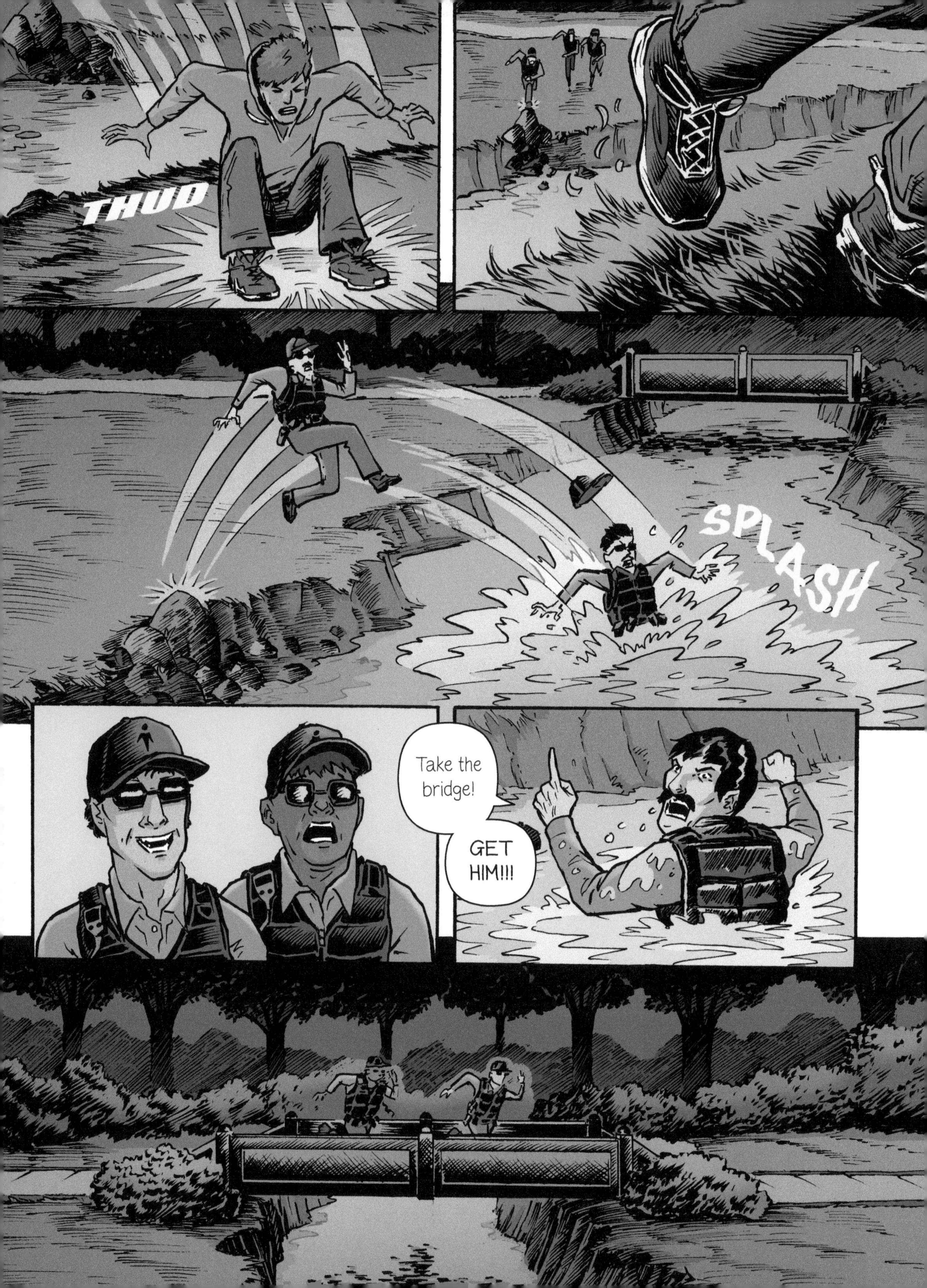
THUD
SPLASH
Take the bridge!
GET HIM!!!

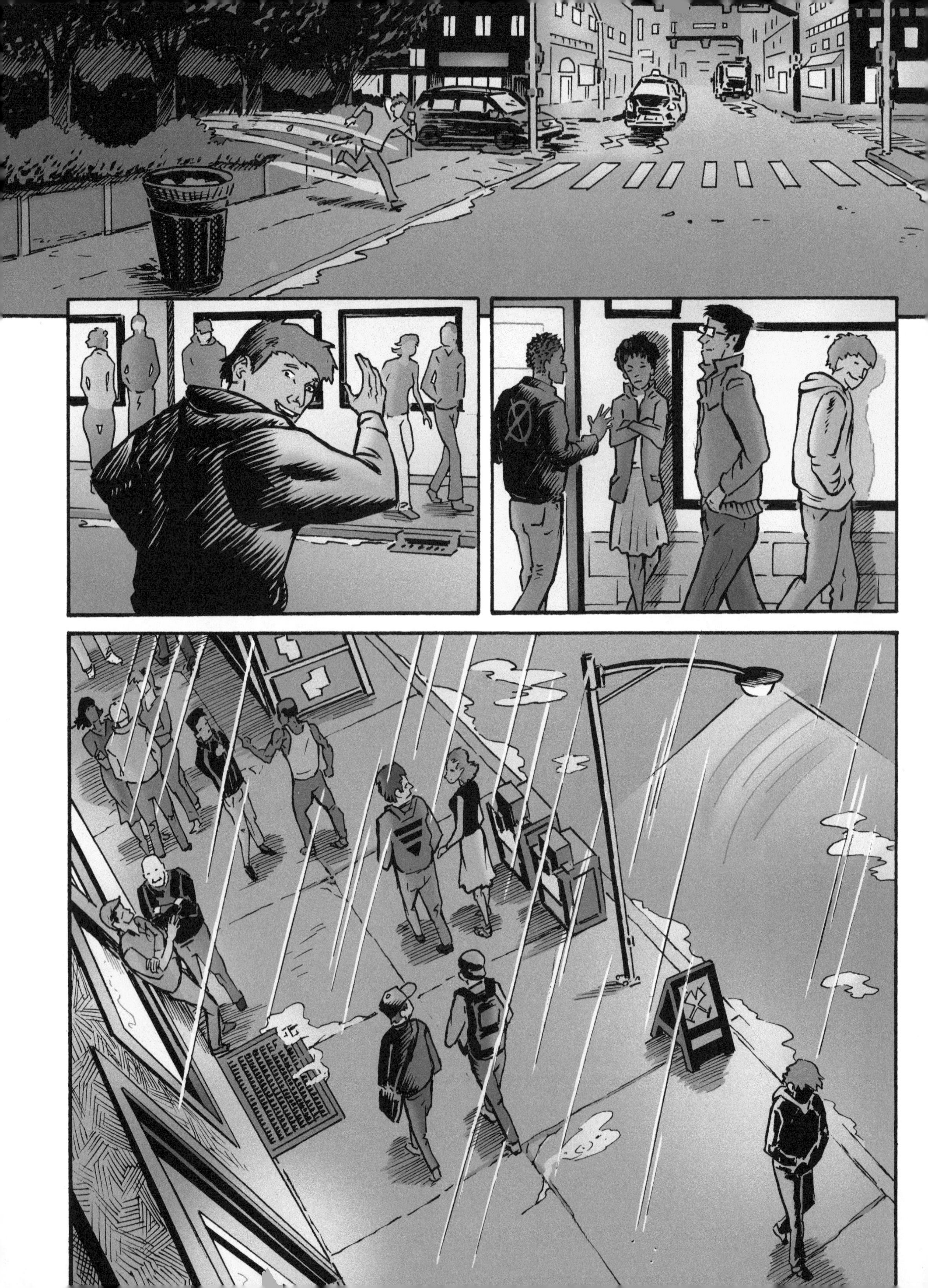

DAY FIVE

What's In a Name?

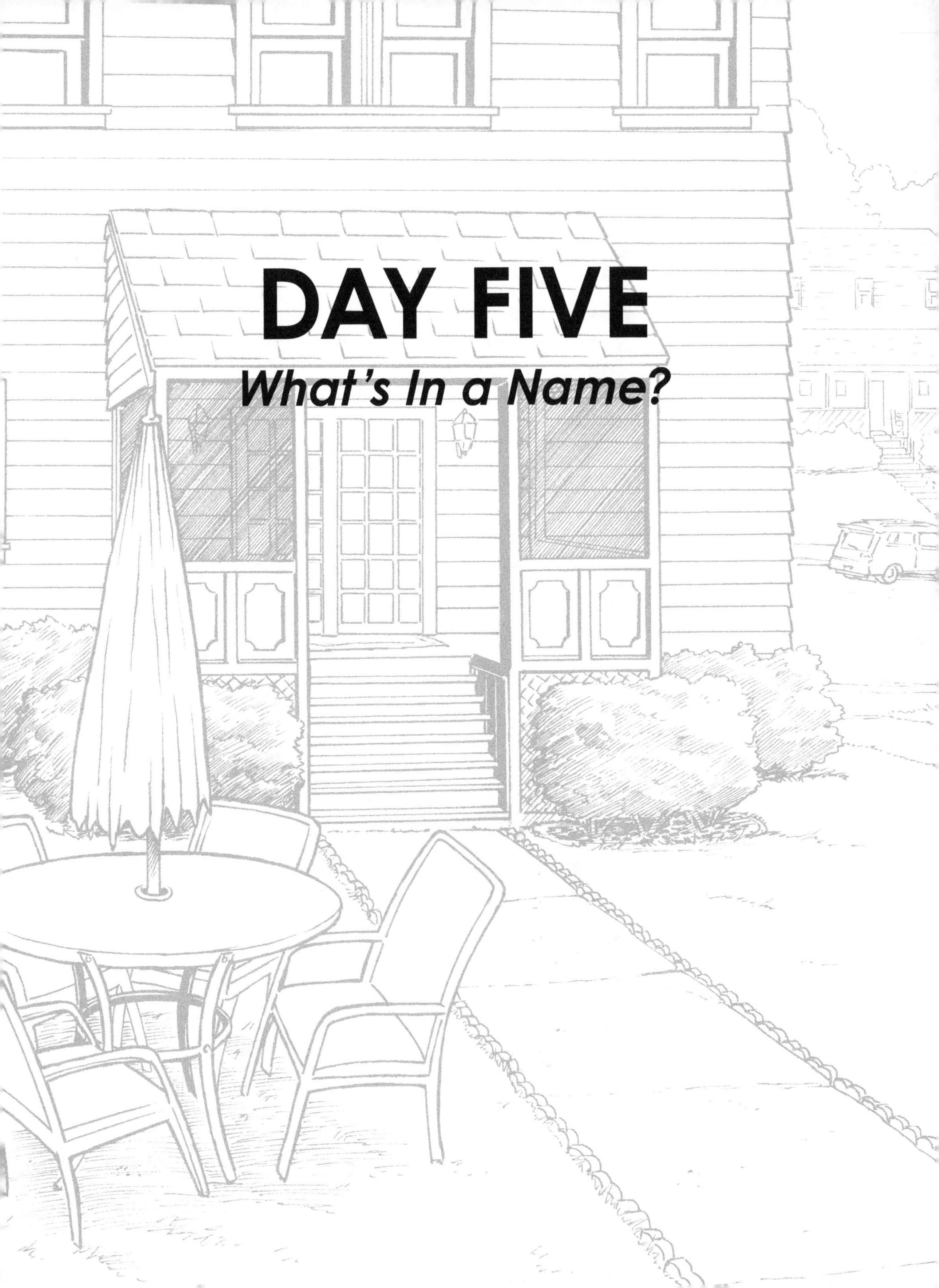

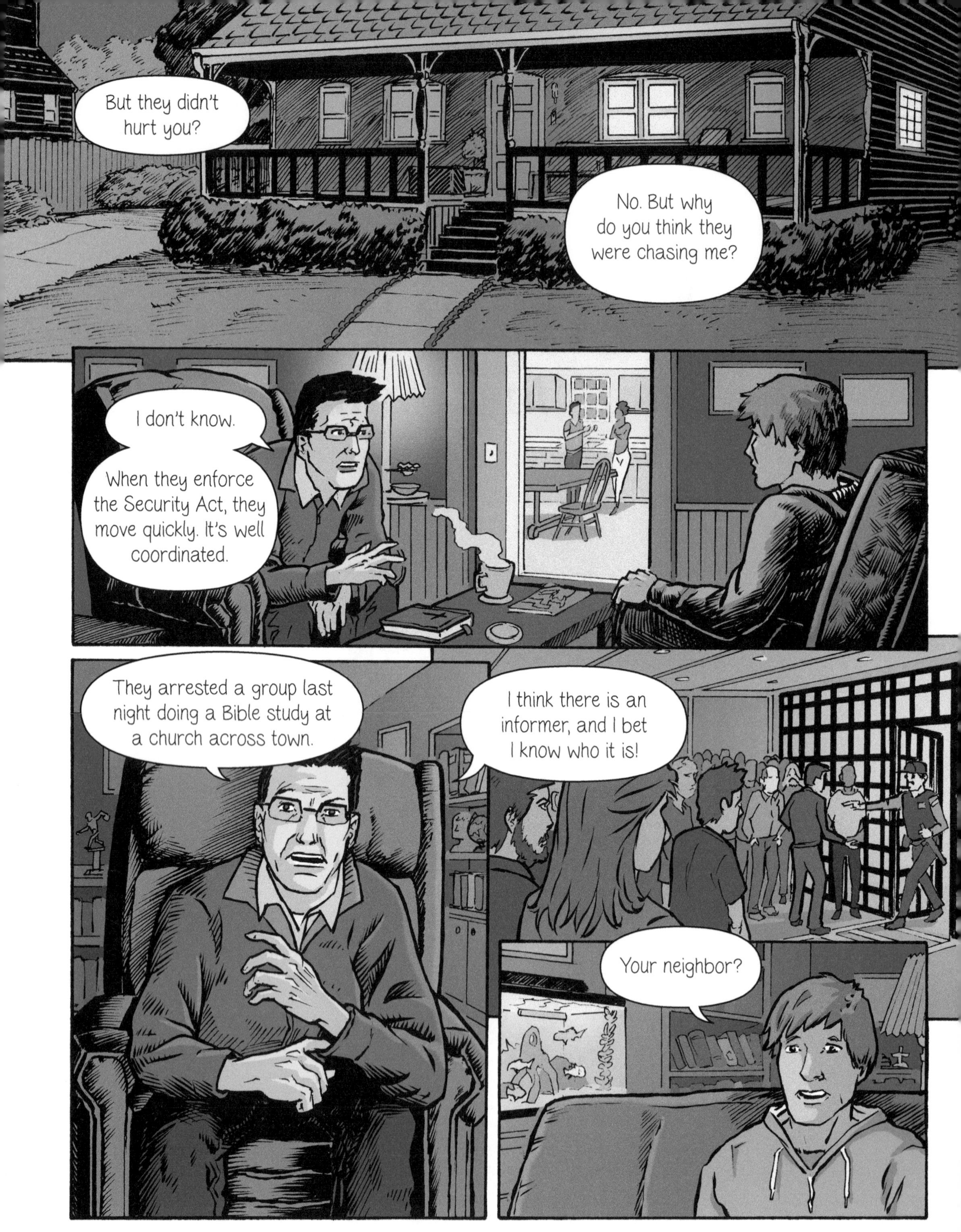
But they didn't hurt you?
No. But why do you think they were chasing me?
I don't know.
When they enforce the Security Act, they move quickly. It's well coordinated.
They arrested a group last night doing a Bible study at a church across town.
I think there is an informer, and I bet I know who it is!
Your neighbor?

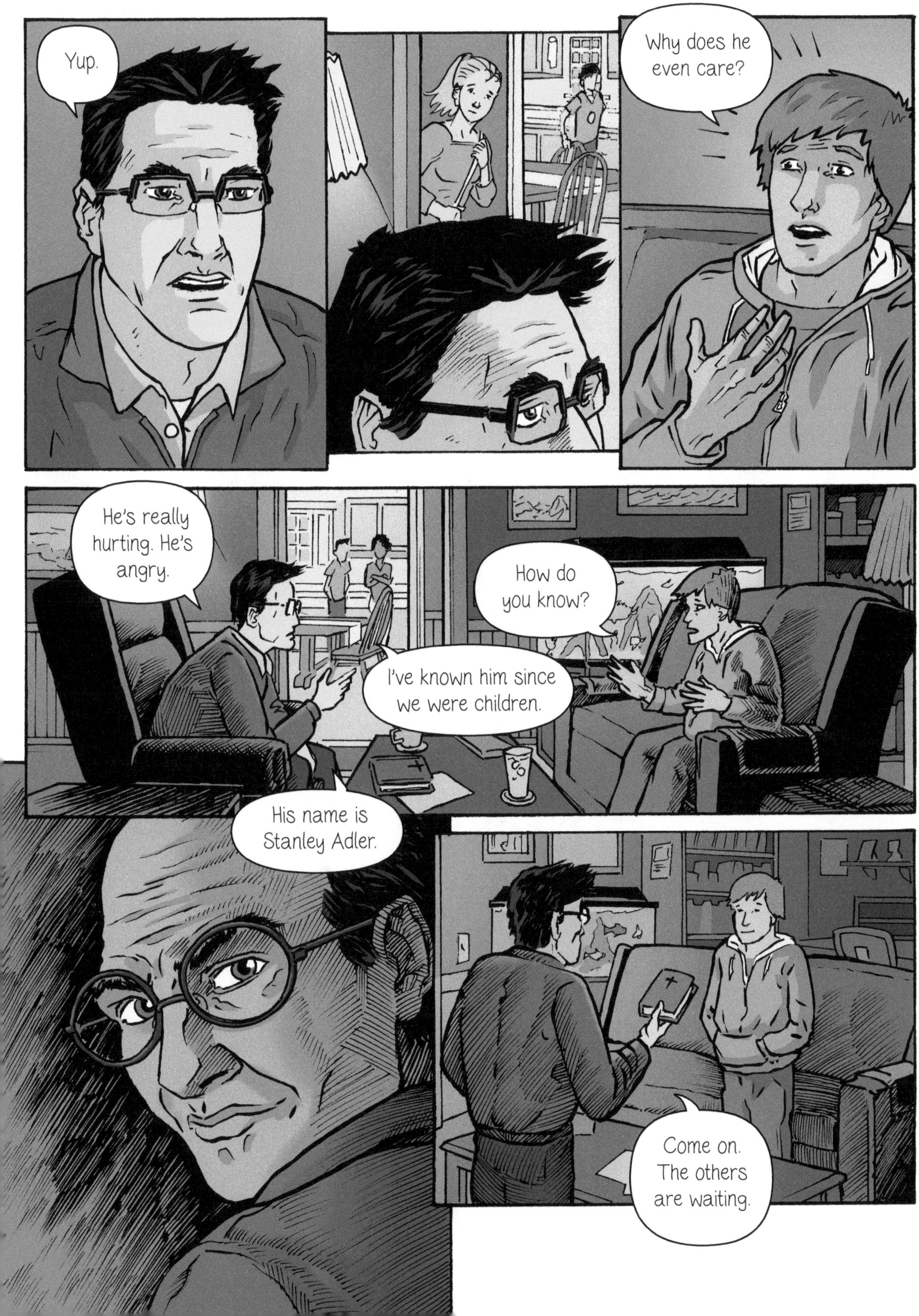

Yup.
Why does he even care?
He's really hurting. He's angry.
How do you know?
I've known him since we were children.
His name is Stanley Adler.
Come on. The others are waiting.

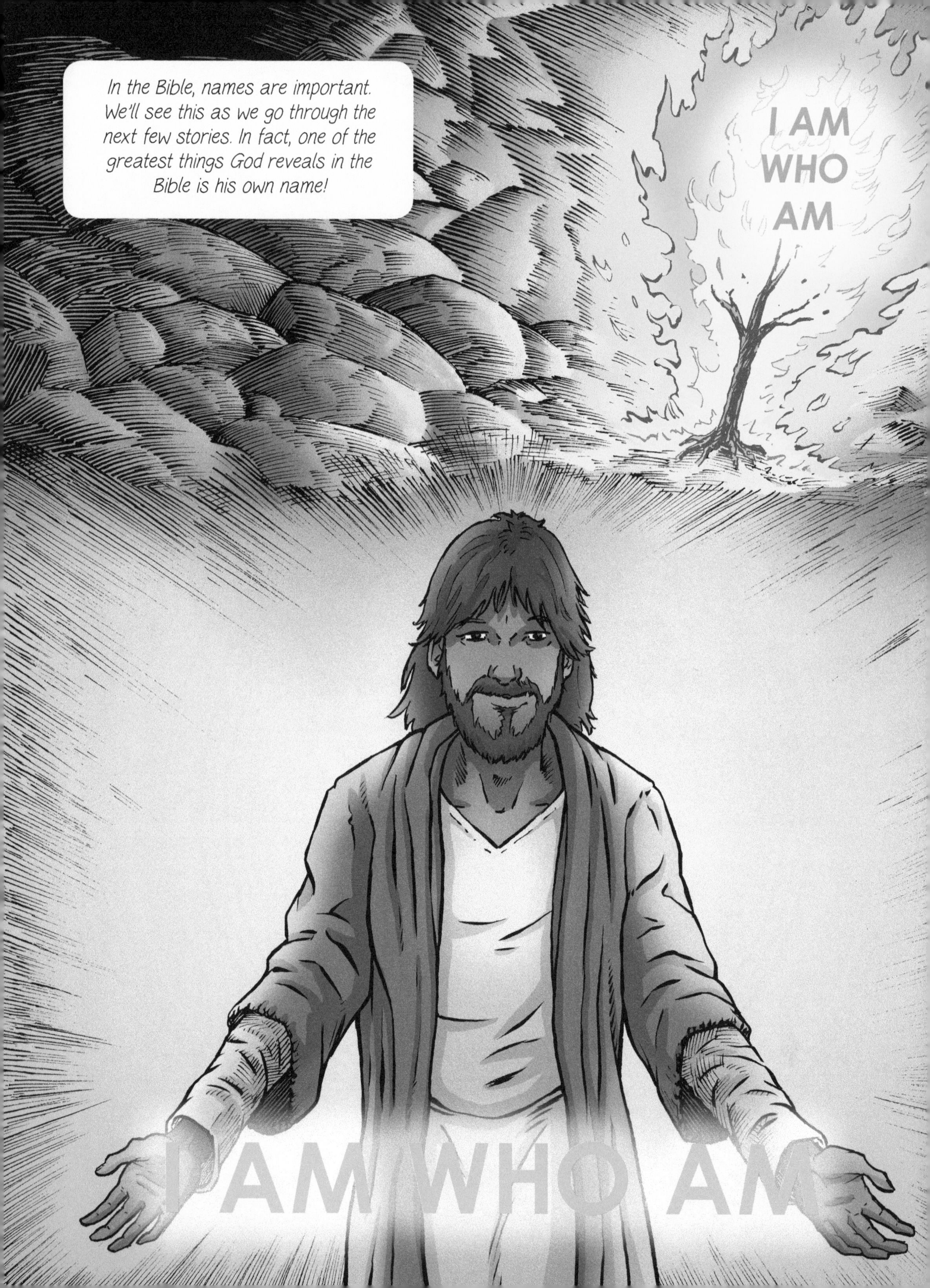
In the Bible, names are important. We'll see this as we go through the next few stories. In fact, one of the greatest things God reveals in the Bible is his own name!
I AM WHO AM
I AM WHO AM

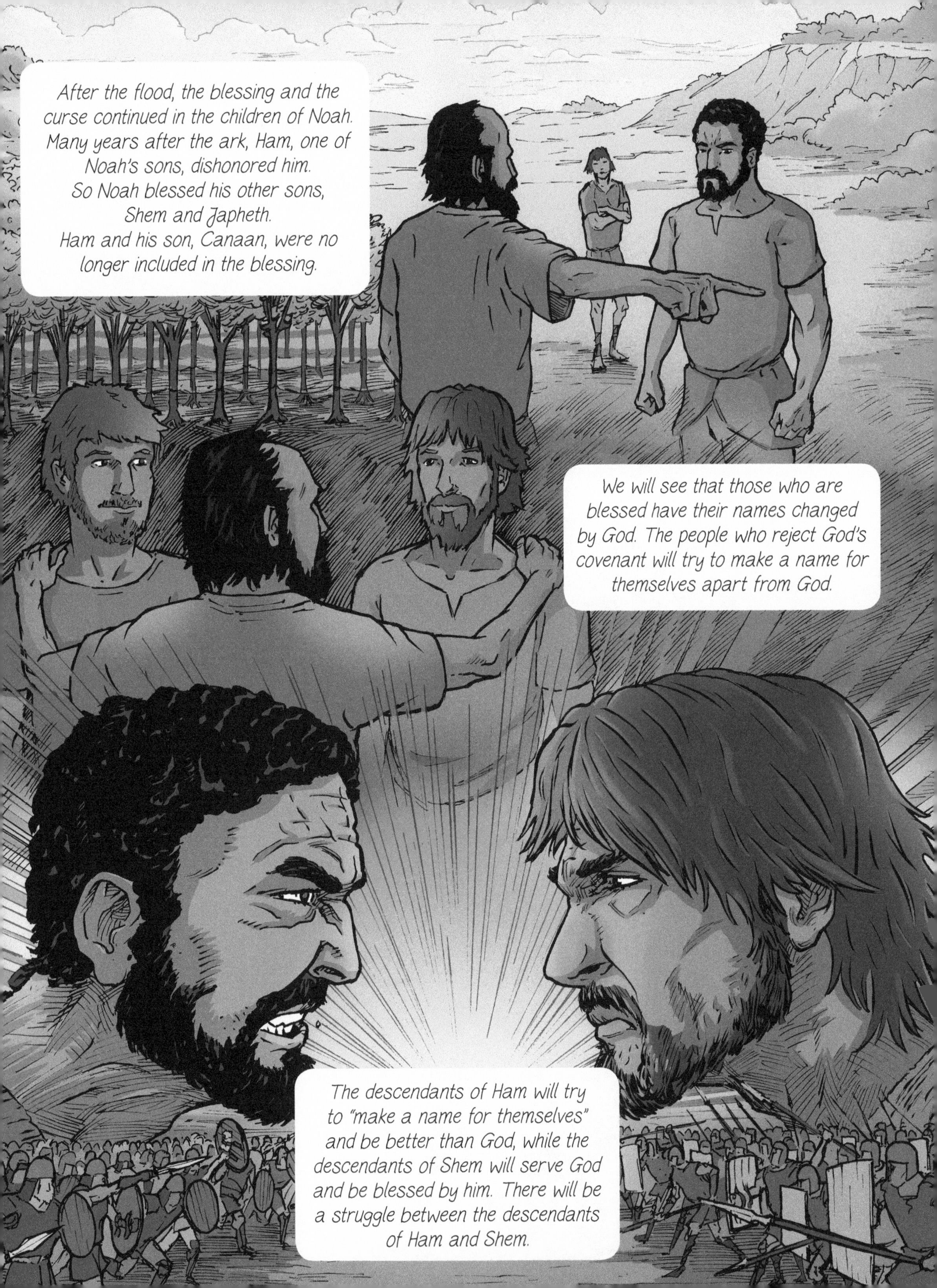
After the flood, the blessing and the curse continued in the children of Noah. Many years after the ark, Ham, one of Noah's sons, dishonored him. So Noah blessed his other sons, Shem and Japheth. Ham and his son, Canaan, were no longer included in the blessing.
We will see that those who are blessed have their names changed by God. The people who reject God's covenant will try to make a name for themselves apart from God.
The descendants of Ham will try to "make a name for themselves" and be better than God, while the descendants of Shem will serve God and be blessed by him. There will be a struggle between the descendants of Ham and Shem.

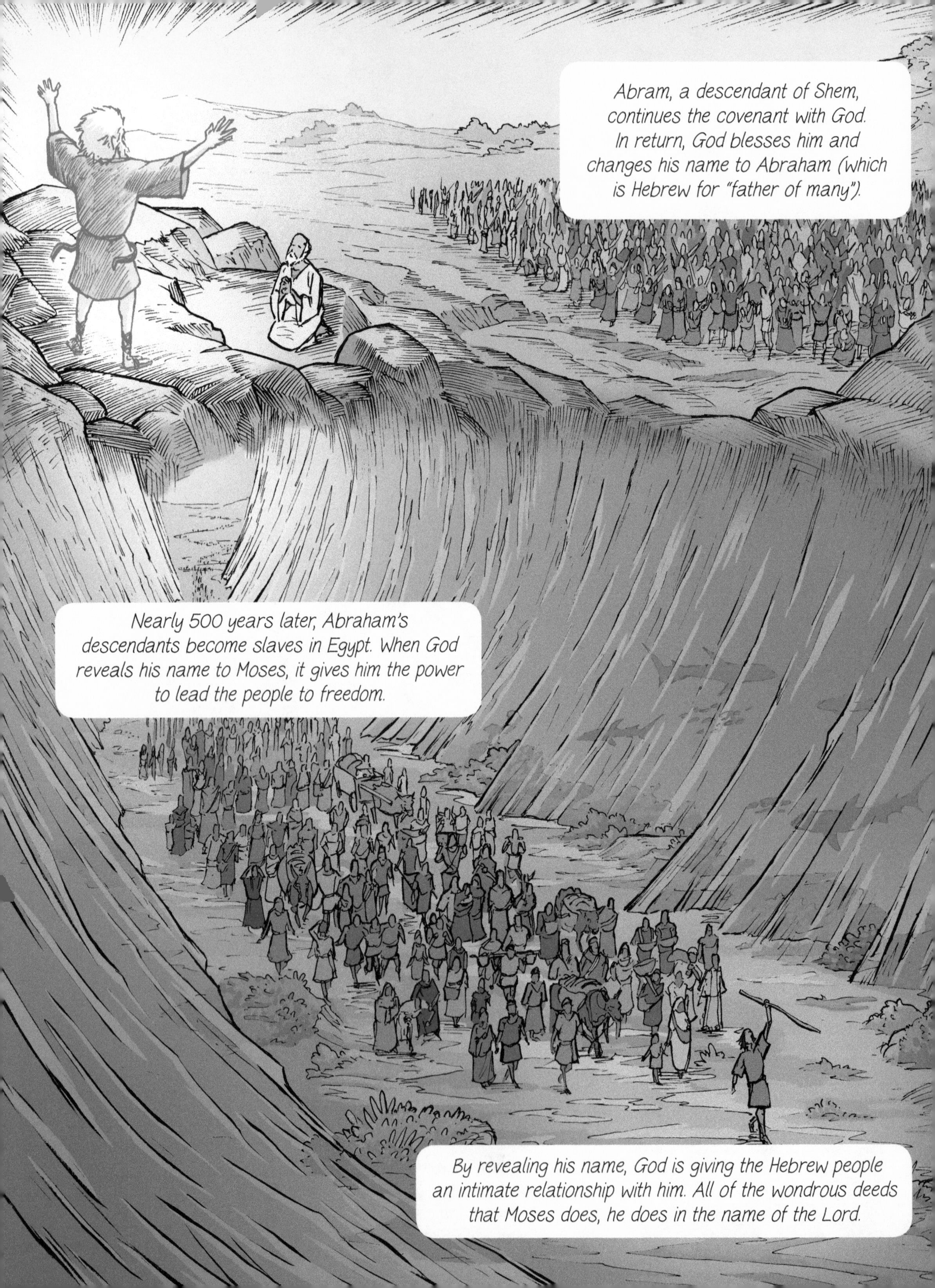
Abram, a descendant of Shem, continues the covenant with God. In return, God blesses him and changes his name to Abraham (which is Hebrew for "father of many").
Nearly 500 years later, Abraham's descendants become slaves in Egypt. When God reveals his name to Moses, it gives him the power to lead the people to freedom.
By revealing his name, God is giving the Hebrew people an intimate relationship with him. All of the wondrous deeds that Moses does, he does in the name of the Lord.

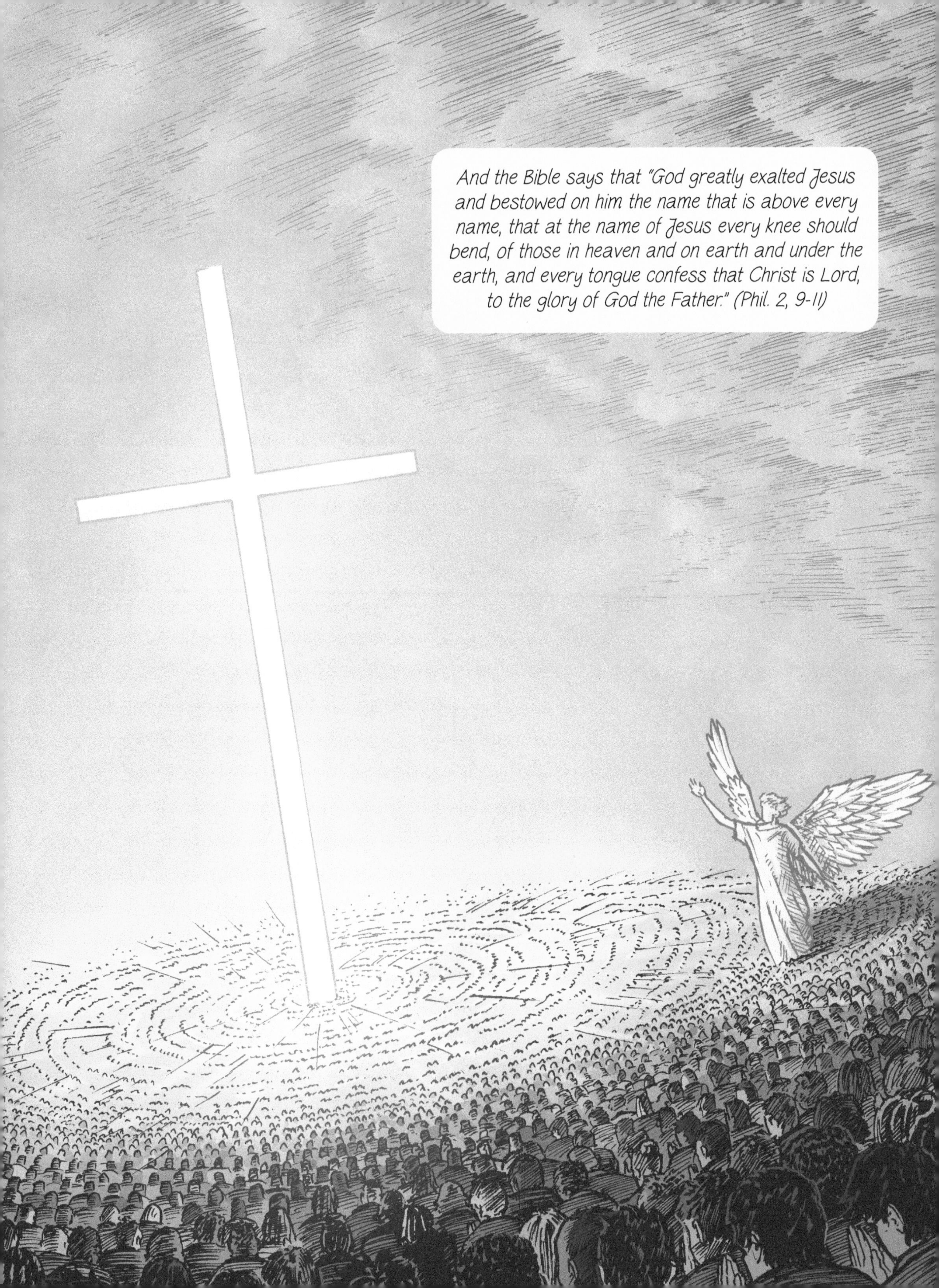
And the Bible says that "God greatly exalted Jesus and bestowed on him the name that is above every name, that at the name of Jesus every knee should bend, of those in heaven and on earth and under the earth, and every tongue confess that Christ is Lord, to the glory of God the Father." (Phil. 2, 9-11)

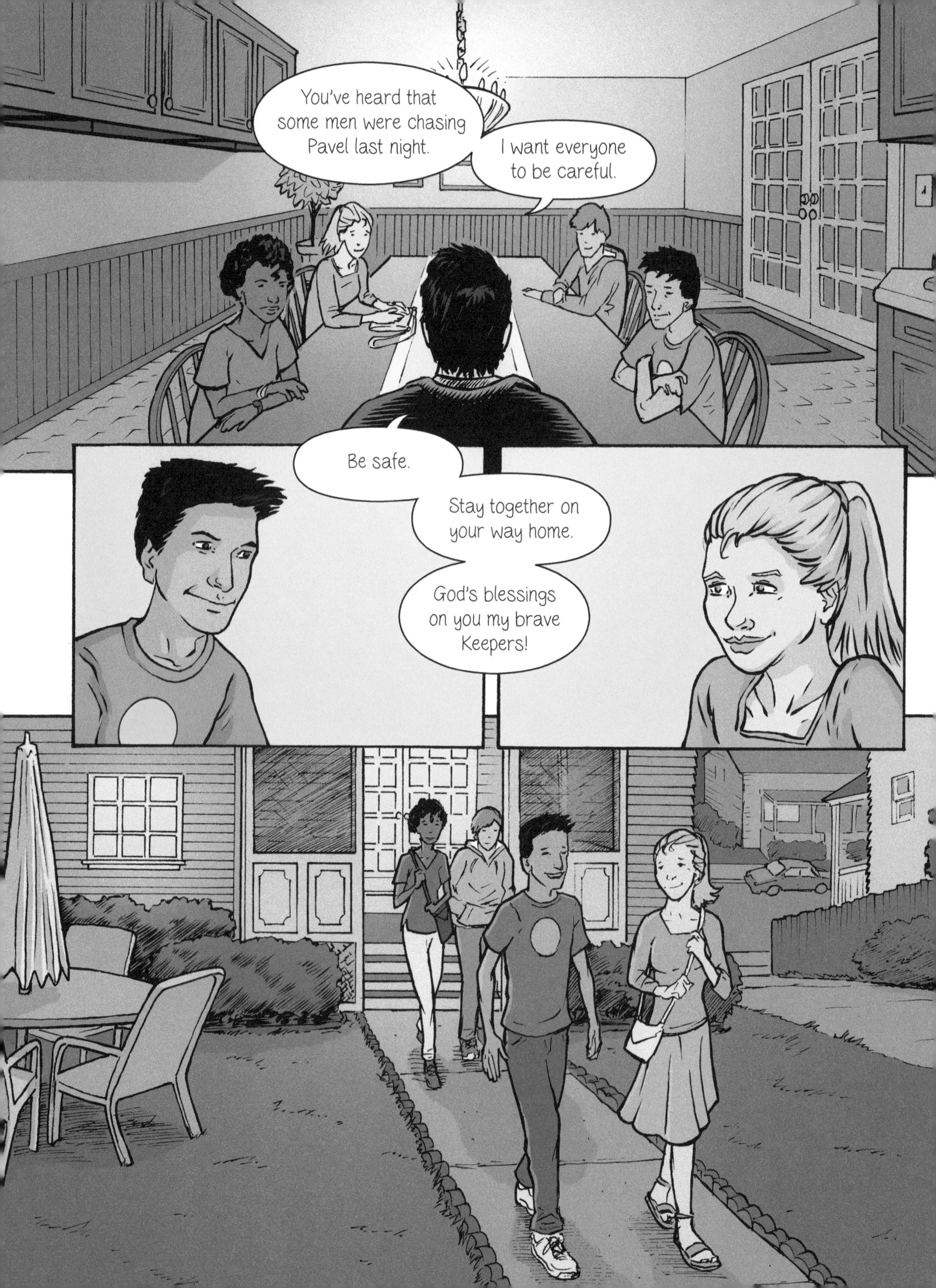
You've heard that some men were chasing Pavel last night.
I want everyone to be careful.
Be safe.
Stay together on your way home.
God's blessings on you my brave Keepers!

DAY SIX

Babel

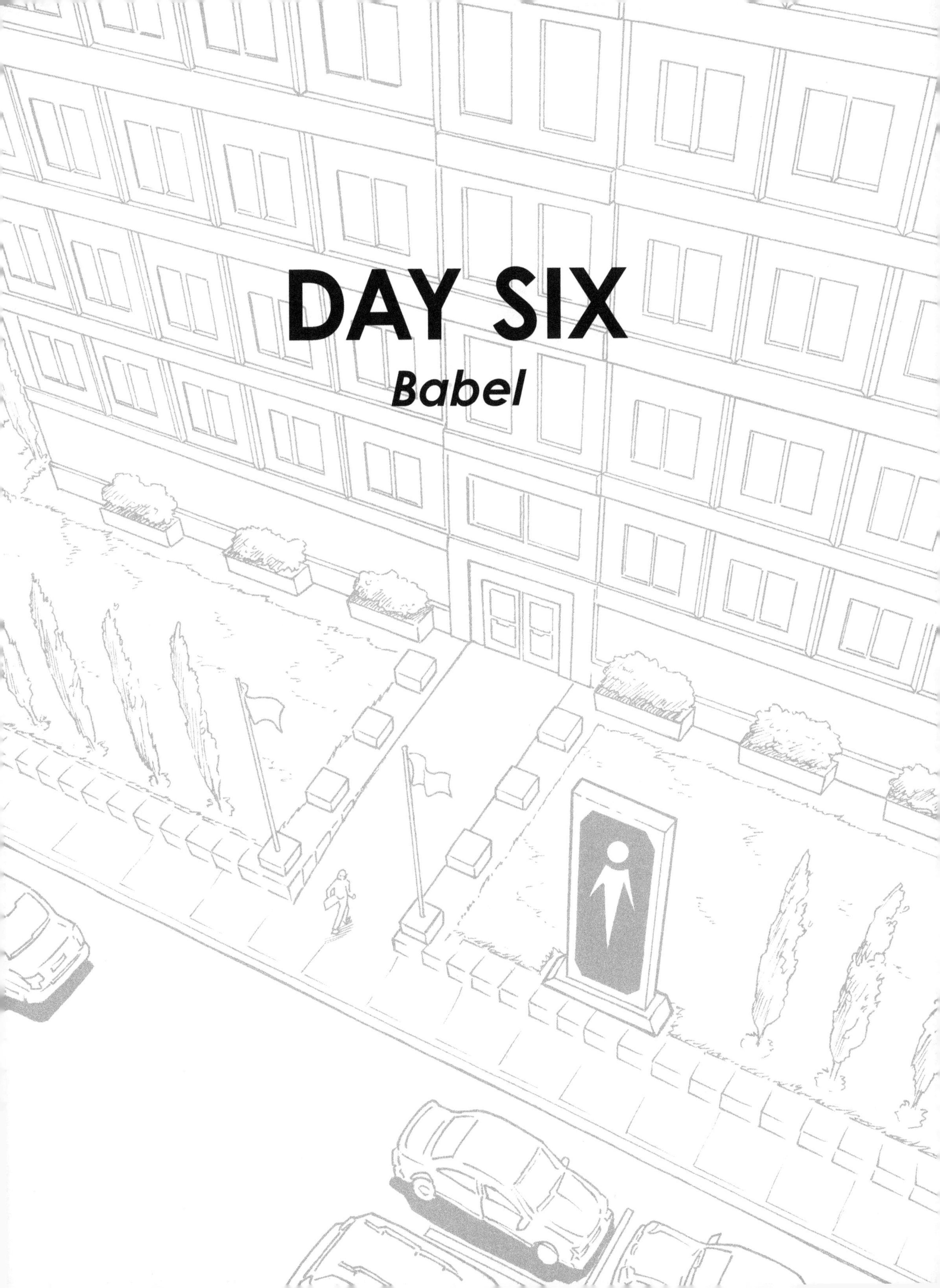

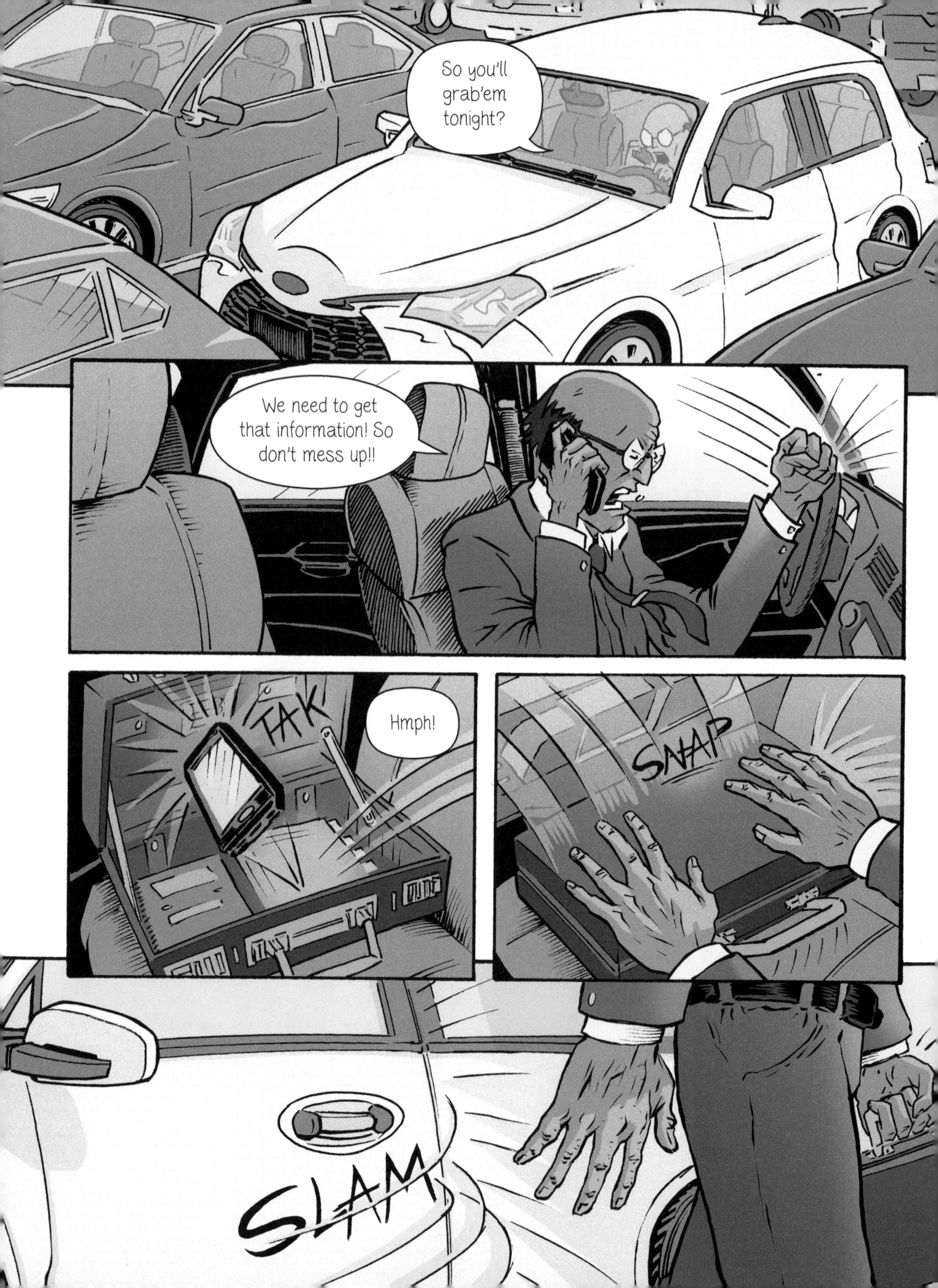
So you'll grab'em tonight?
We need to get that information! So don't mess up!!
TAK
Hmph!
SNAP
SLAM

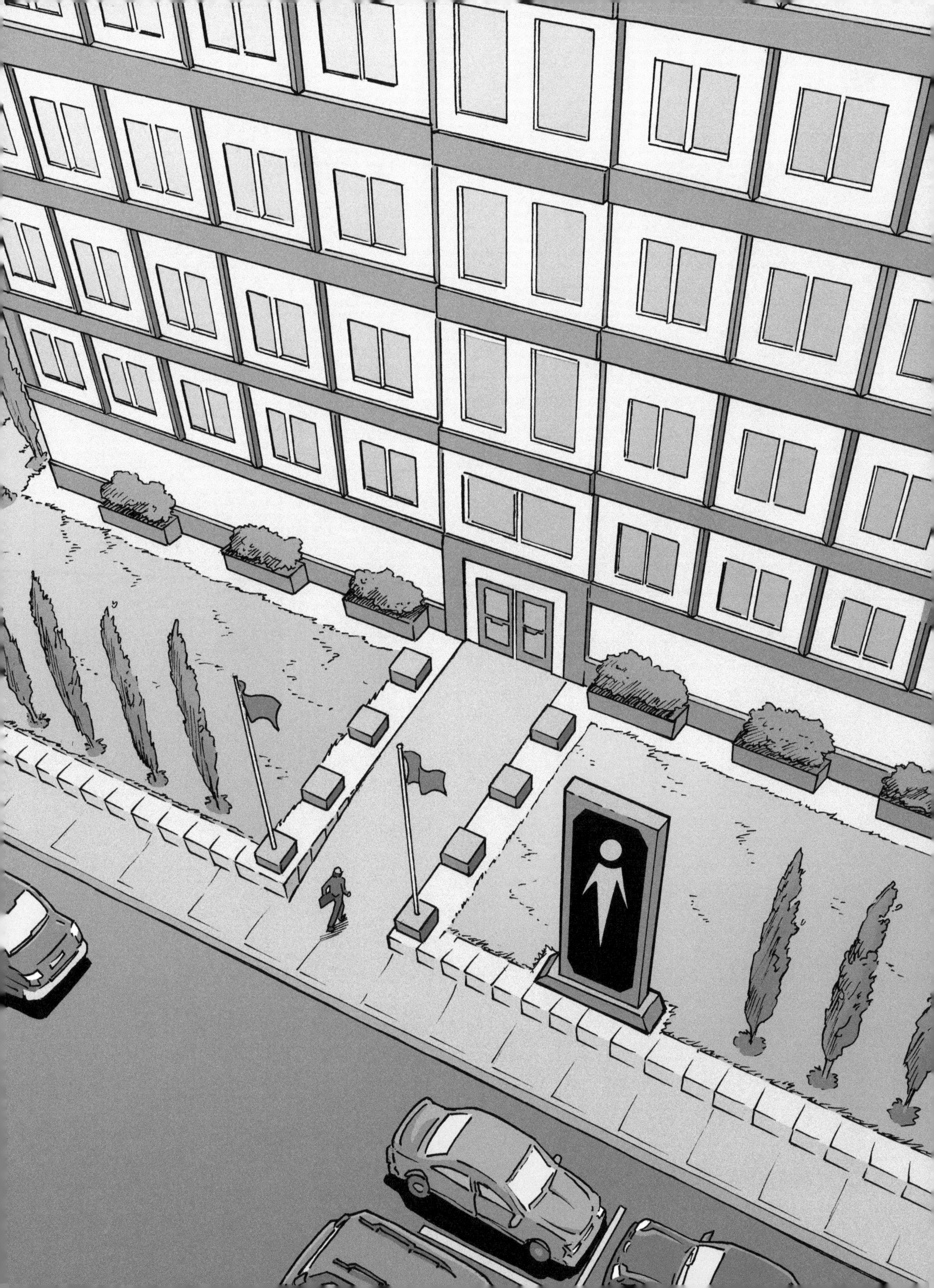

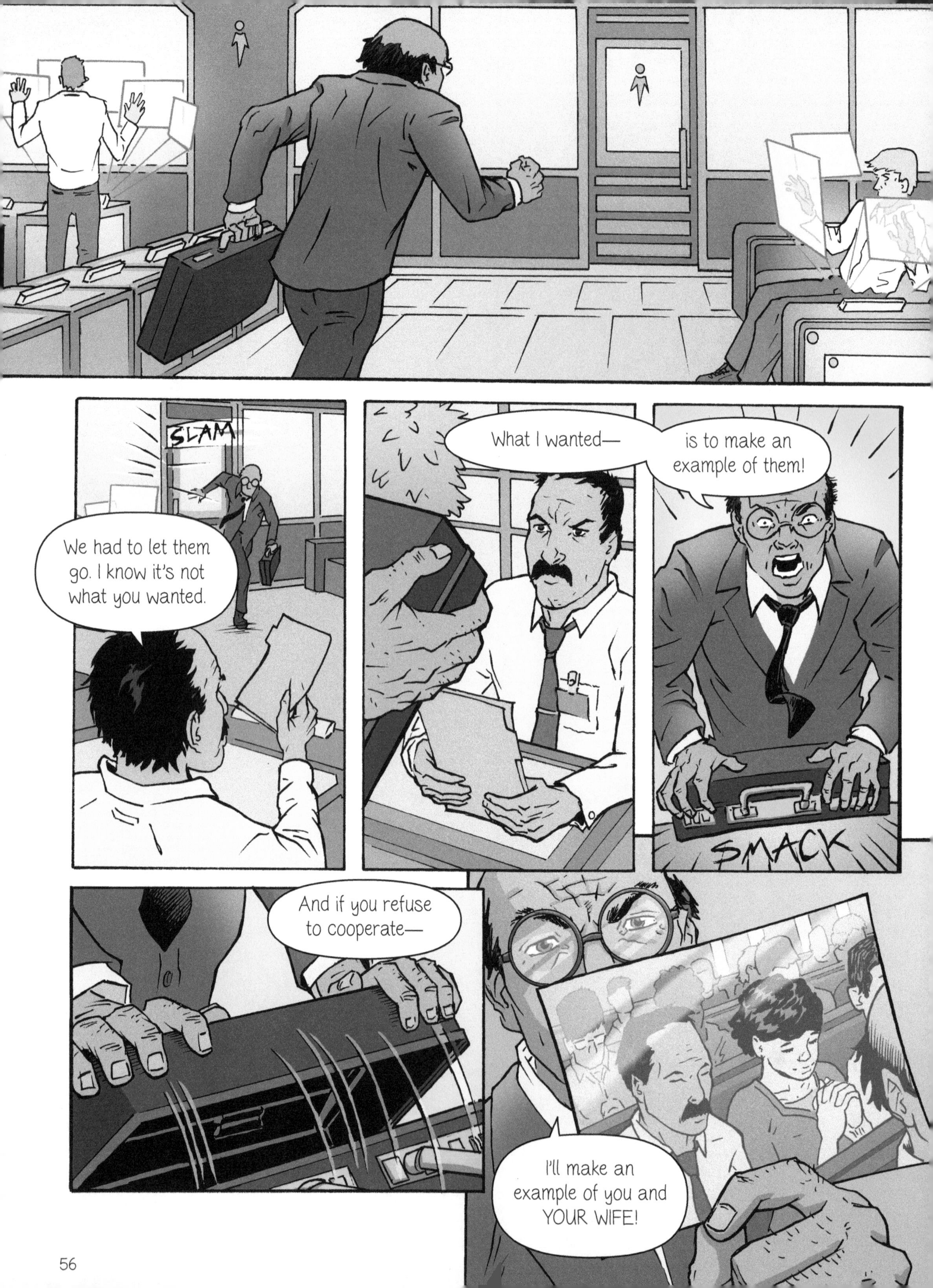
SLAM
We had to let them go. I know it's not what you wanted.
What I wanted—
is to make an example of them!
SMACK
And if you refuse to cooperate—
I'll make an example of you and YOUR WIFE!

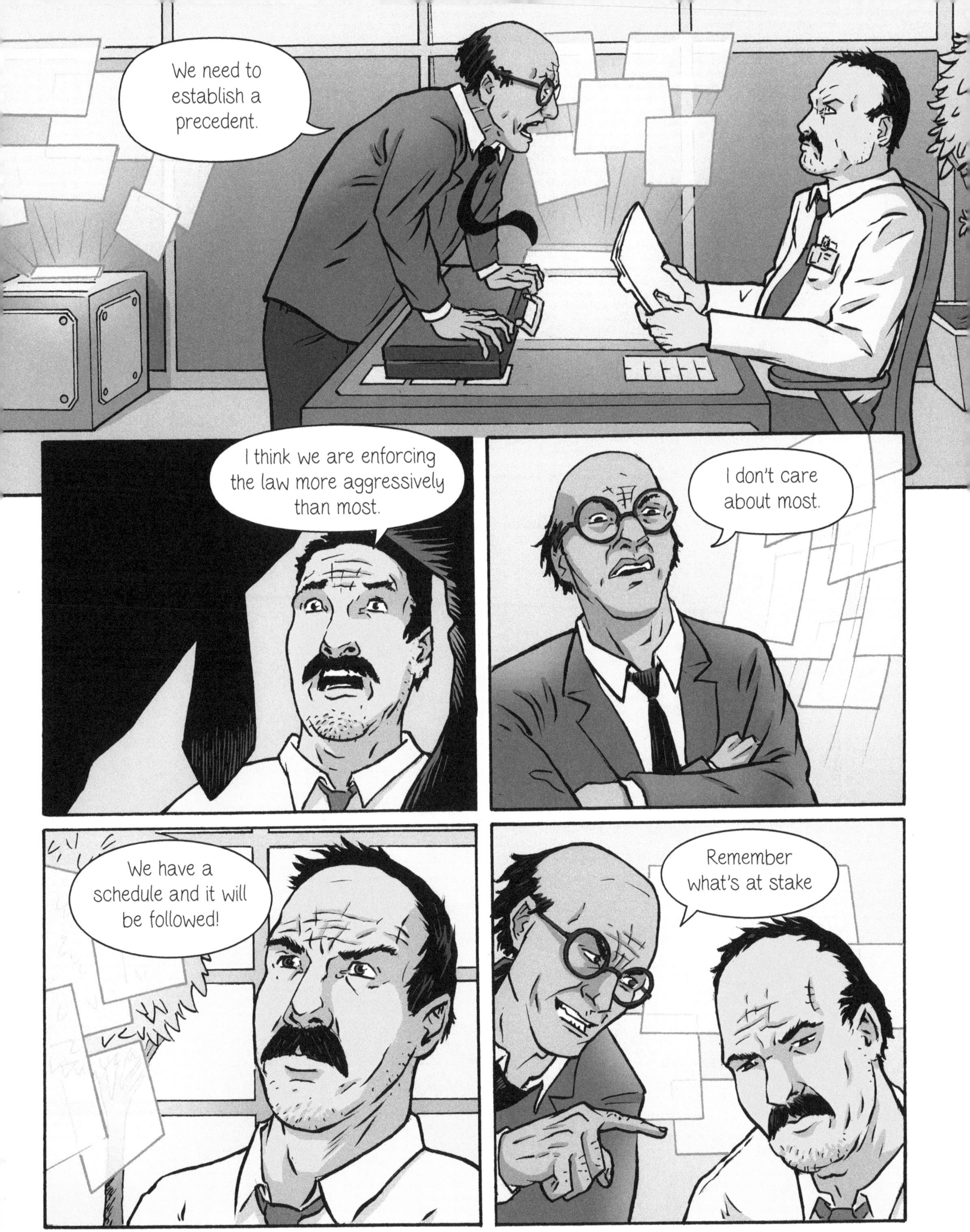
We need to establish a precedent.
I think we are enforcing the law more aggressively than most.
I don't care about most.
We have a schedule and it will be followed!
Remember what's at stake

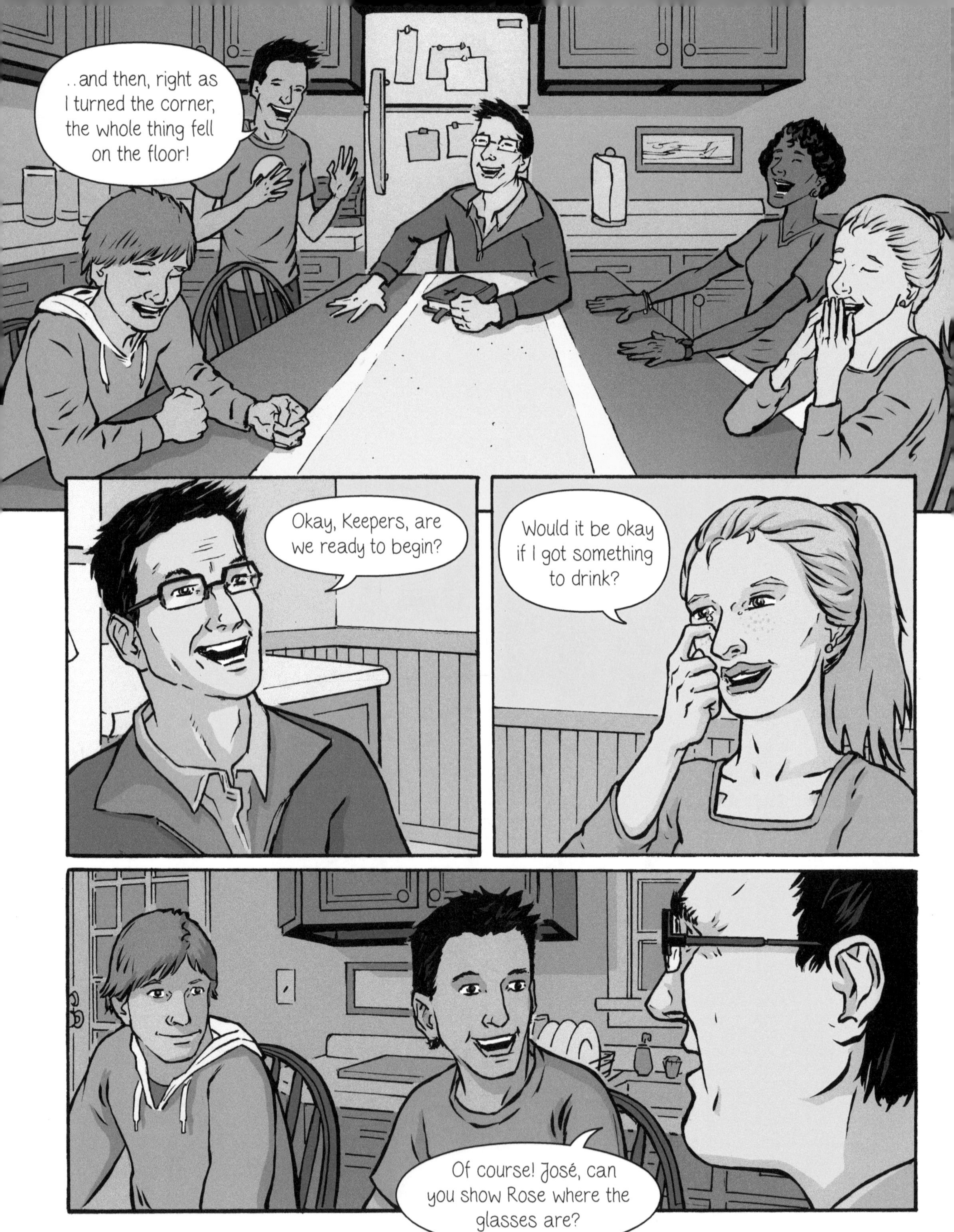
..and then, right as I turned the corner, the whole thing fell on the floor!
Okay, Keepers, are we ready to begin?
Would it be okay if I got something to drink?
Of course! José, can you show Rose where the glasses are?

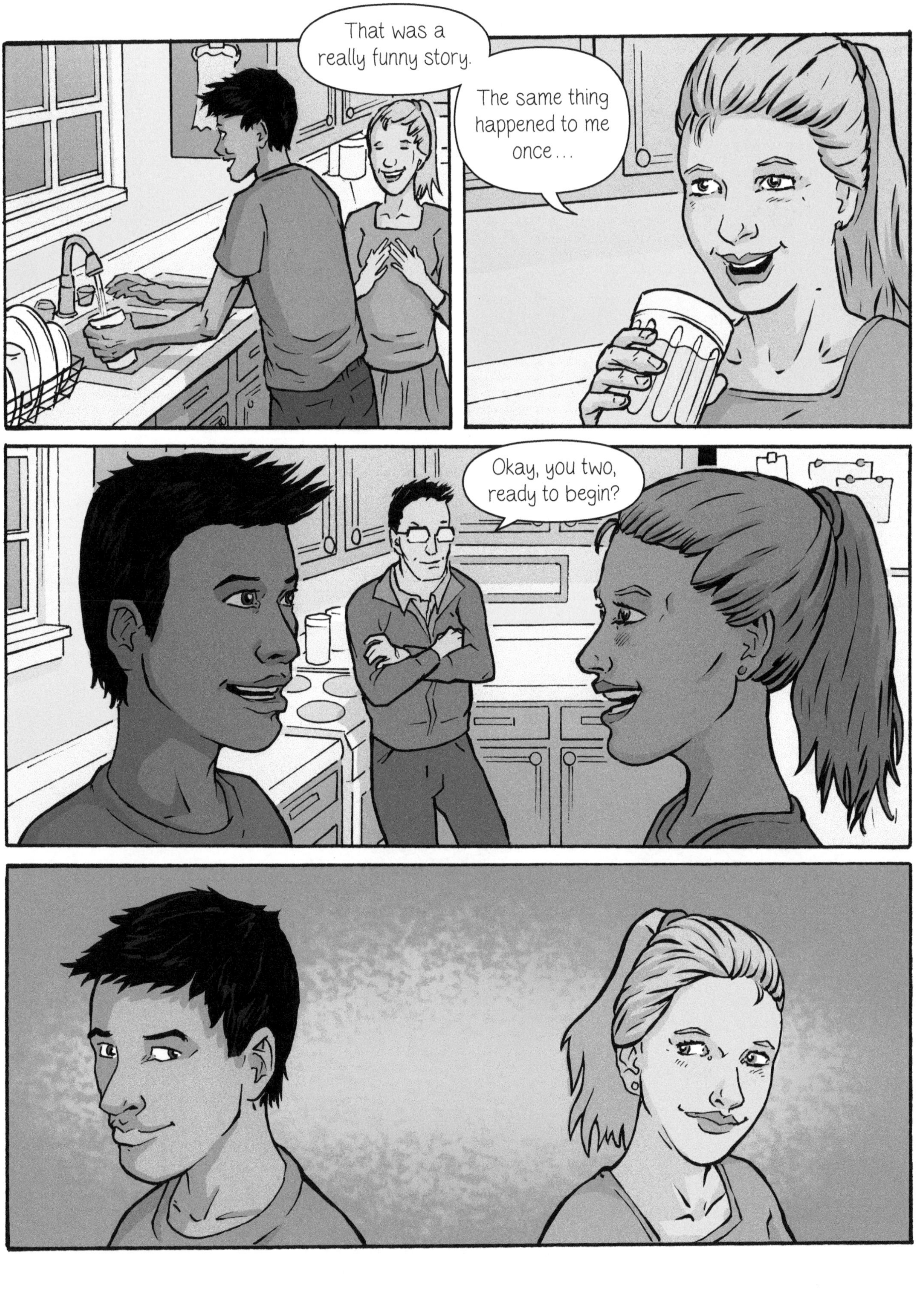
That was a really funny story.
The same thing happened to me once…
Okay, you two, ready to begin?

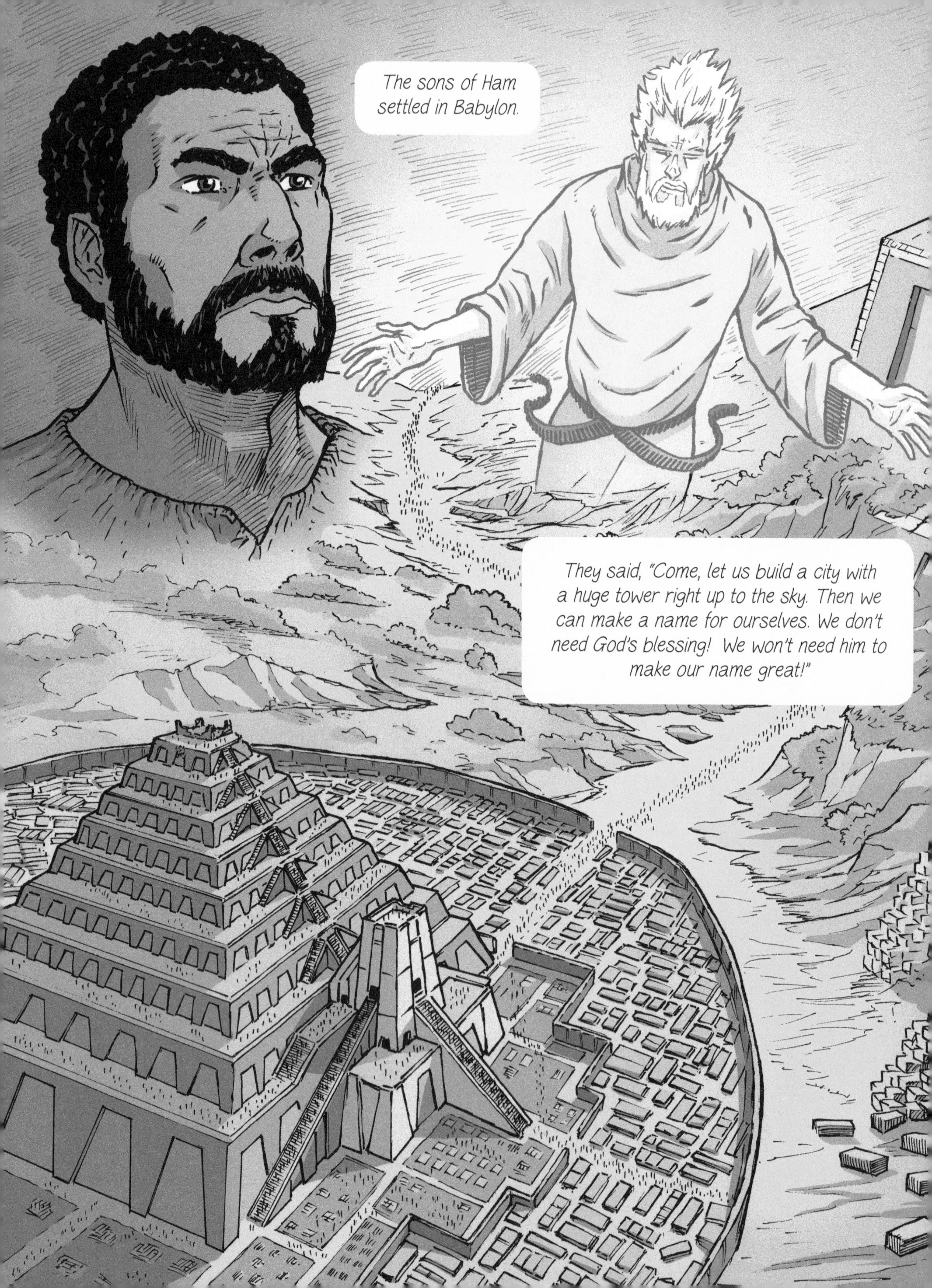
The sons of Ham settled in Babylon.
They said, "Come, let us build a city with a huge tower right up to the sky. Then we can make a name for ourselves. We don't need God's blessing! We won't need him to make our name great!"

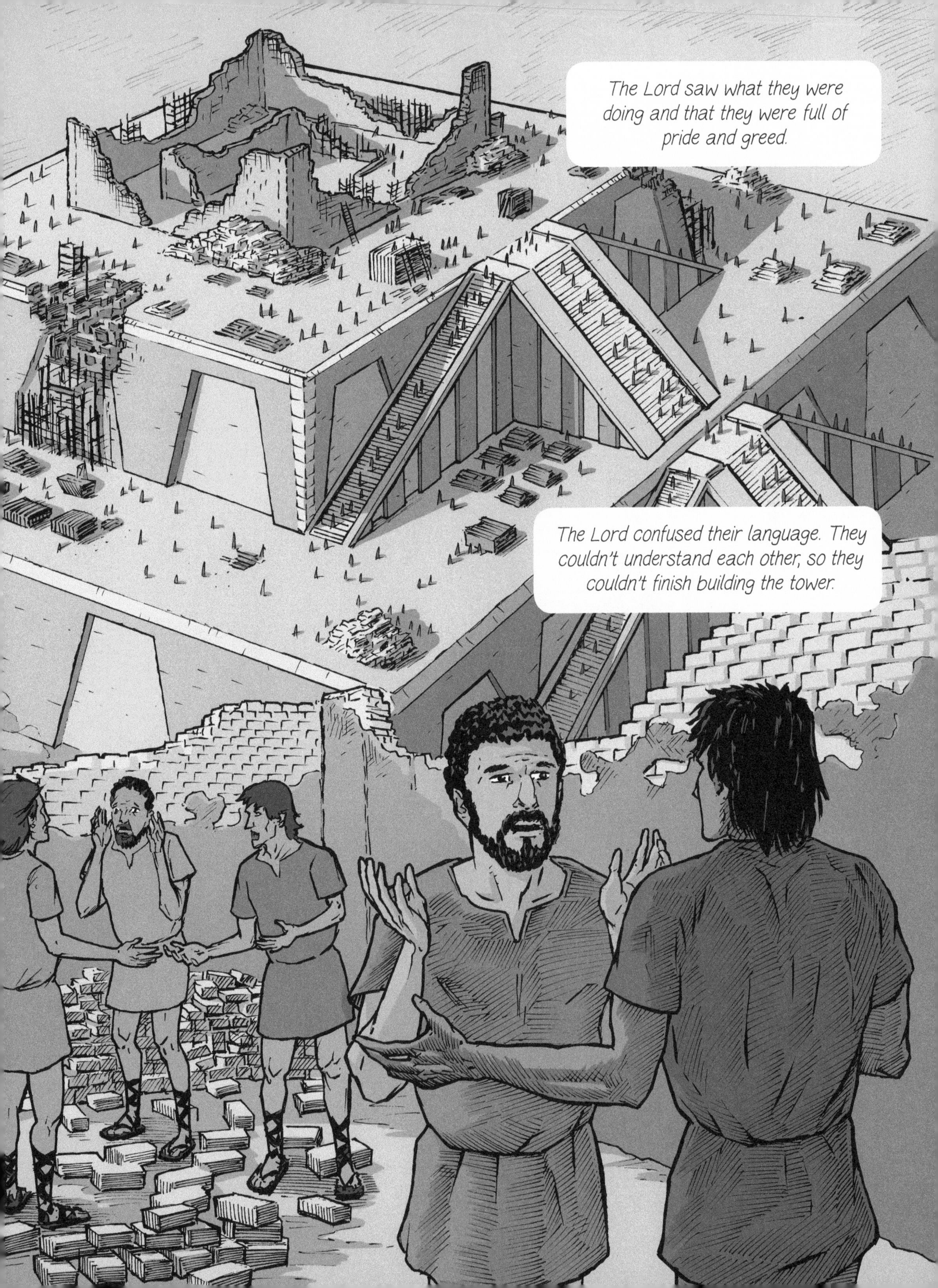
The Lord saw what they were doing and that they were full of pride and greed.
The Lord confused their language. They couldn't understand each other, so they couldn't finish building the tower.

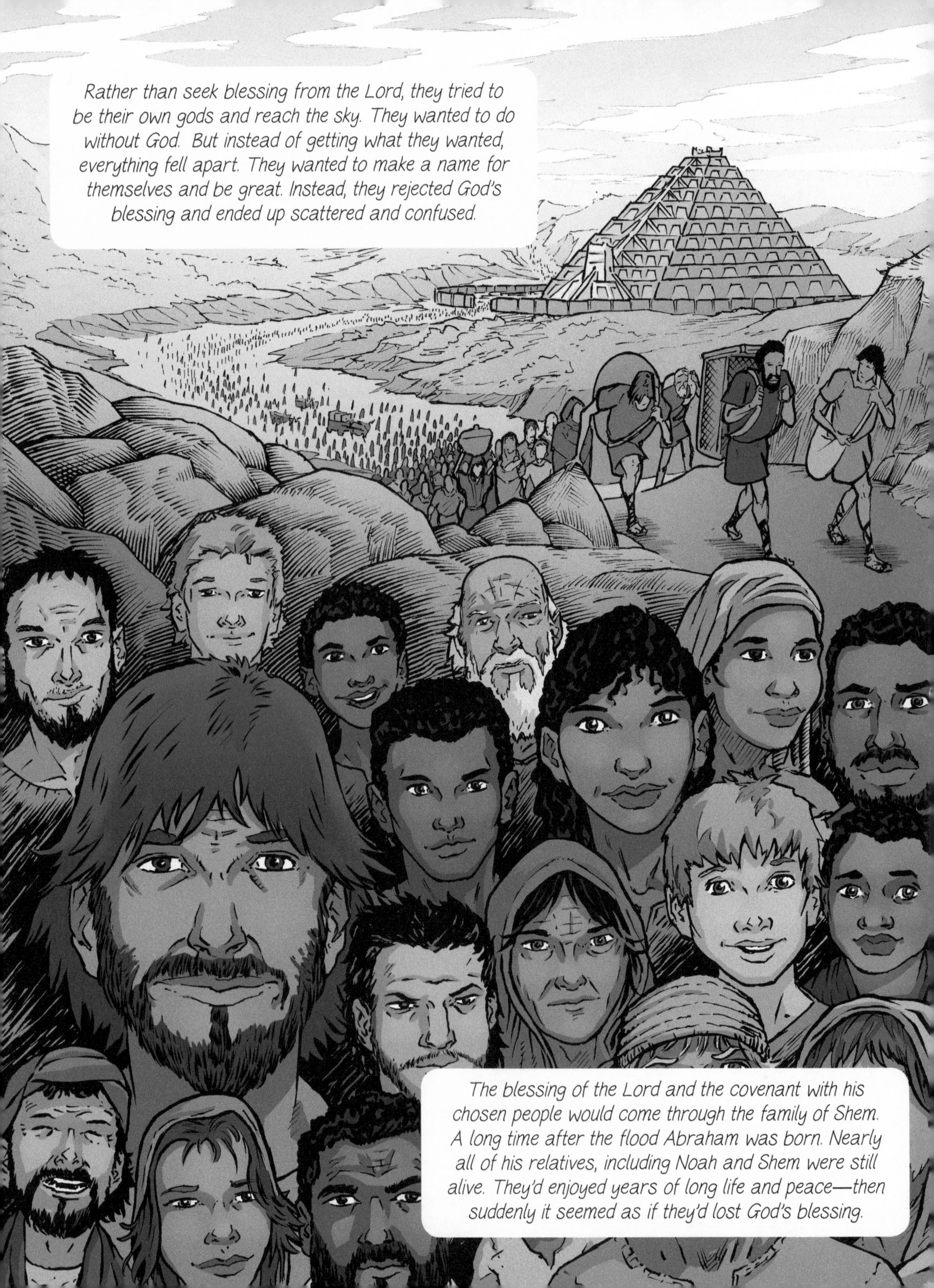
Rather than seek blessing from the Lord, they tried to be their own gods and reach the sky. They wanted to do without God. But instead of getting what they wanted, everything fell apart. They wanted to make a name for themselves and be great. Instead, they rejected God's blessing and ended up scattered and confused.
The blessing of the Lord and the covenant with his chosen people would come through the family of Shem. A long time after the flood Abraham was born. Nearly all of his relatives, including Noah and Shem were still alive. They'd enjoyed years of long life and peace—then suddenly it seemed as if they'd lost God's blessing.

DAY SEVEN

Death and Life

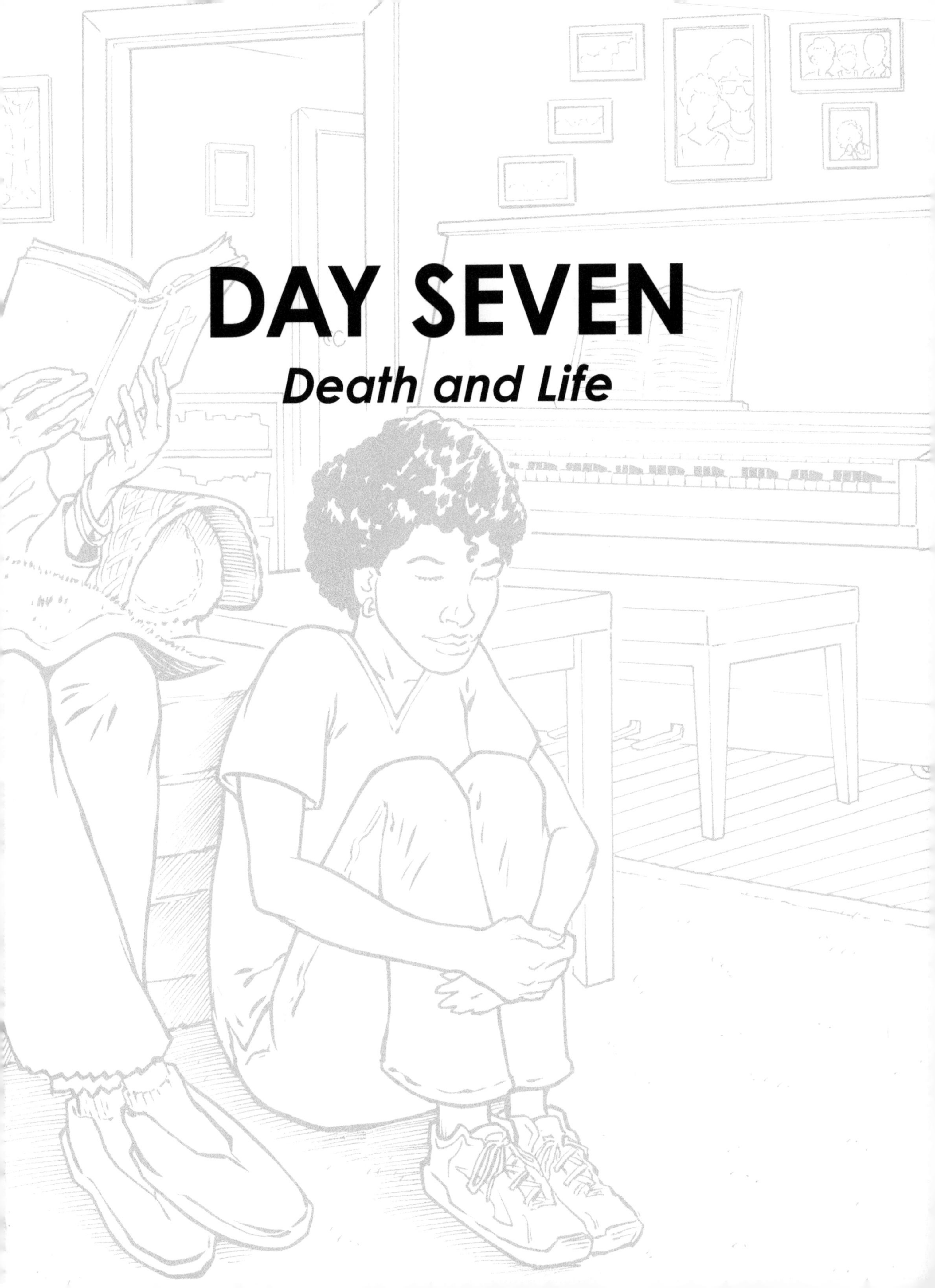

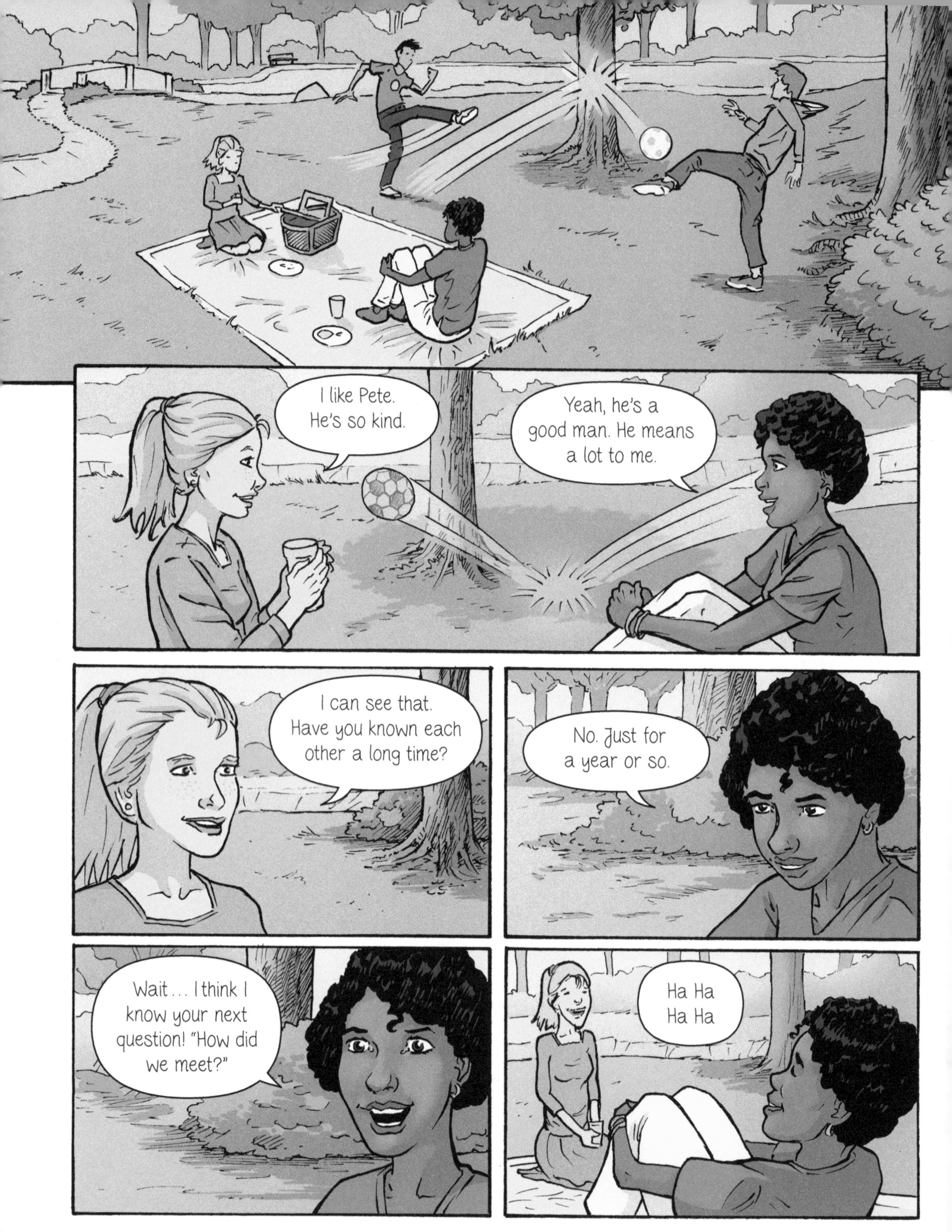
I like Pete. He's so kind.
Yeah, he's a good man. He means a lot to me.
I can see that. Have you known each other a long time?
No. Just for a year or so.
Wait... I think I know your next question! "How did we meet?"
Ha Ha Ha Ha

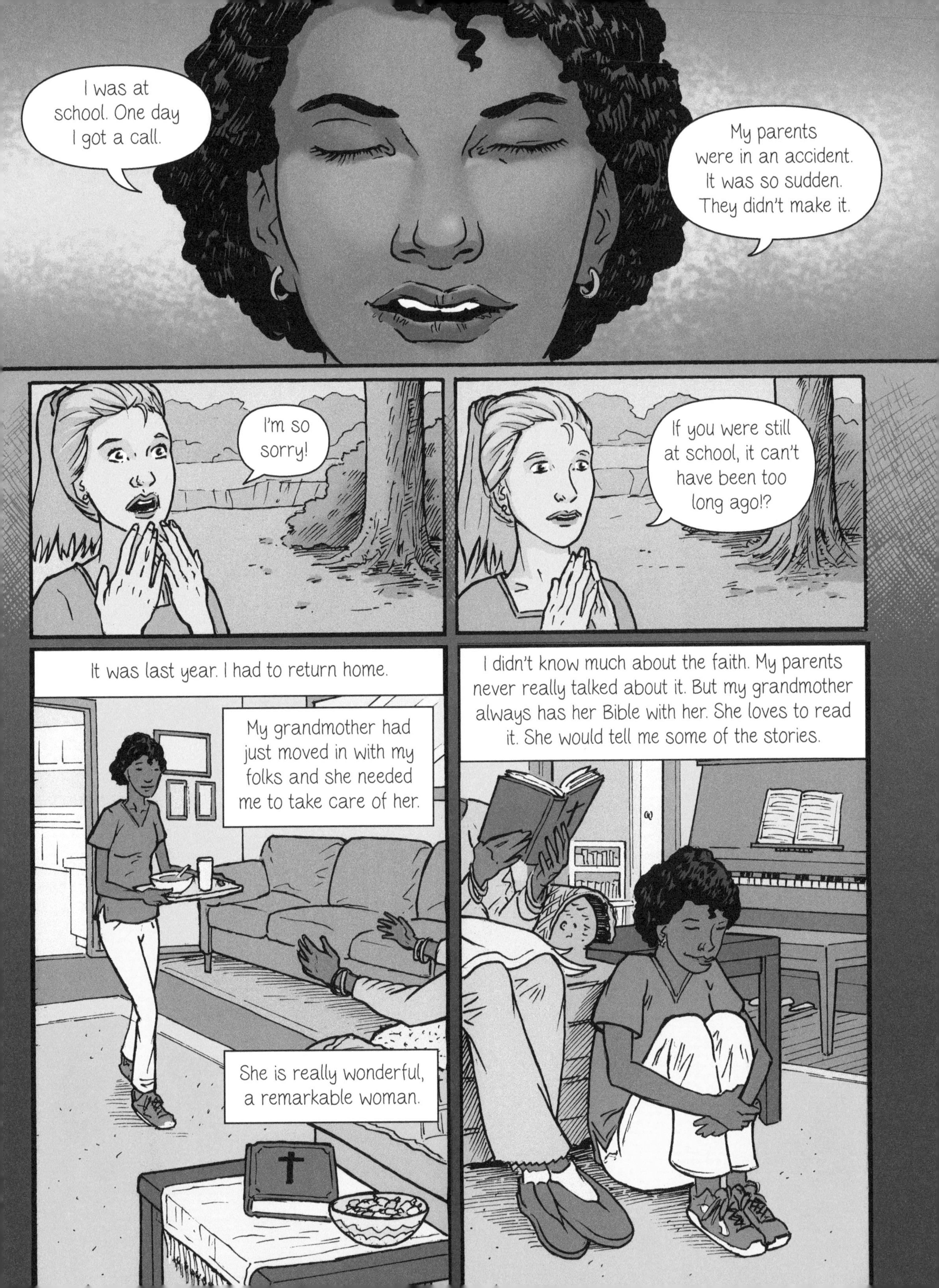
I was at school. One day I got a call.
My parents were in an accident. It was so sudden. They didn't make it.
I'm so sorry!
If you were still at school, it can't have been too long ago!?
It was last year. I had to return home.
My grandmother had just moved in with my folks and she needed me to take care of her.
She is really wonderful, a remarkable woman.
I didn't know much about the faith. My parents never really talked about it. But my grandmother always has her Bible with her. She loves to read it. She would tell me some of the stories.

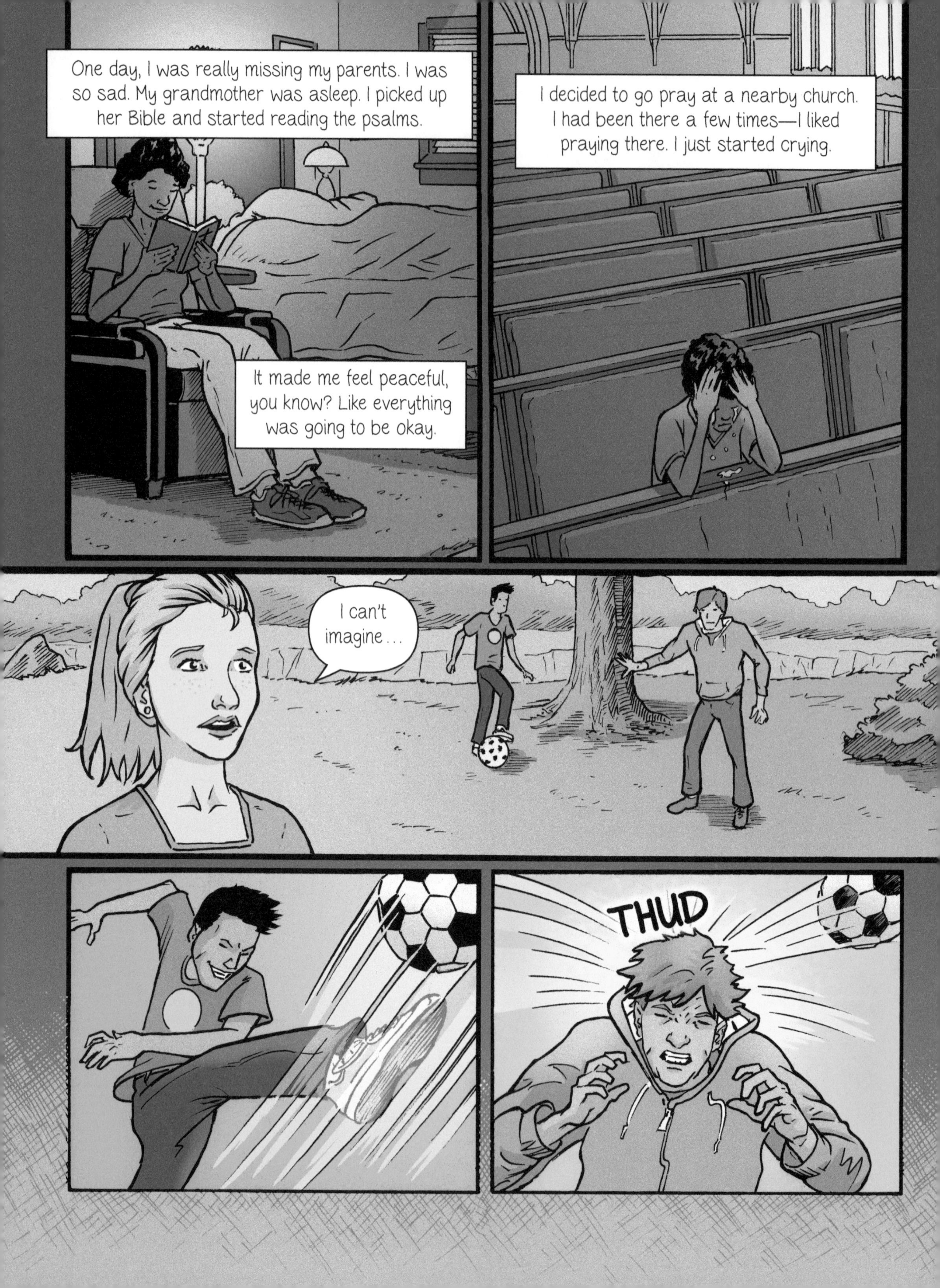
One day, I was really missing my parents. I was so sad. My grandmother was asleep. I picked up her Bible and started reading the psalms.
It made me feel peaceful, you know? Like everything was going to be okay.
I decided to go pray at a nearby church. I had been there a few times—I liked praying there. I just started crying.
I can't imagine . . .
THUD

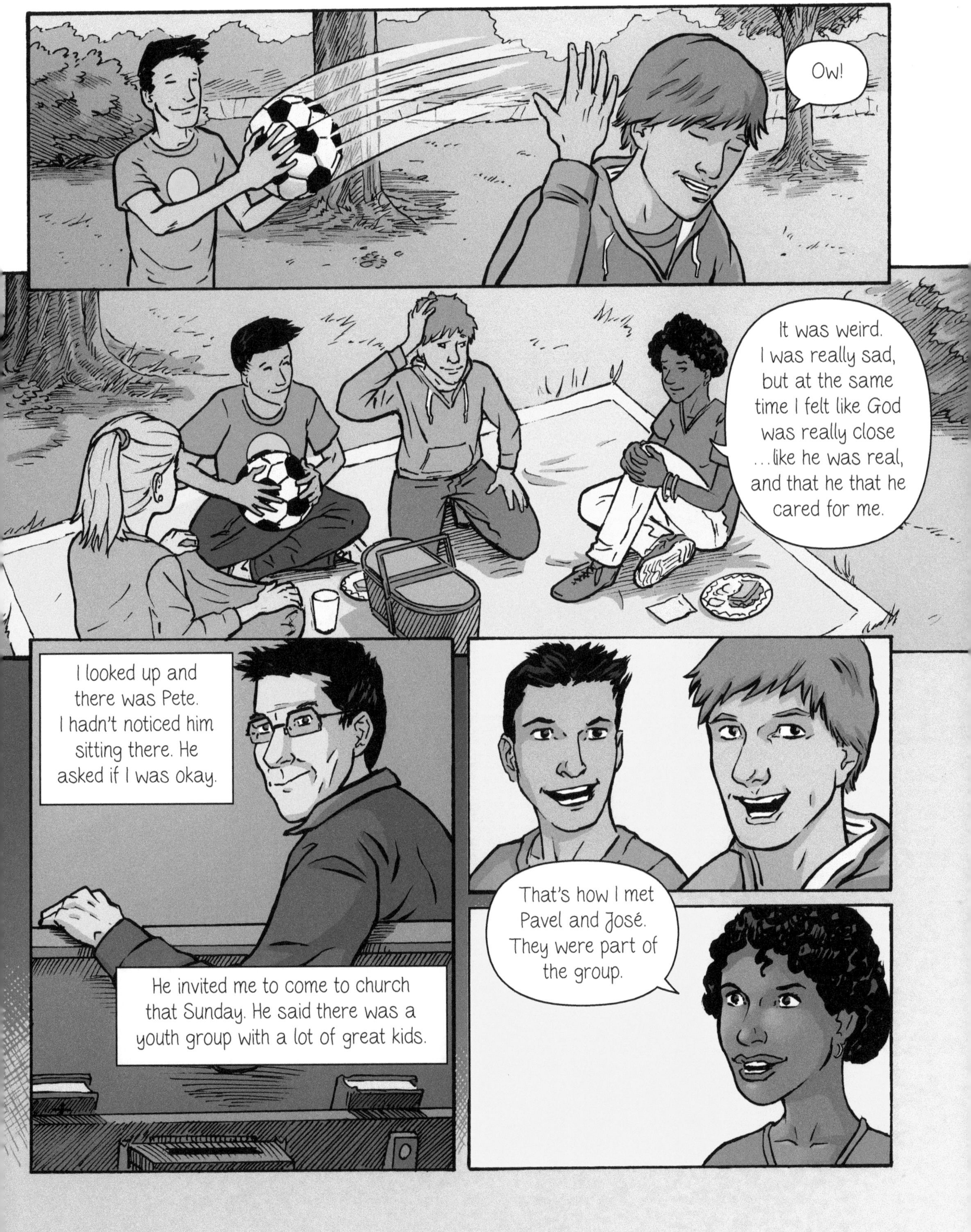
Ow!
It was weird. I was really sad, but at the same time I felt like God was really close . . . like he was real, and that he that he cared for me.
I looked up and there was Pete. I hadn't noticed him sitting there. He asked if I was okay.
He invited me to come to church that Sunday. He said there was a youth group with a lot of great kids.
That's how I met Pavel and José. They were part of the group.

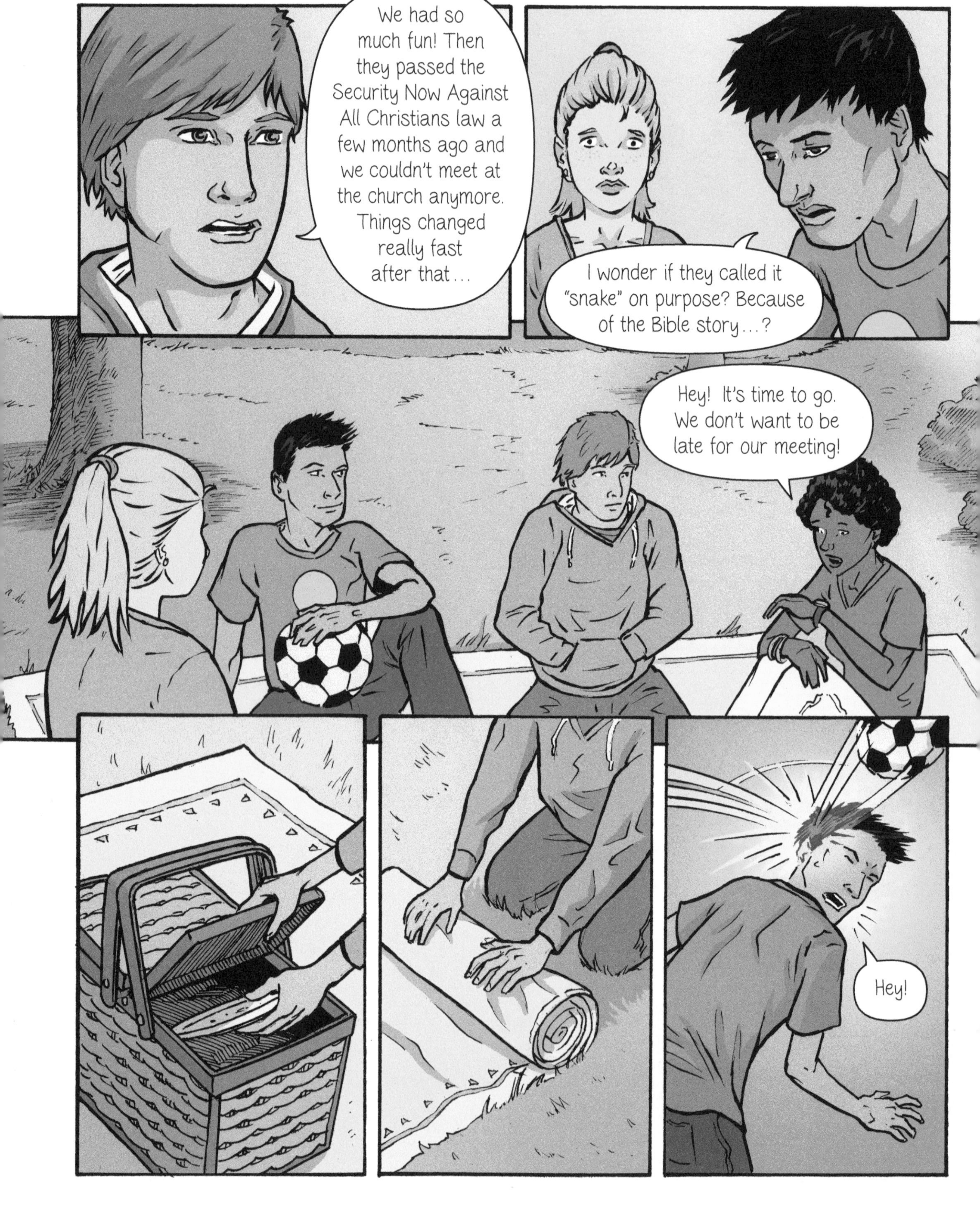
We had so much fun! Then they passed the Security Now Against All Christians law a few months ago and we couldn't meet at the church anymore. Things changed really fast after that...
I wonder if they called it "snake" on purpose? Because of the Bible story...?
Hey! It's time to go. We don't want to be late for our meeting!
Hey!

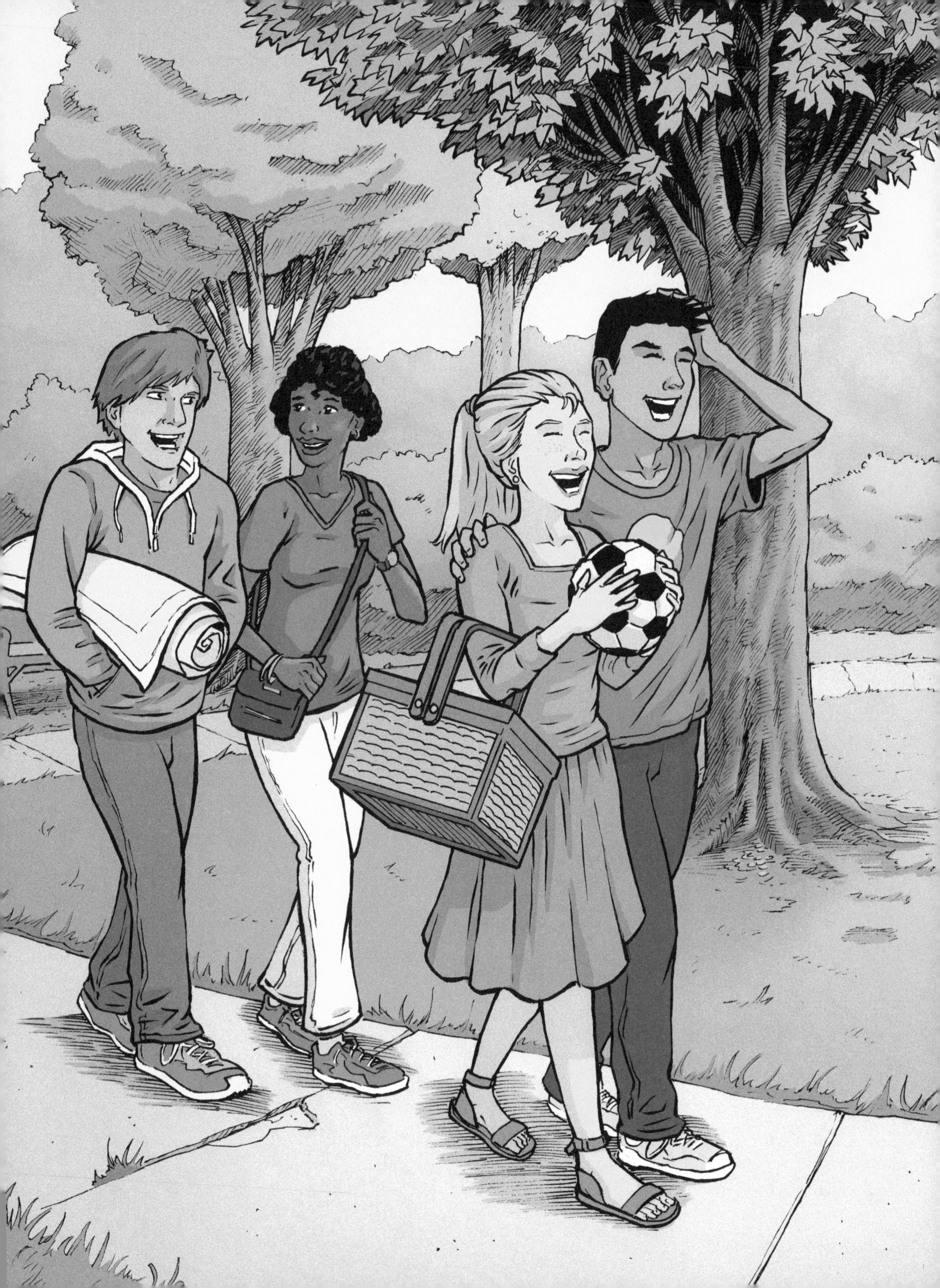

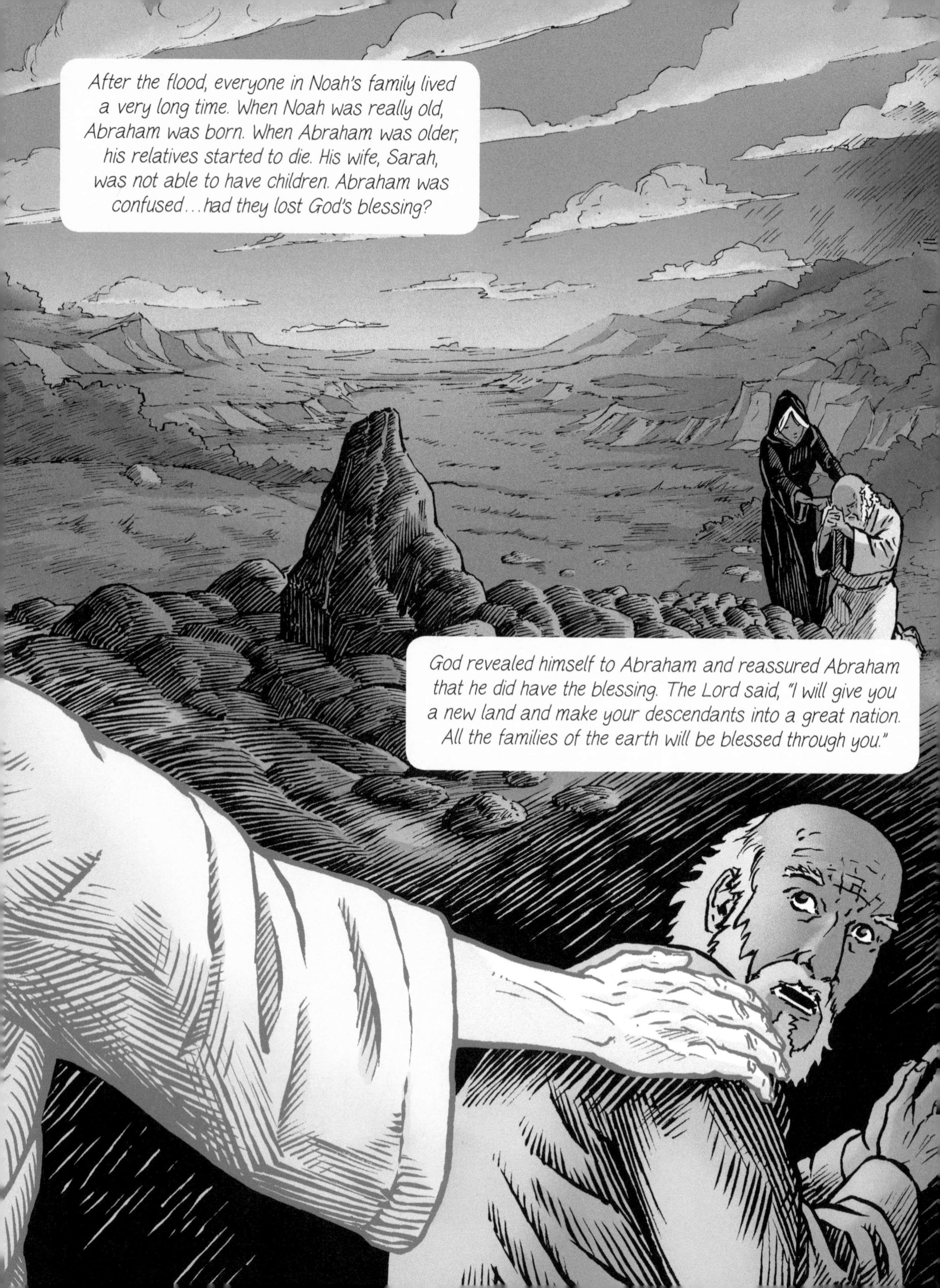
After the flood, everyone in Noah's family lived a very long time. When Noah was really old, Abraham was born. When Abraham was older, his relatives started to die. His wife, Sarah, was not able to have children. Abraham was confused...had they lost God's blessing?
God revealed himself to Abraham and reassured Abraham that he did have the blessing. The Lord said, "I will give you a new land and make your descendants into a great nation. All the families of the earth will be blessed through you."

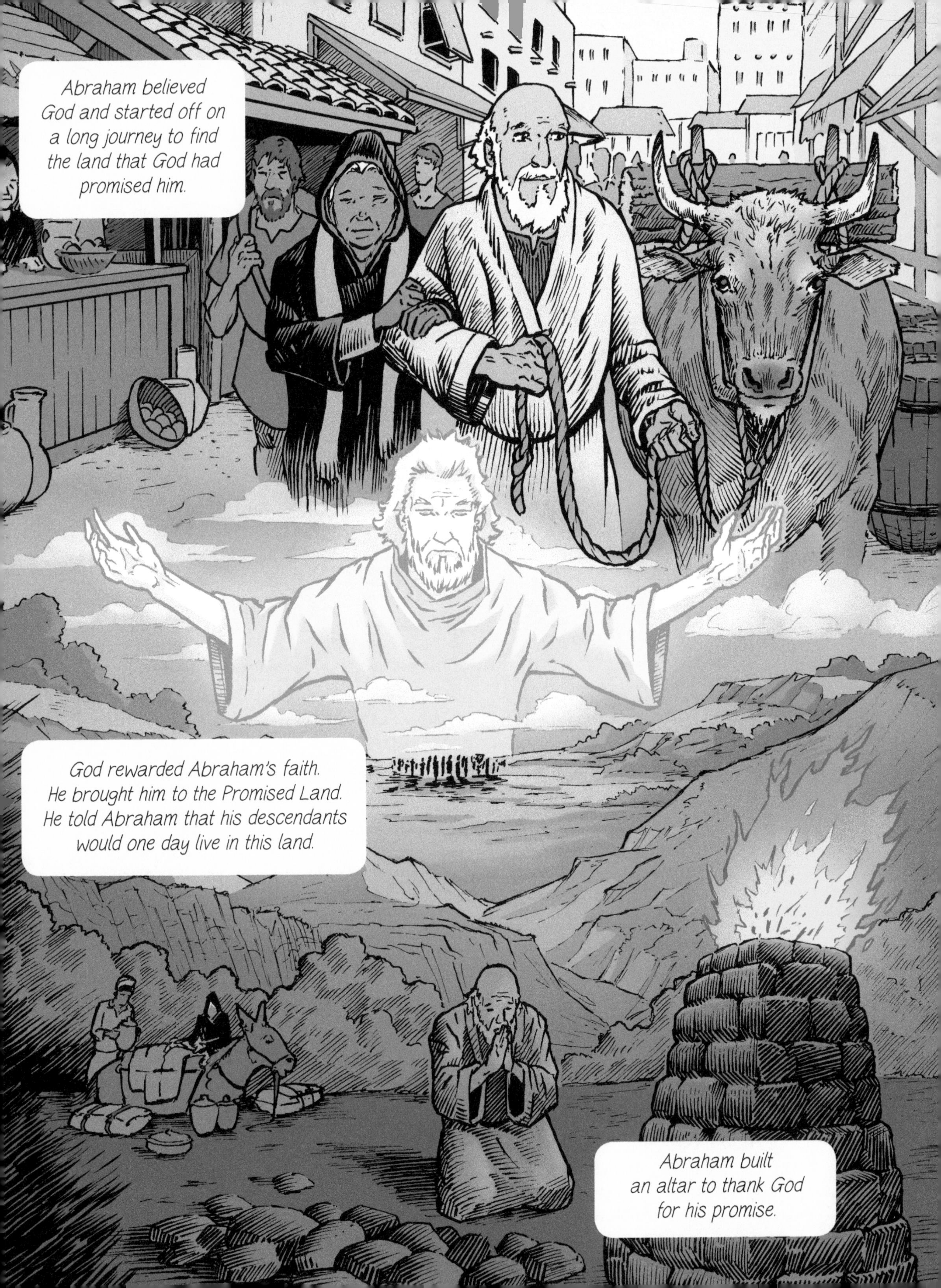
Abraham believed God and started off on a long journey to find the land that God had promised him.
God rewarded Abraham's faith. He brought him to the Promised Land. He told Abraham that his descendants would one day live in this land.
Abraham built an altar to thank God for his promise.

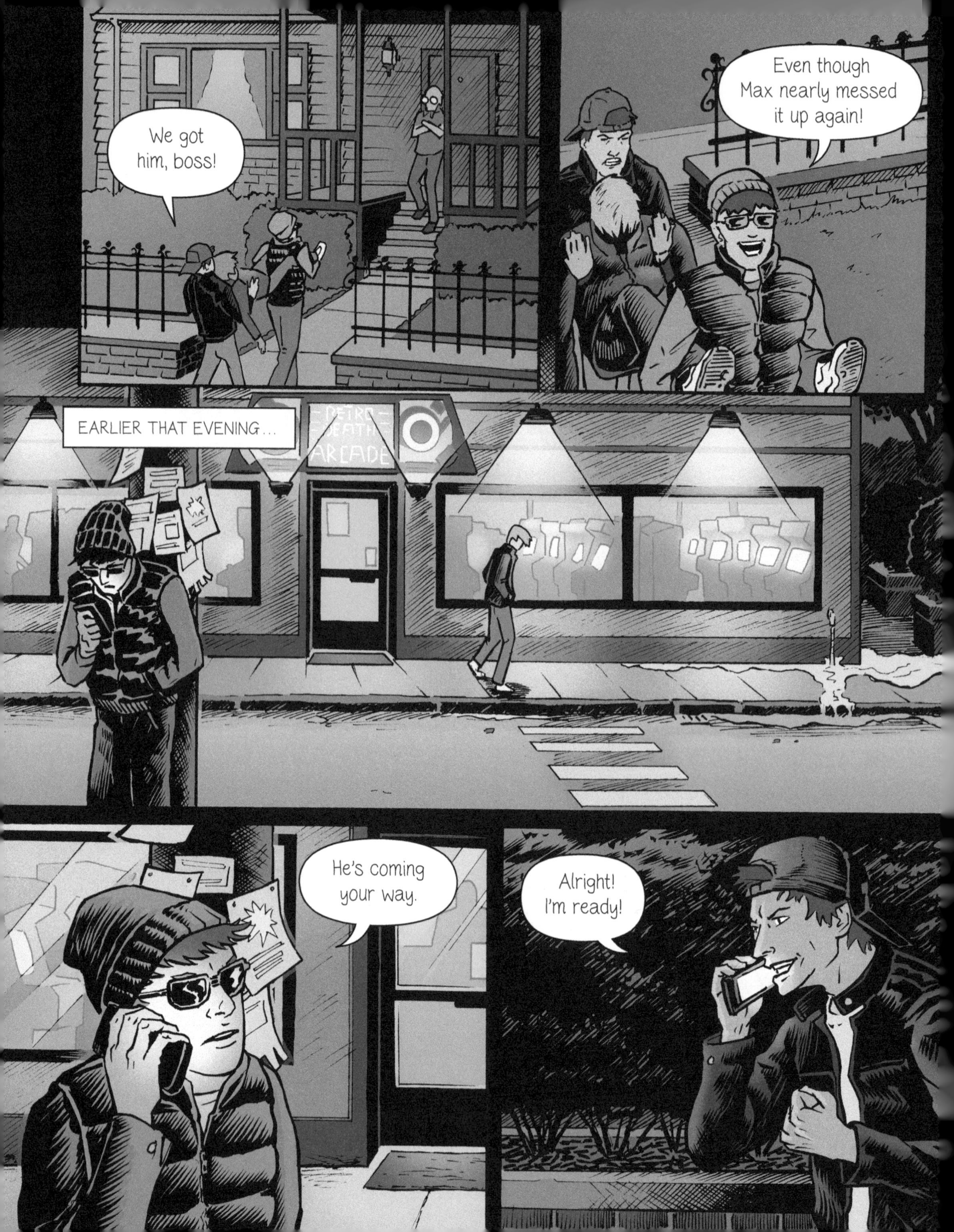
We got him, boss!
Even though Max nearly messed it up again!
EARLIER THAT EVENING...
RETRO DEATH ARCADE
He's coming your way.
Alright! I'm ready!

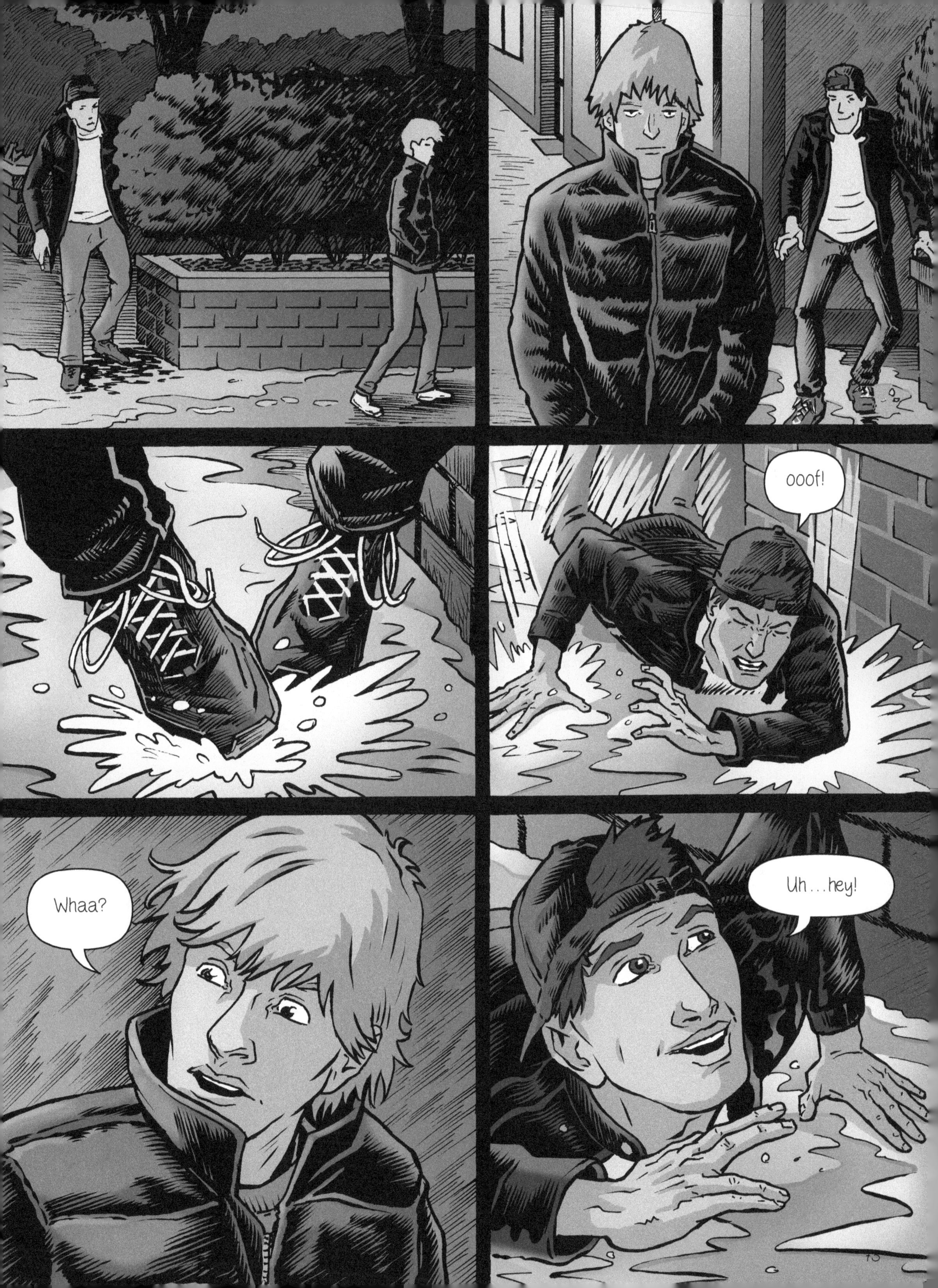
ooof!
Whaa?
Uh...hey!

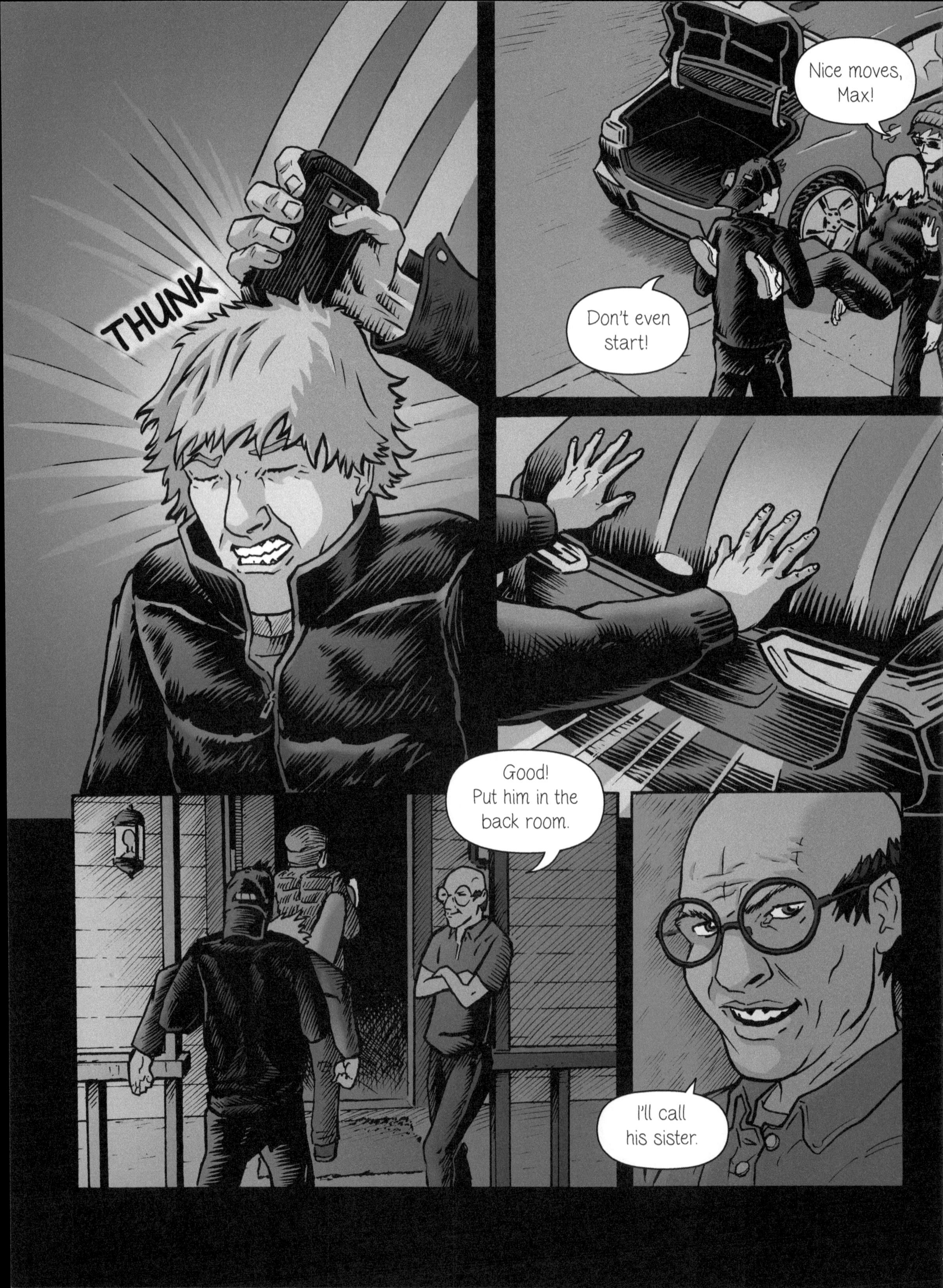
THUNK
Nice moves, Max!
Don't even start!
Good! Put him in the back room.
I'll call his sister.

DAY EIGHT
Time to Go

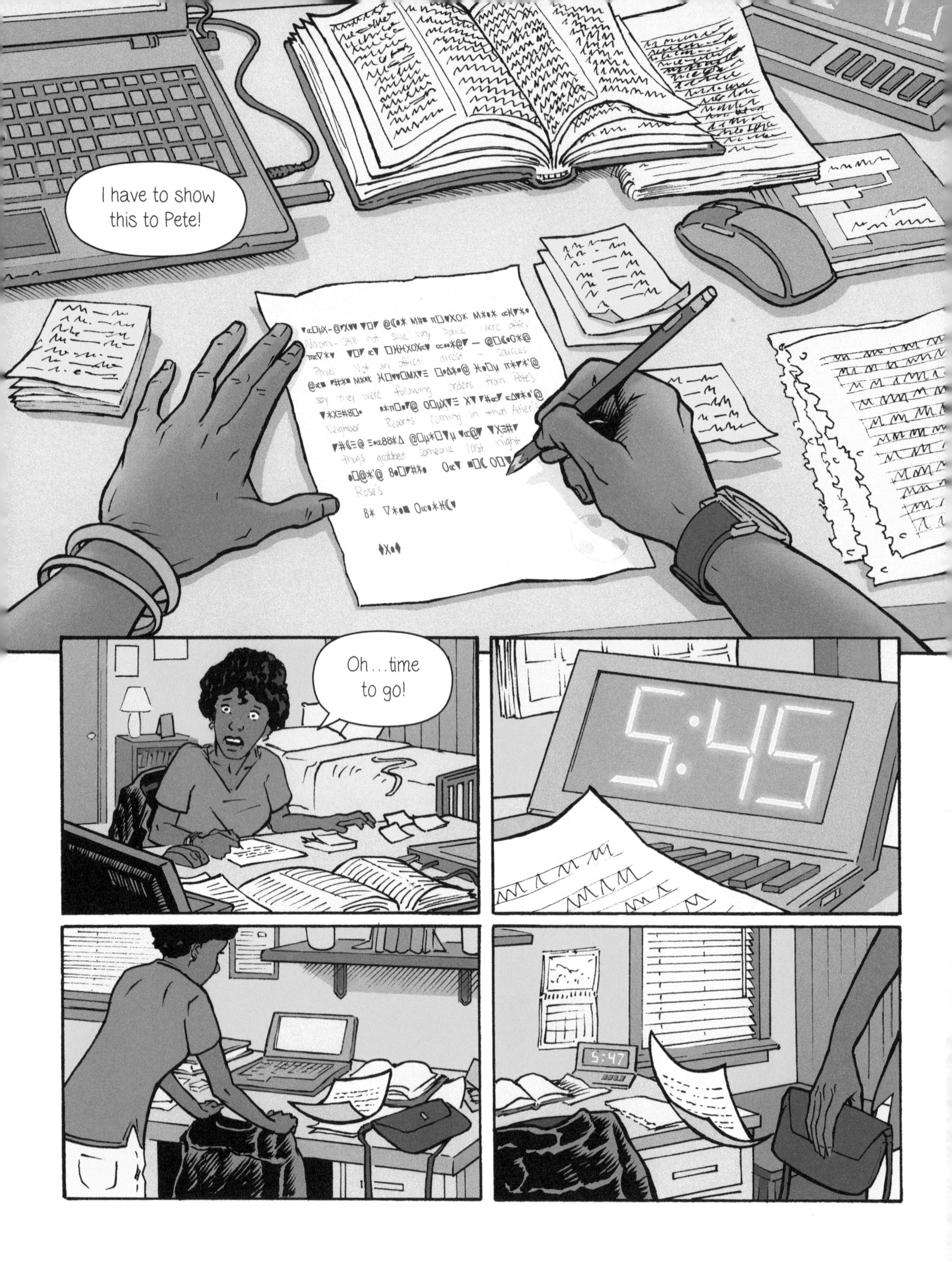
I have to show this to Pete!
Naomi- Still not sure why police were after
Pavel. Not an official arrest - sources
say they were following orders from Pete's
Neighbor. Reports coming in that Adler's
thugs grabbed someone last night
Rose's
Oh…time to go!
5:45
5:47

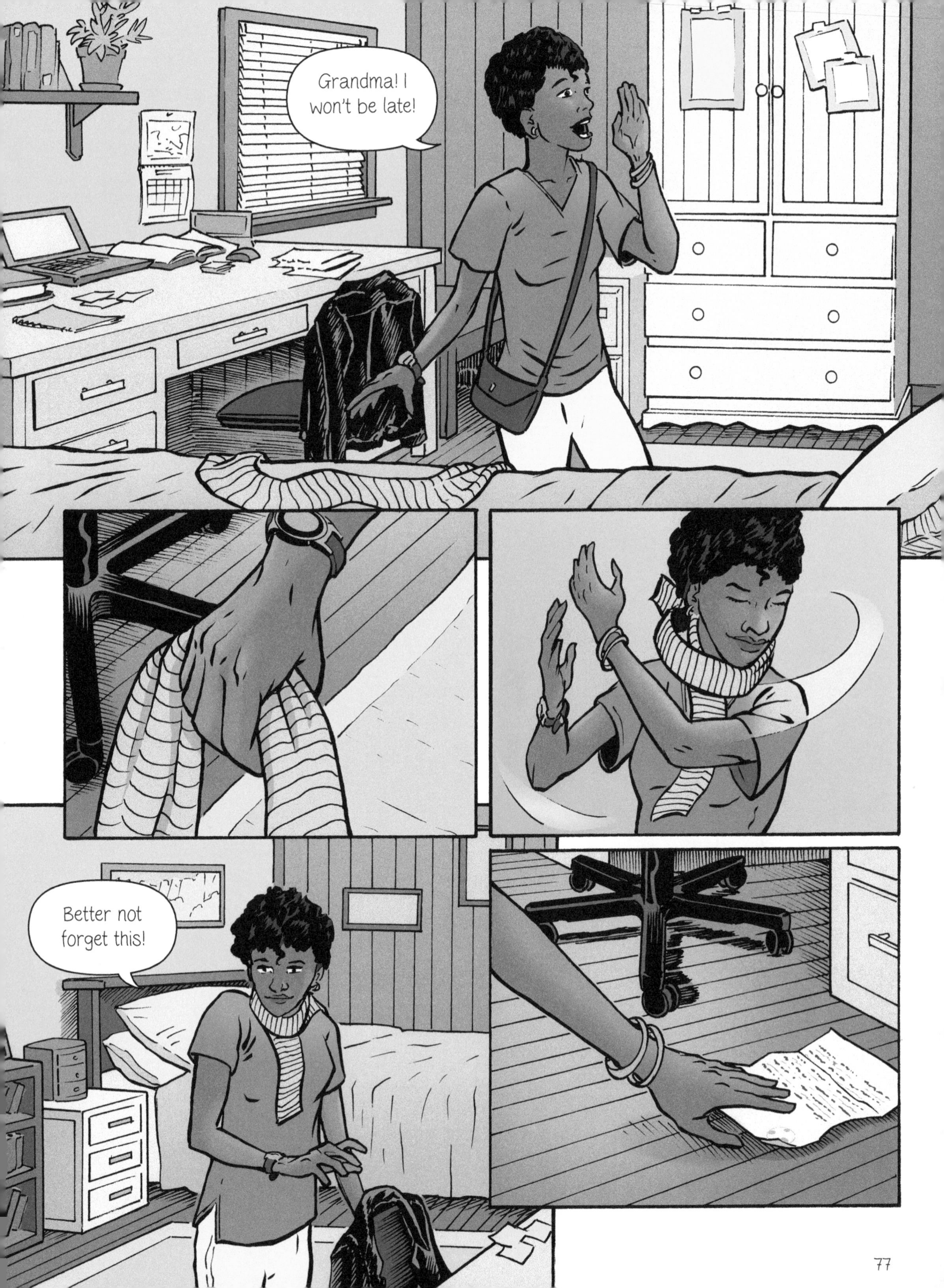

Grandma! I won't be late!
Better not forget this!

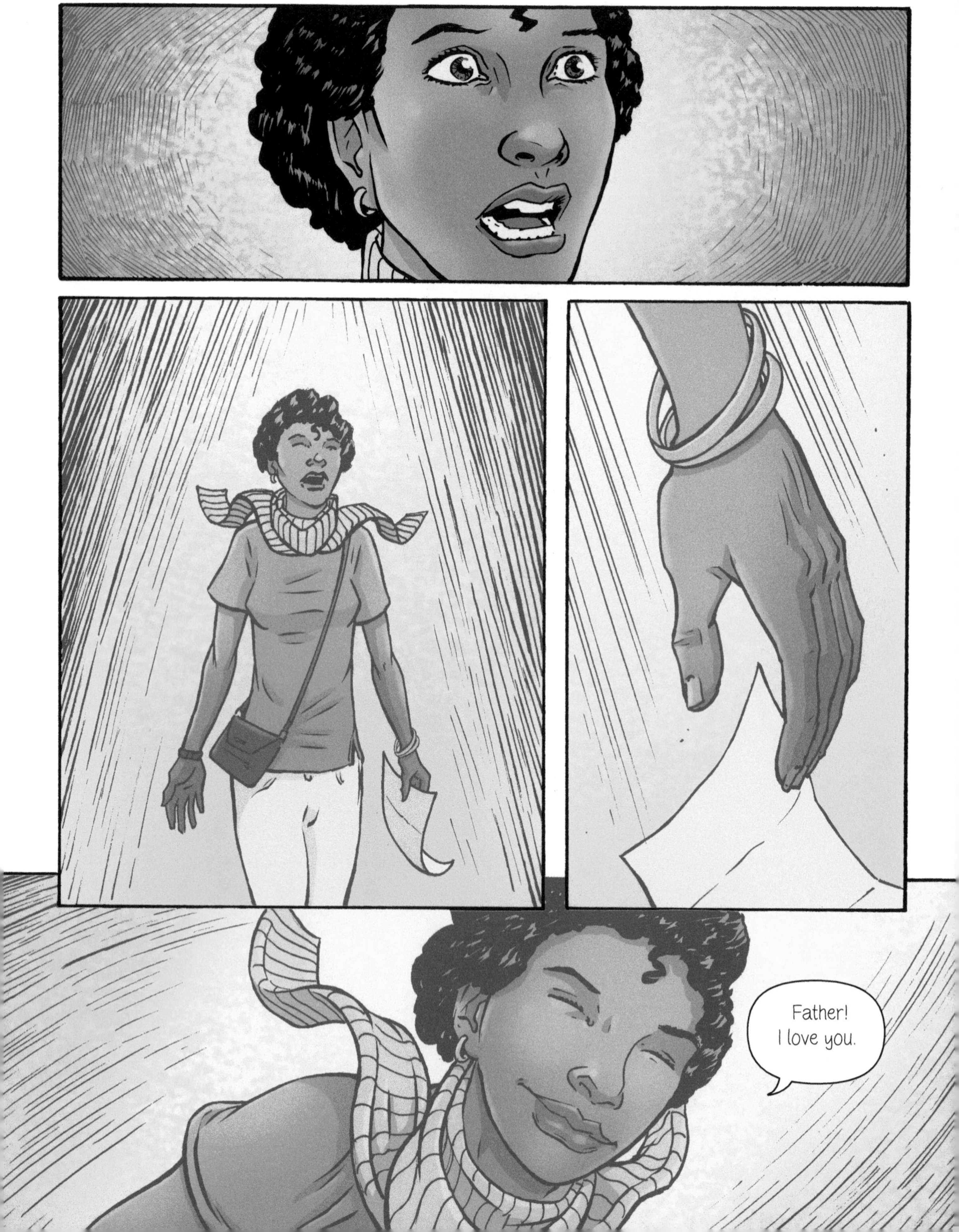
Father!
I love you.

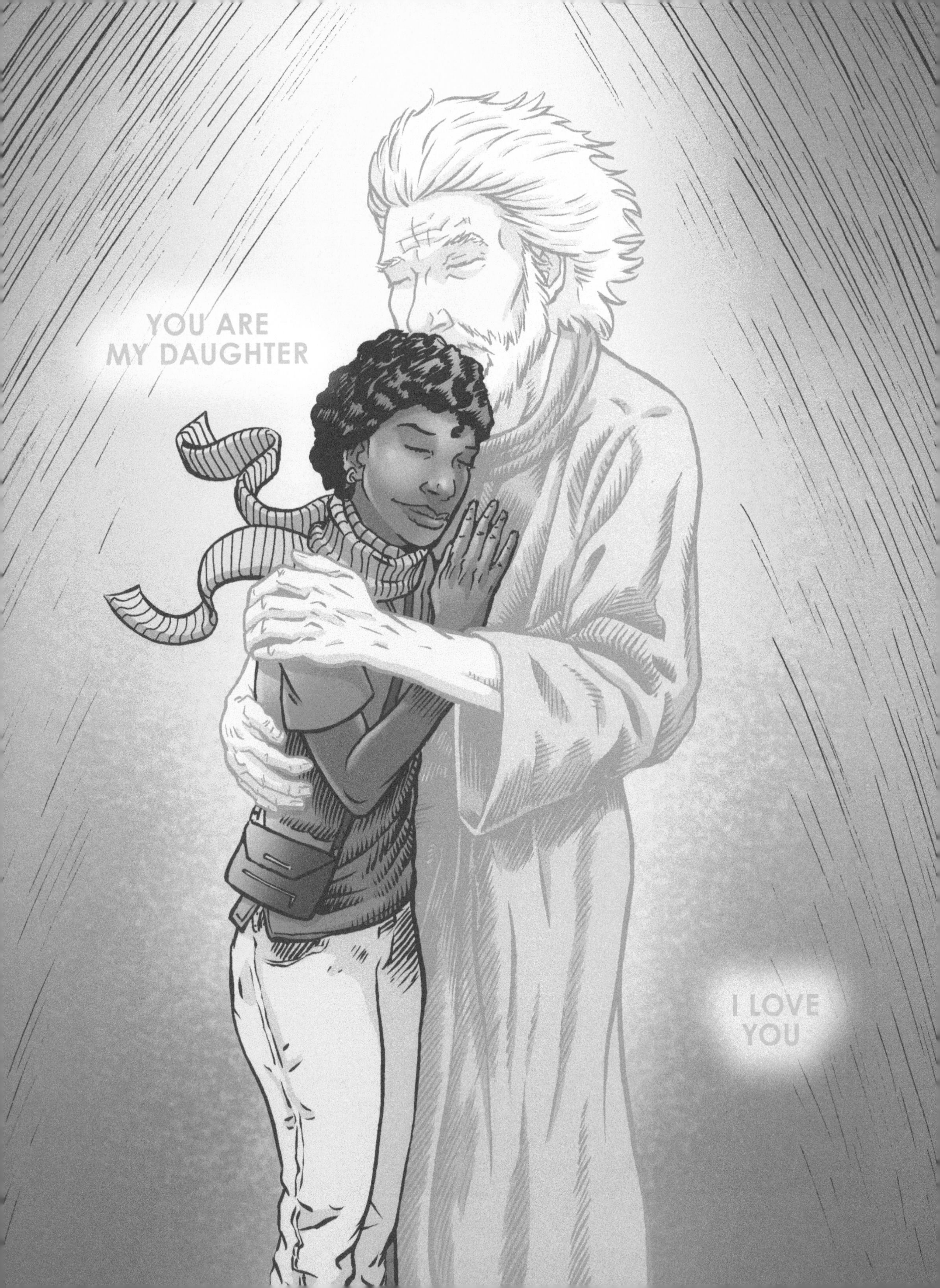
YOU ARE MY DAUGHTER
I LOVE YOU

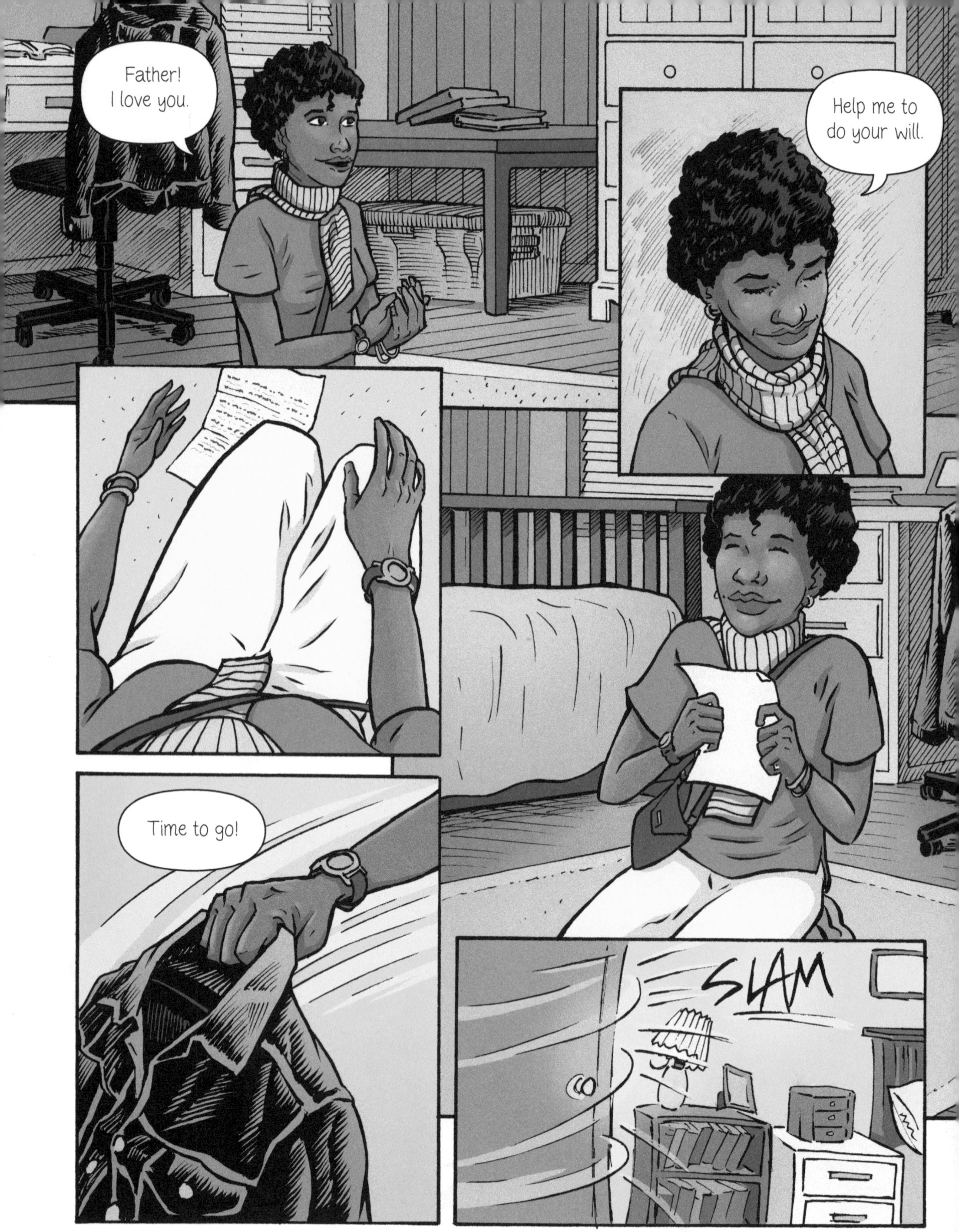
Father!
I love you.
Help me to
do your will.
Time to go!
SLAM

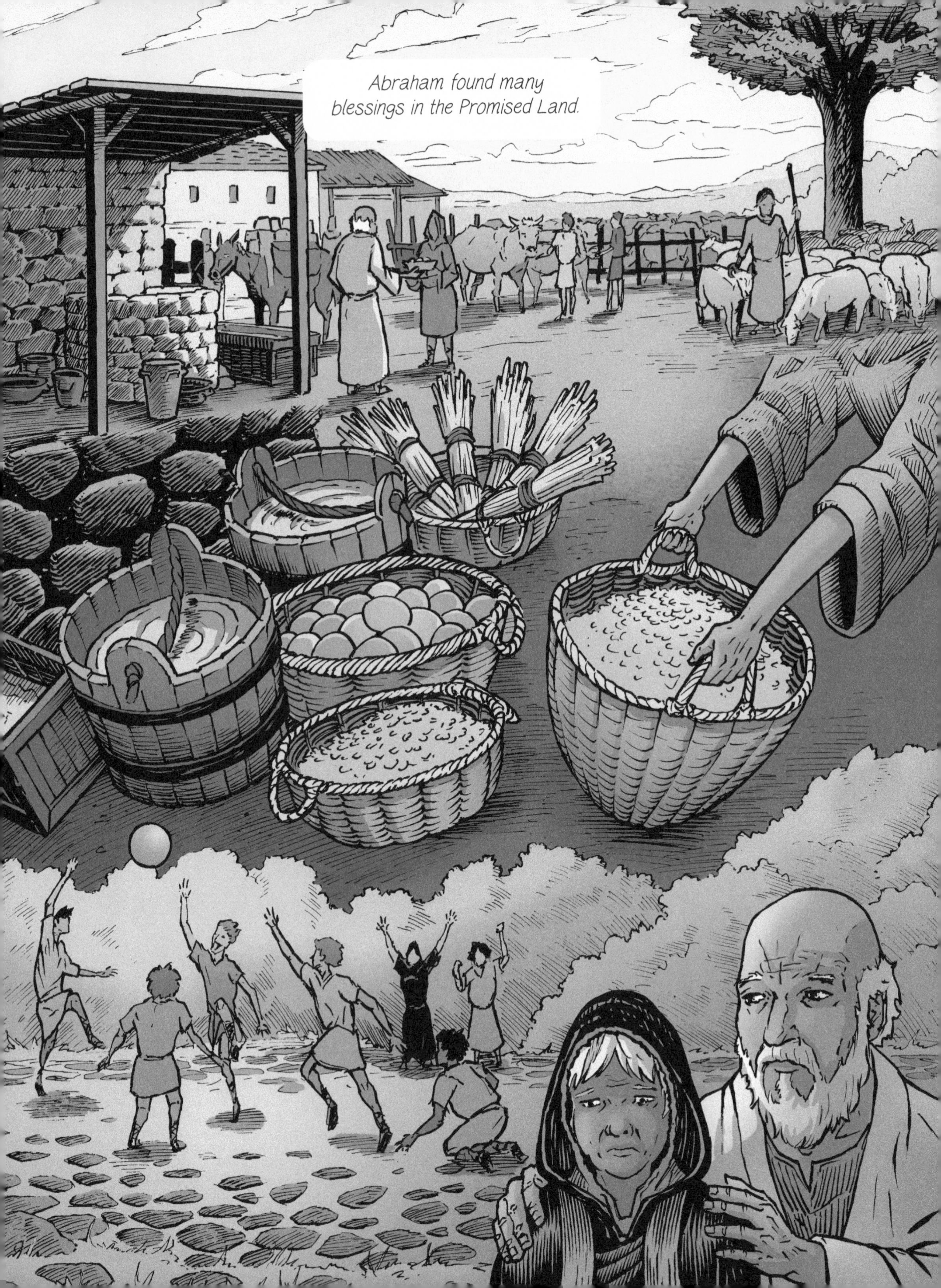
Abraham found many blessings in the Promised Land.

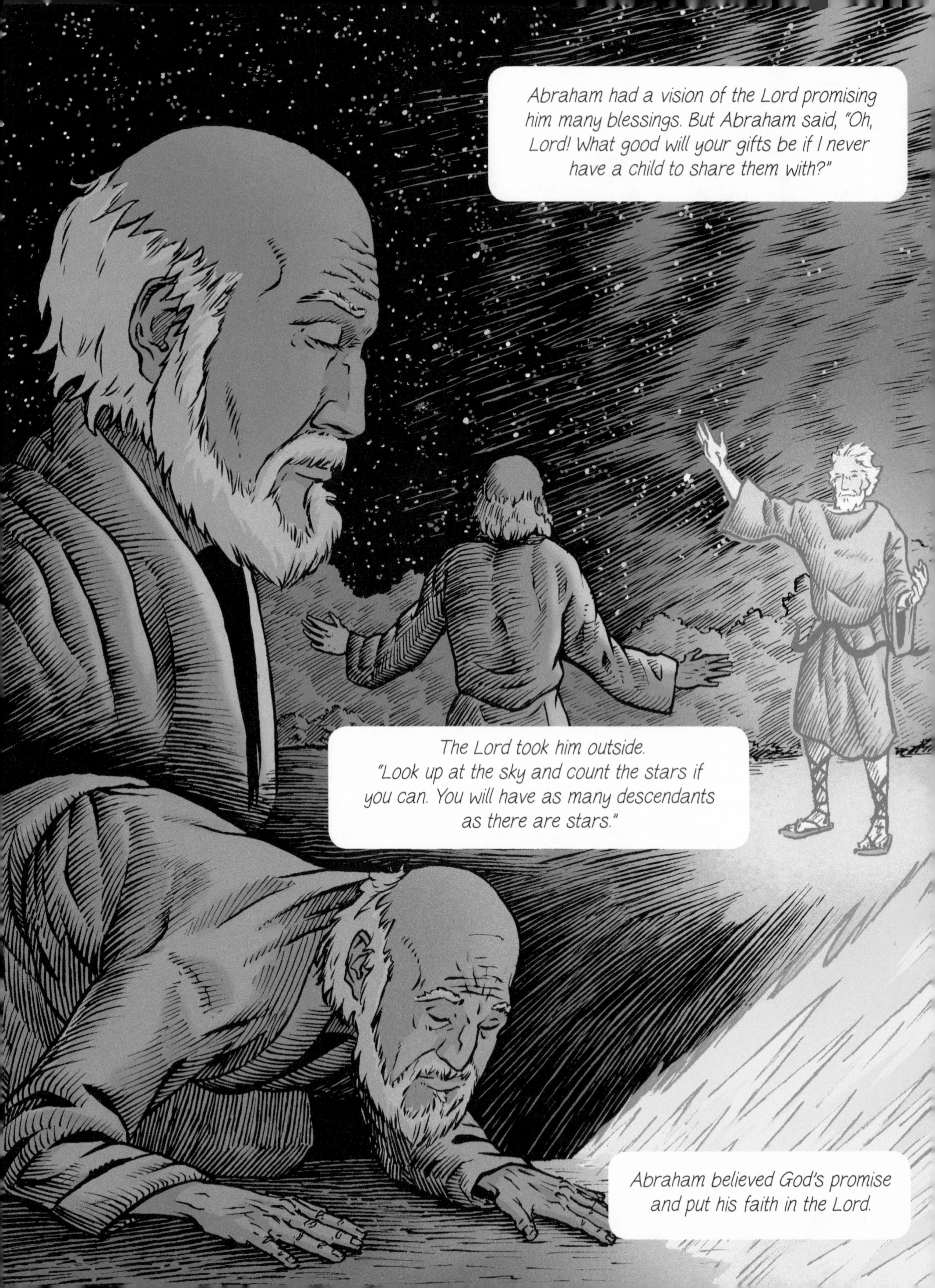
Abraham had a vision of the Lord promising him many blessings. But Abraham said, "Oh, Lord! What good will your gifts be if I never have a child to share them with?"
The Lord took him outside. "Look up at the sky and count the stars if you can. You will have as many descendants as there are stars."
Abraham believed God's promise and put his faith in the Lord.

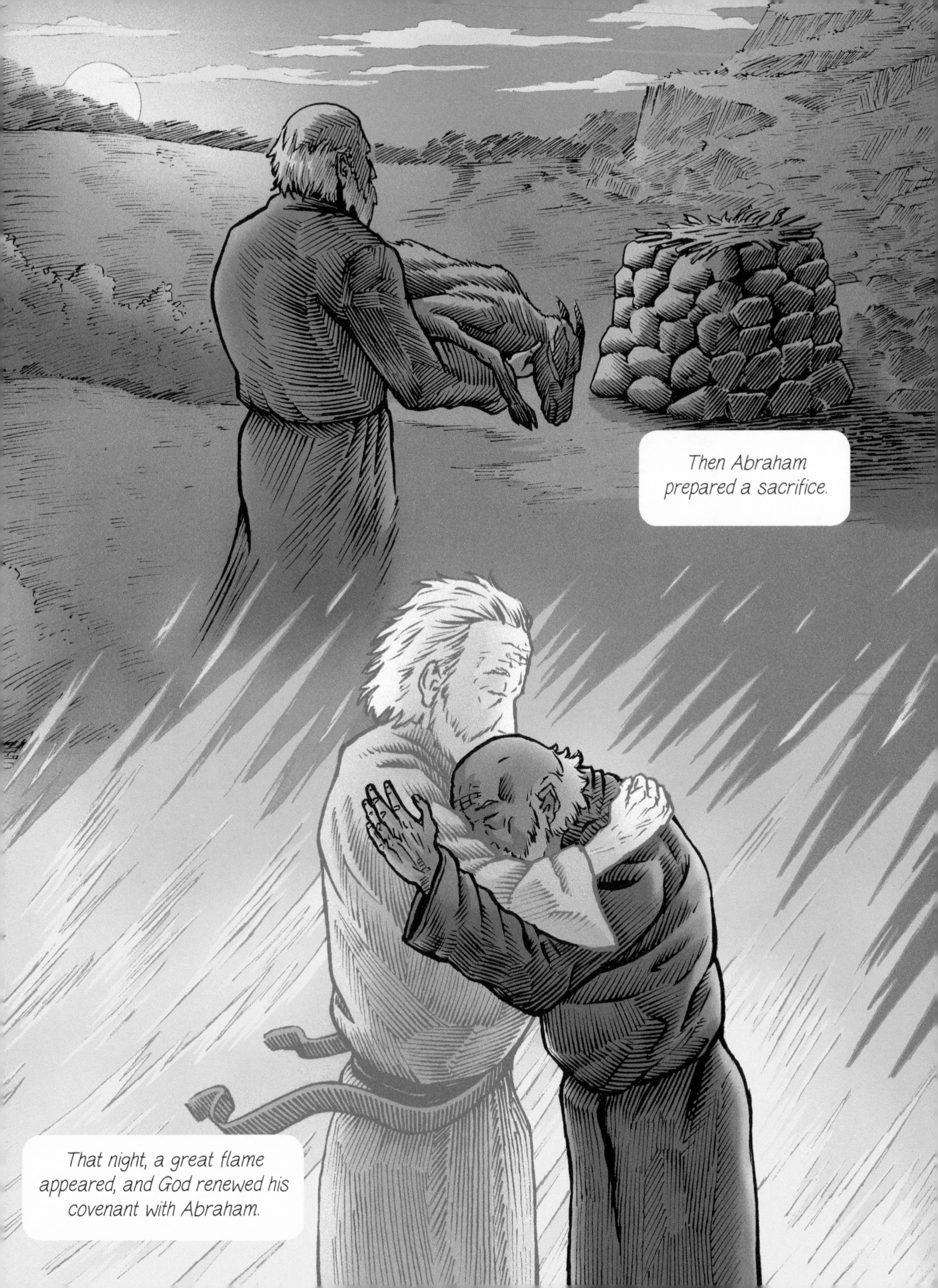
Then Abraham prepared a sacrifice.
That night, a great flame appeared, and God renewed his covenant with Abraham.

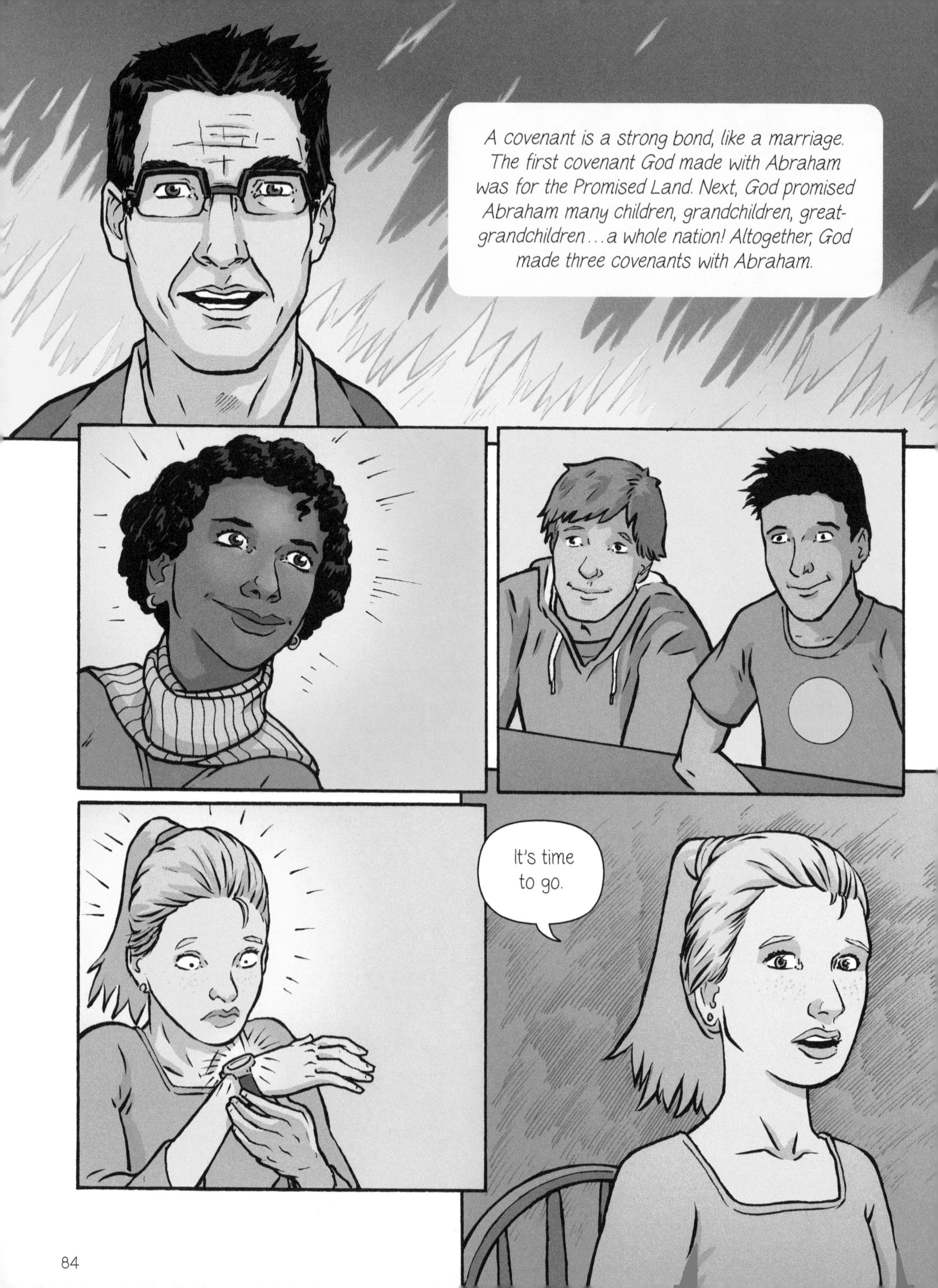
A covenant is a strong bond, like a marriage. The first covenant God made with Abraham was for the Promised Land. Next, God promised Abraham many children, grandchildren, great-grandchildren . . . a whole nation! Altogether, God made three covenants with Abraham.
It's time to go.

DAY NINE

Sisters and Brothers

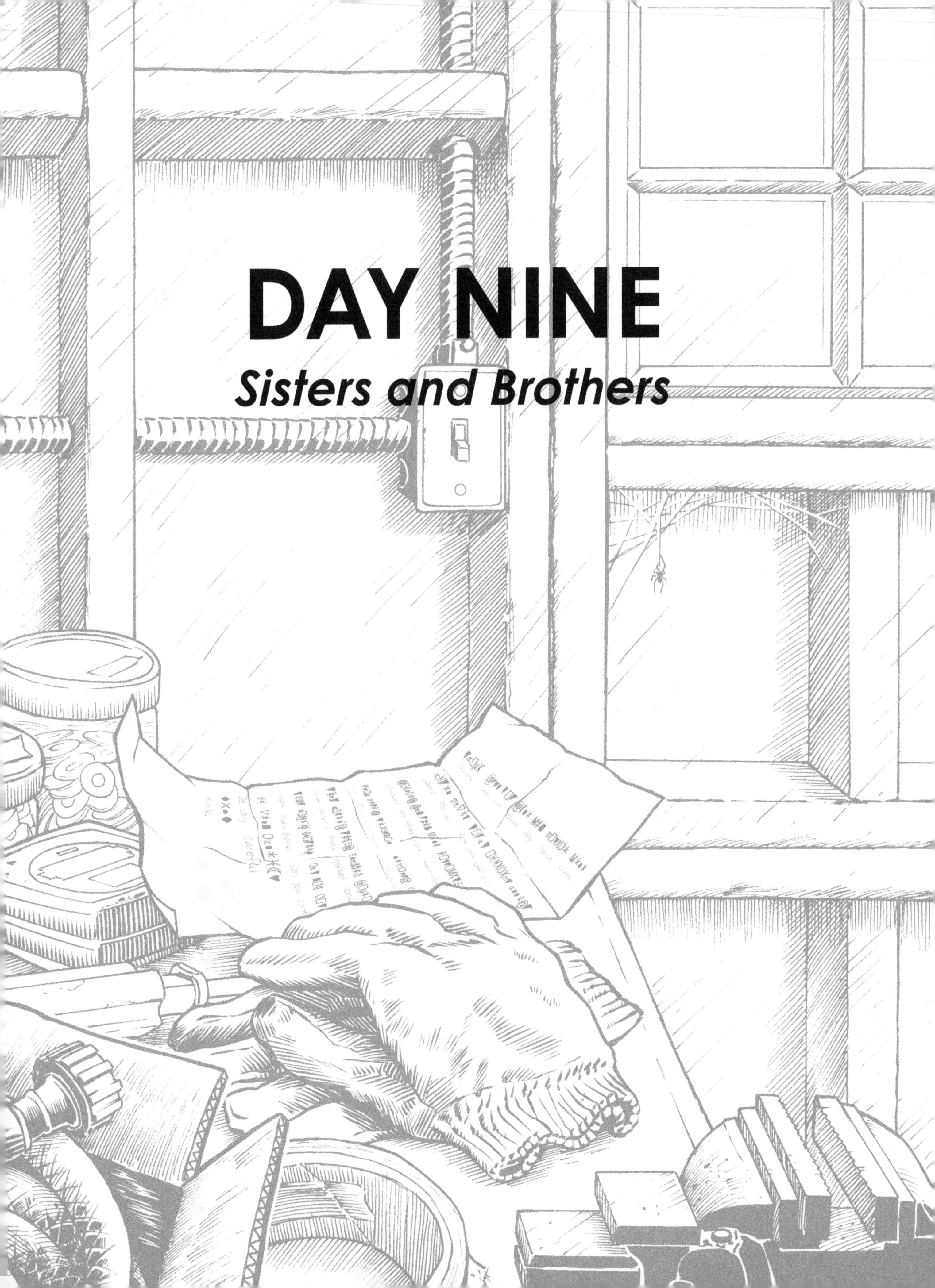

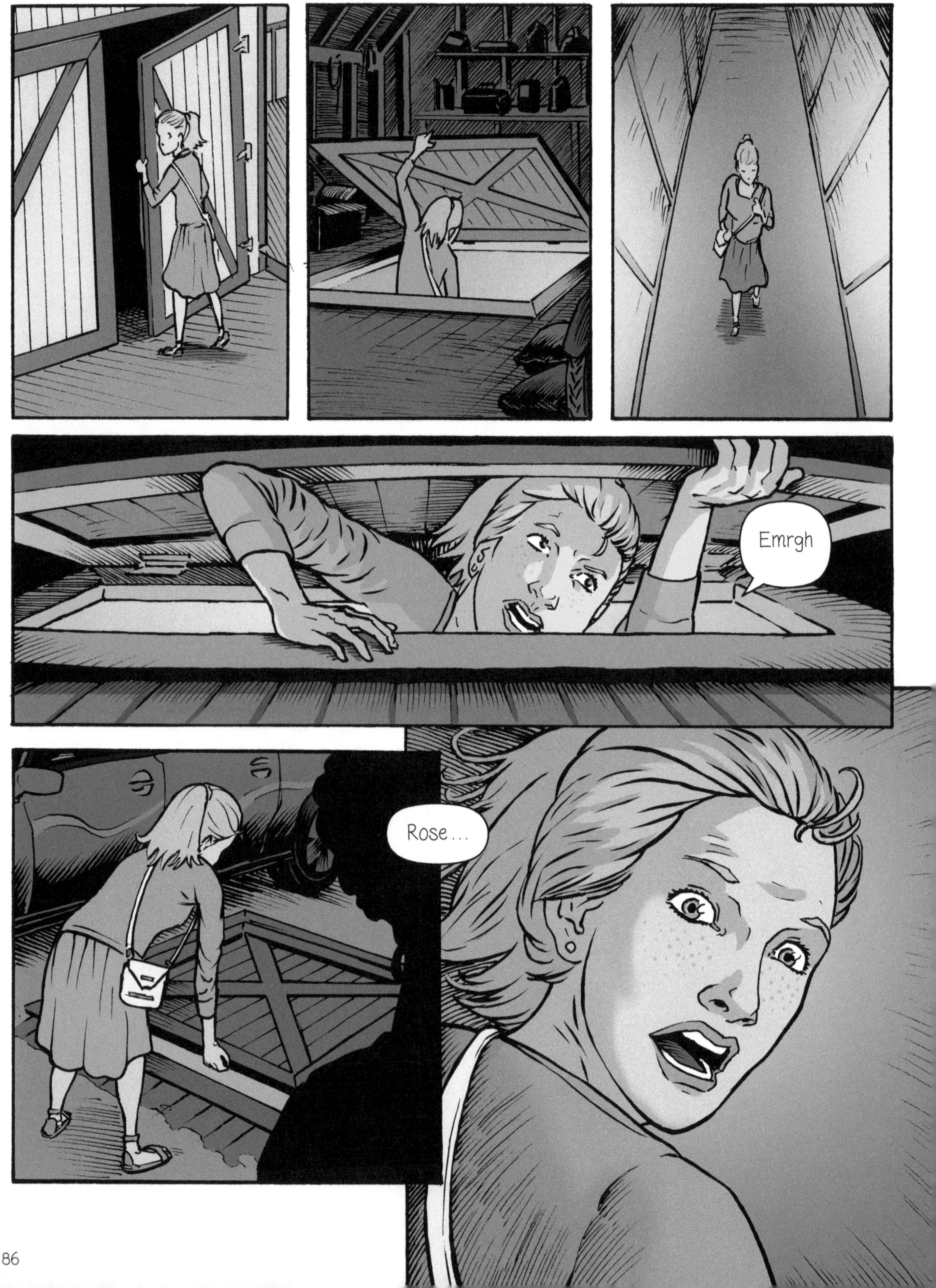
Emrgh
Rose...

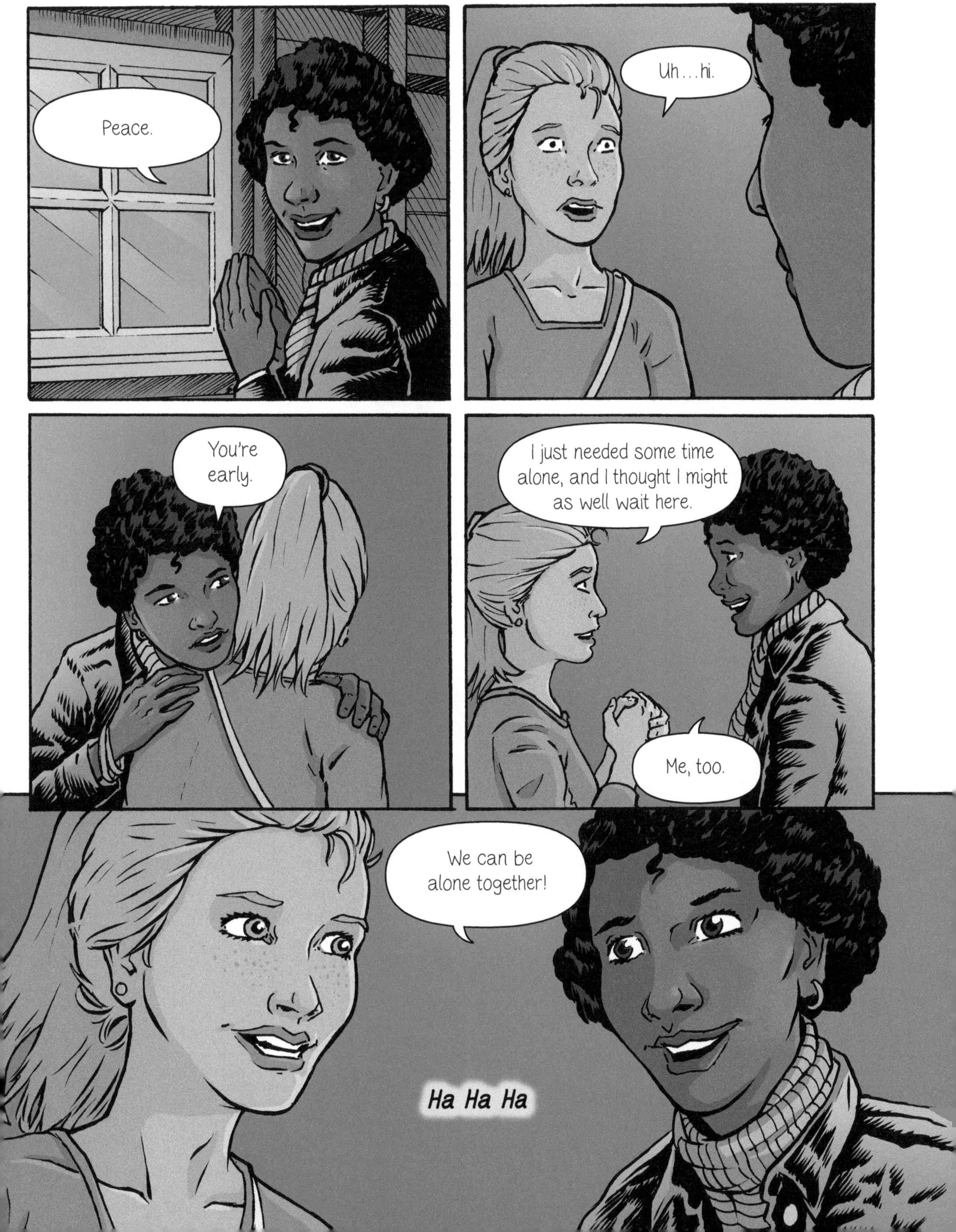
Peace.
Uh...hi.
You're early.
I just needed some time alone, and I thought I might as well wait here.
Me, too.
We can be alone together!
Ha Ha Ha

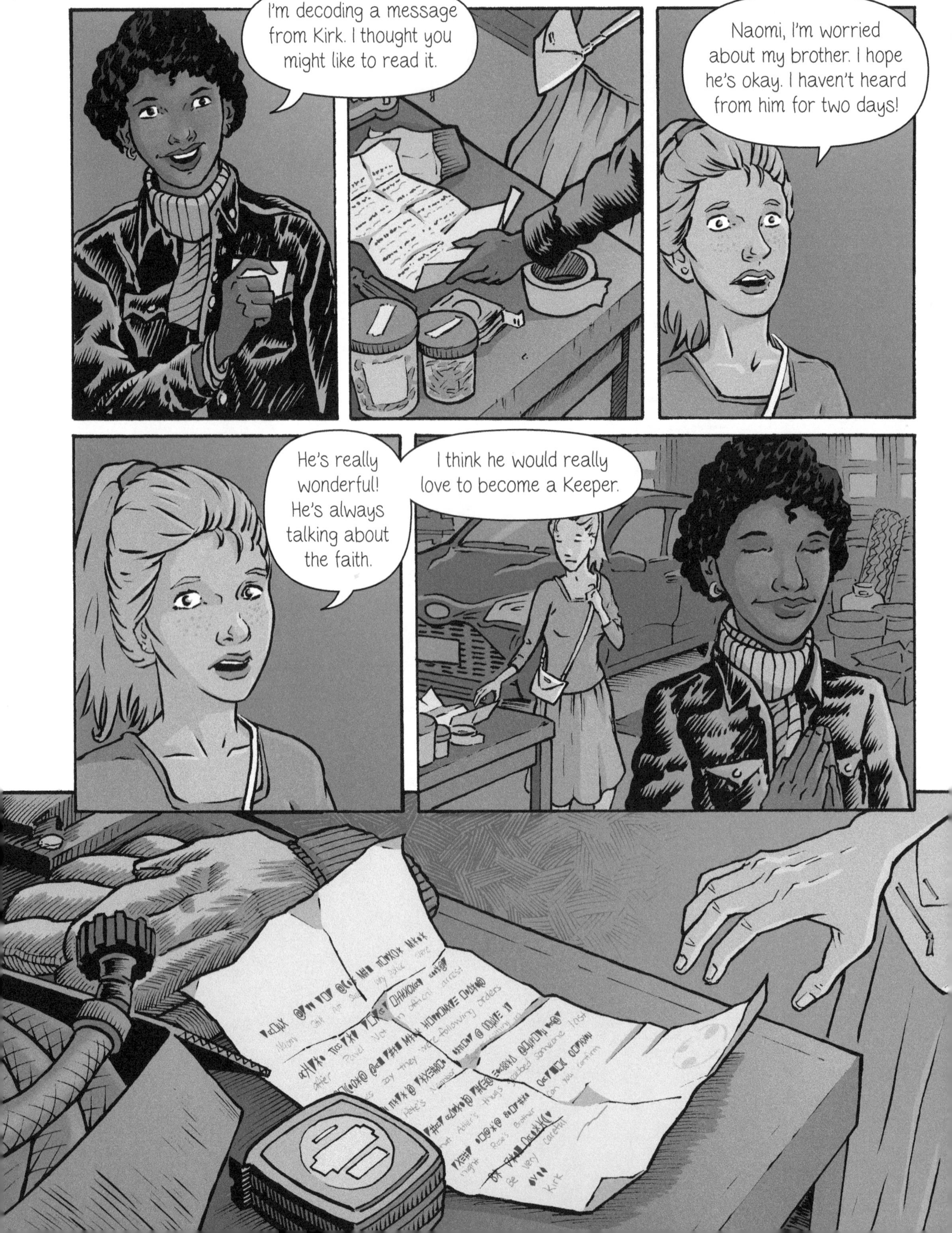
I'm decoding a message from Kirk. I thought you might like to read it.
Naomi, I'm worried about my brother. I hope he's okay. I haven't heard from him for two days!
He's really wonderful! He's always talking about the faith.
I think he would really love to become a Keeper.
Be very careful
Kirk

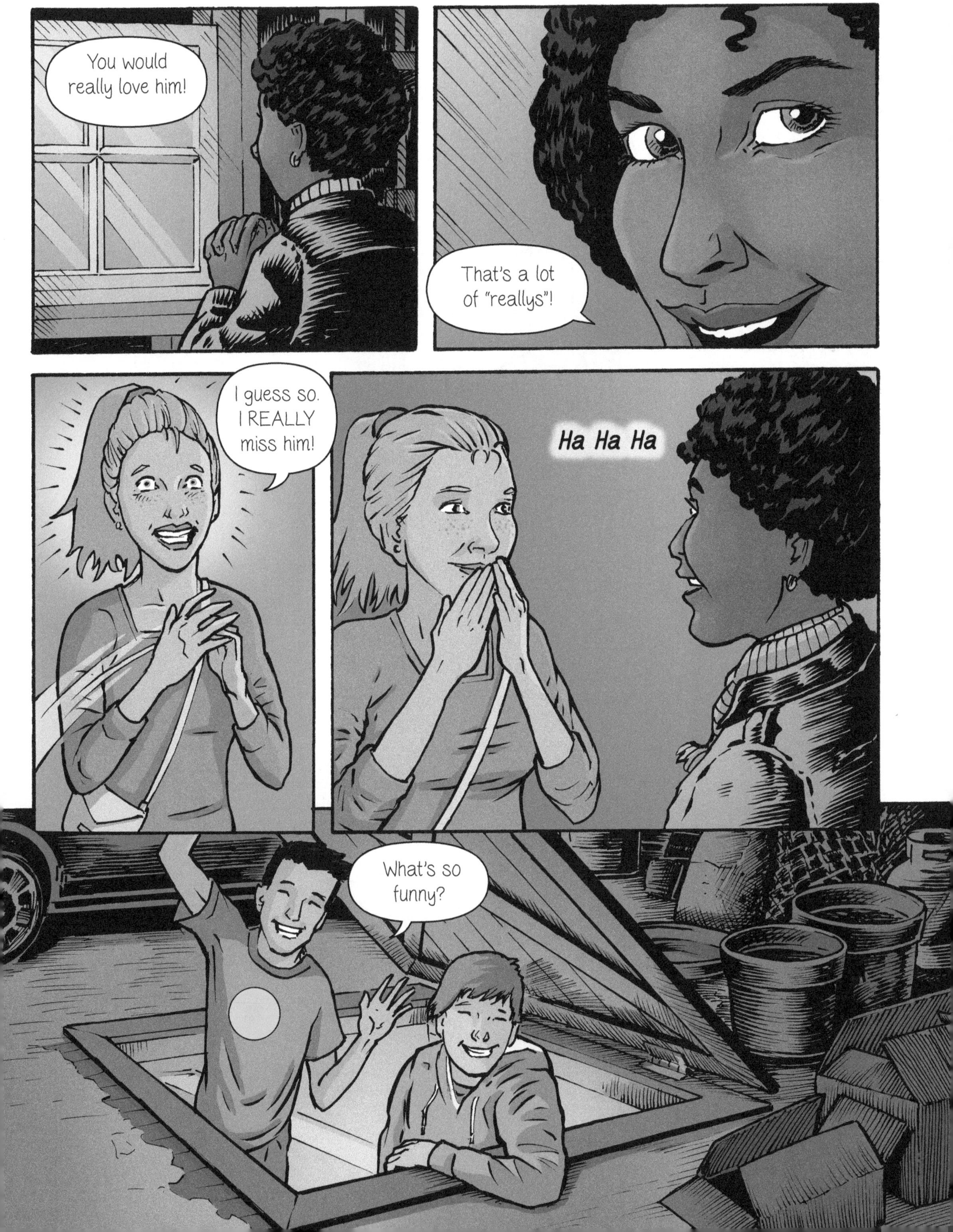
You would really love him!
That's a lot of "reallys"!
I guess so. I REALLY miss him!
Ha Ha Ha
What's so funny?

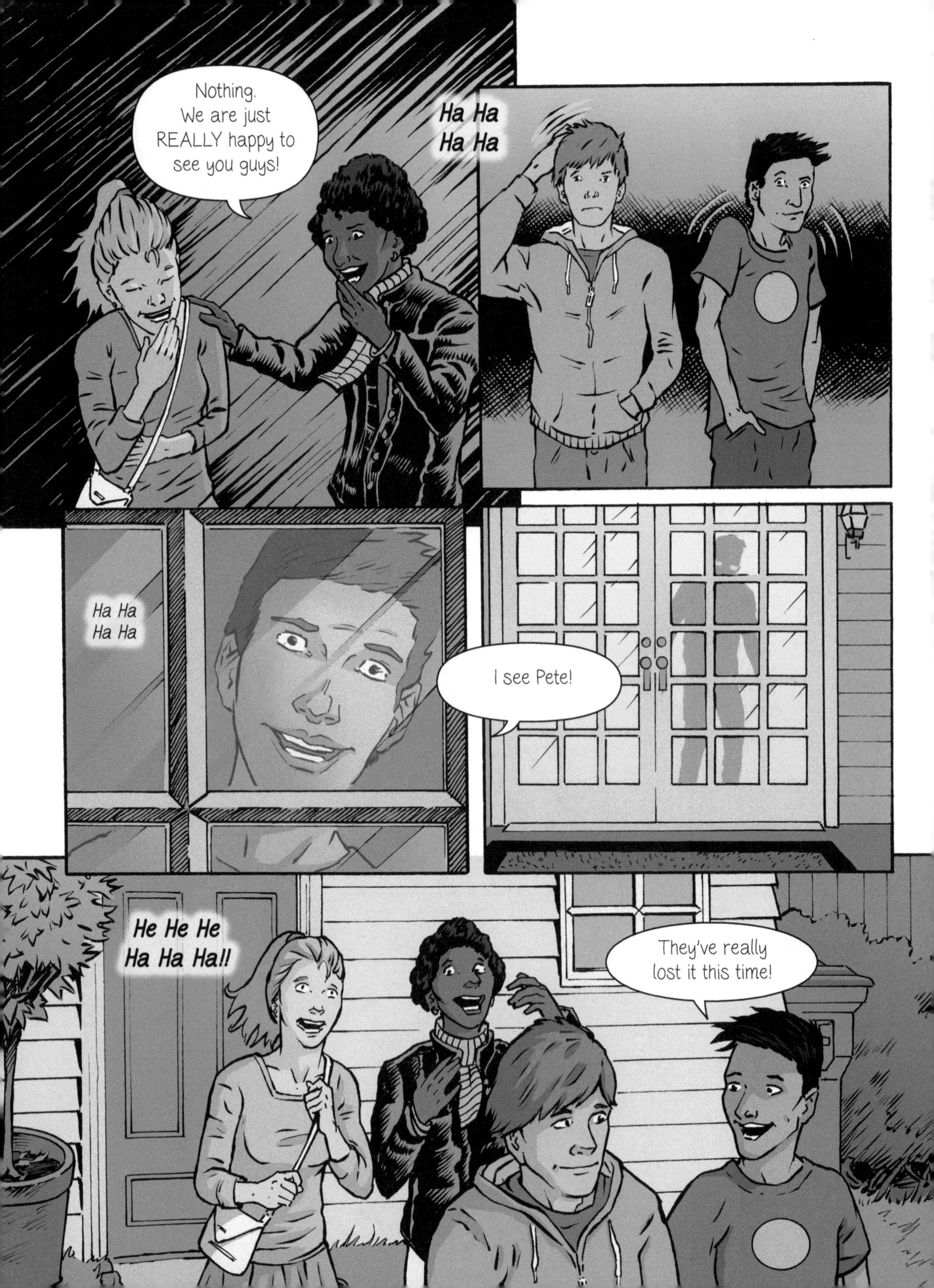
Nothing. We are just REALLY happy to see you guys!
Ha Ha Ha Ha
Ha Ha Ha Ha
I see Pete!
He He He Ha Ha Ha!!
They've really lost it this time!

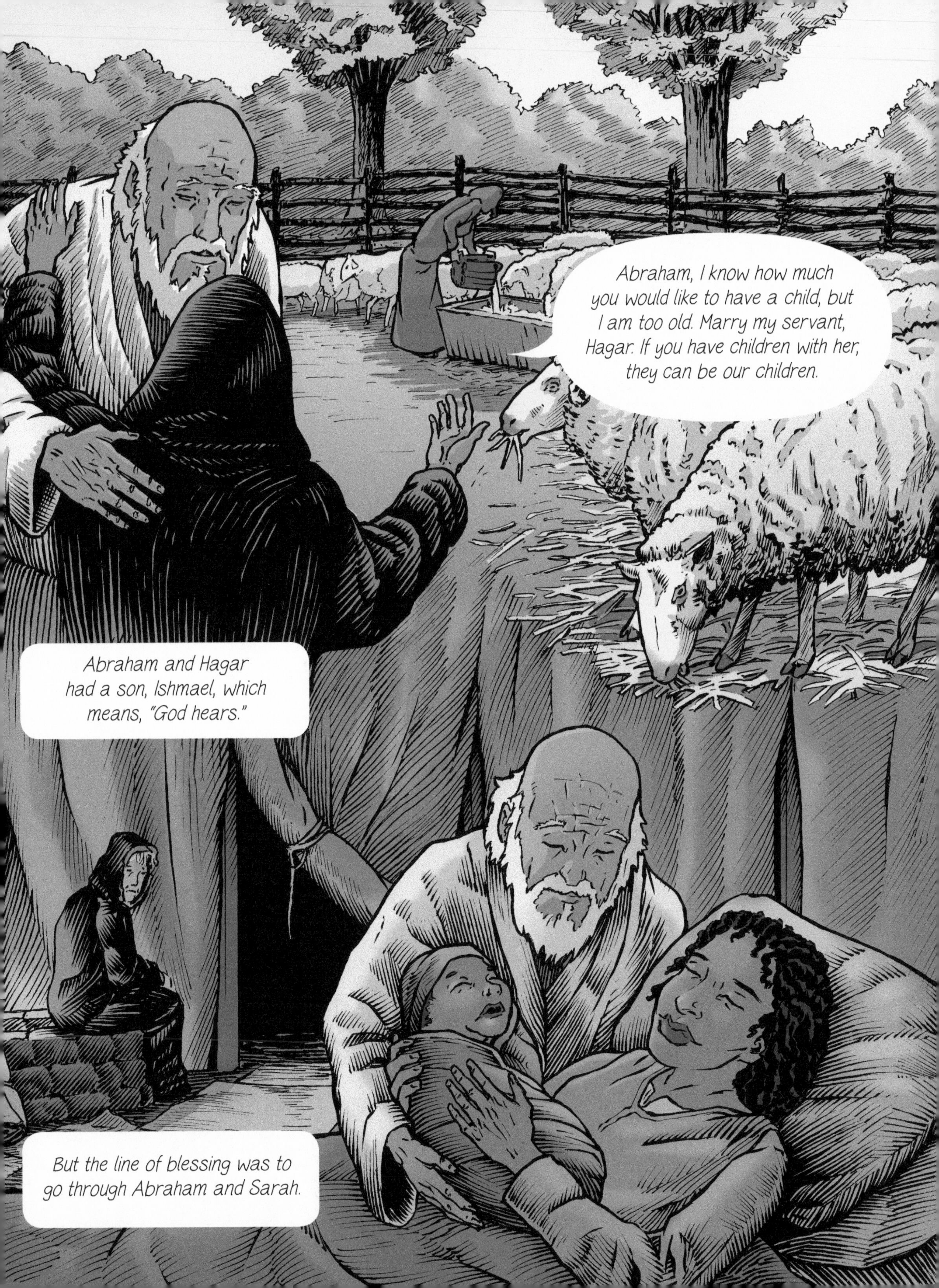
Abraham, I know how much you would like to have a child, but I am too old. Marry my servant, Hagar. If you have children with her, they can be our children.
Abraham and Hagar had a son, Ishmael, which means, "God hears."
But the line of blessing was to go through Abraham and Sarah.

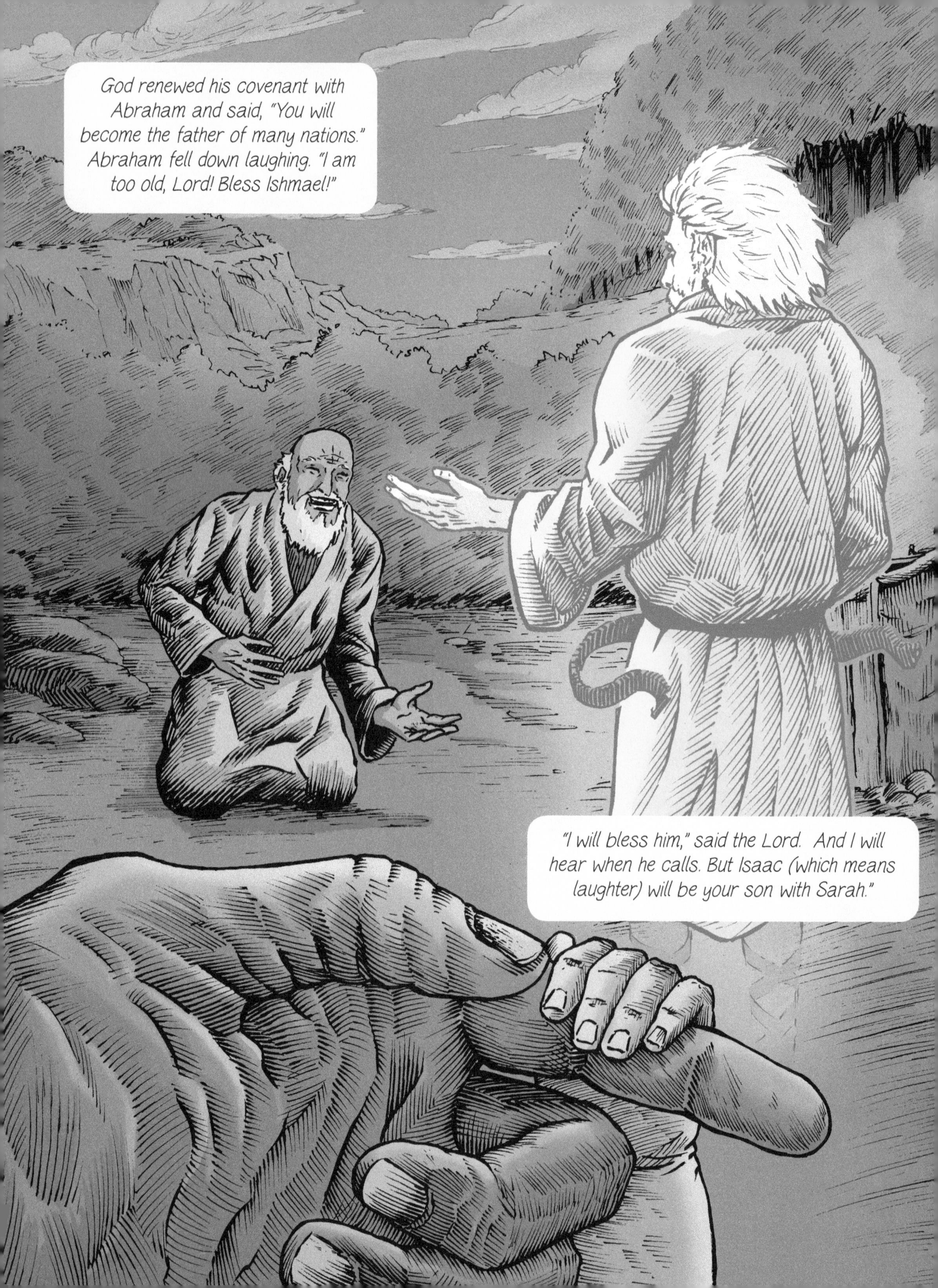
God renewed his covenant with Abraham and said, "You will become the father of many nations." Abraham fell down laughing. "I am too old, Lord! Bless Ishmael!"
"I will bless him," said the Lord. And I will hear when he calls. But Isaac (which means laughter) will be your son with Sarah."

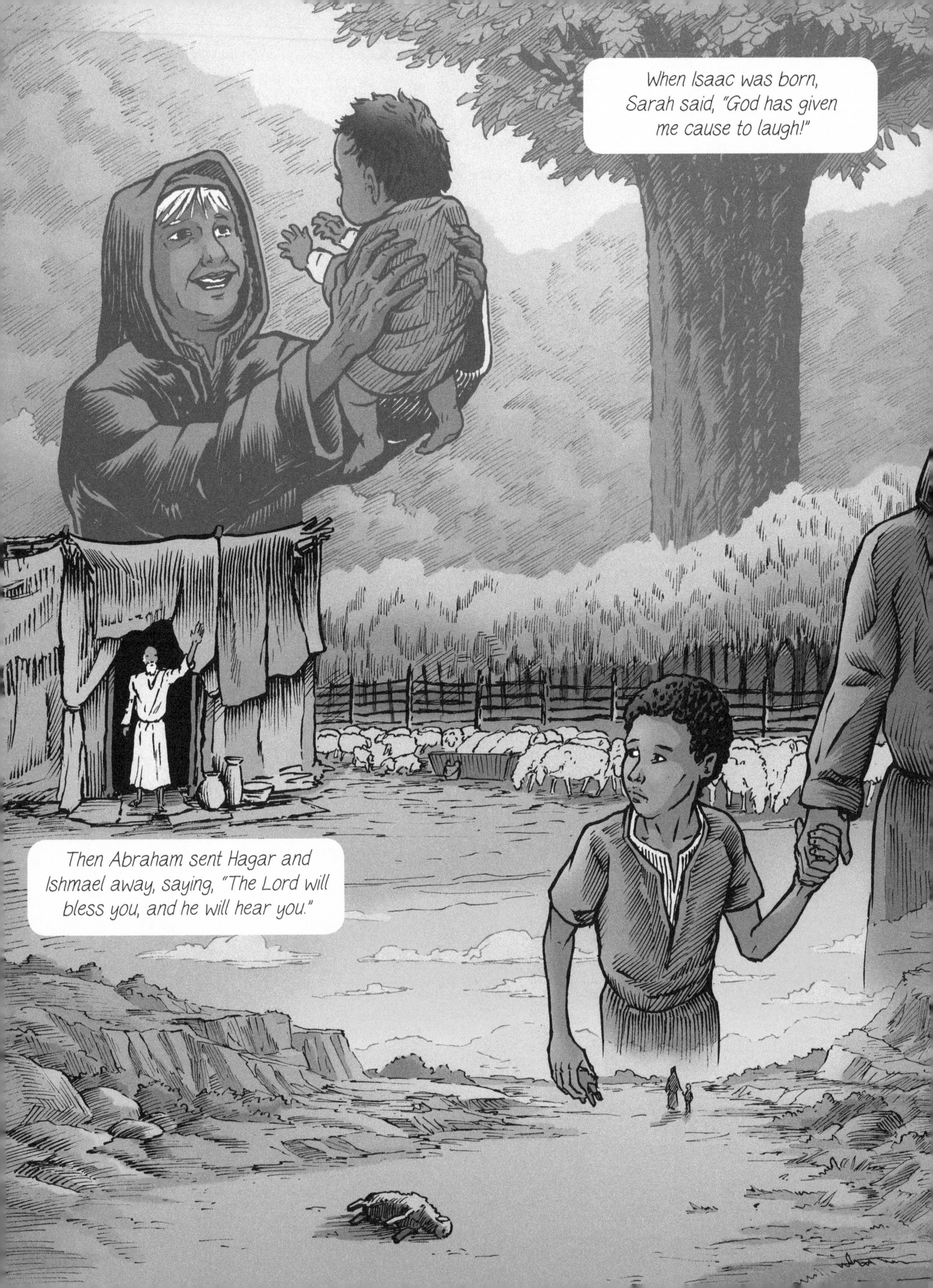
When Isaac was born, Sarah said, "God has given me cause to laugh!"
Then Abraham sent Hagar and Ishmael away, saying, "The Lord will bless you, and he will hear you."

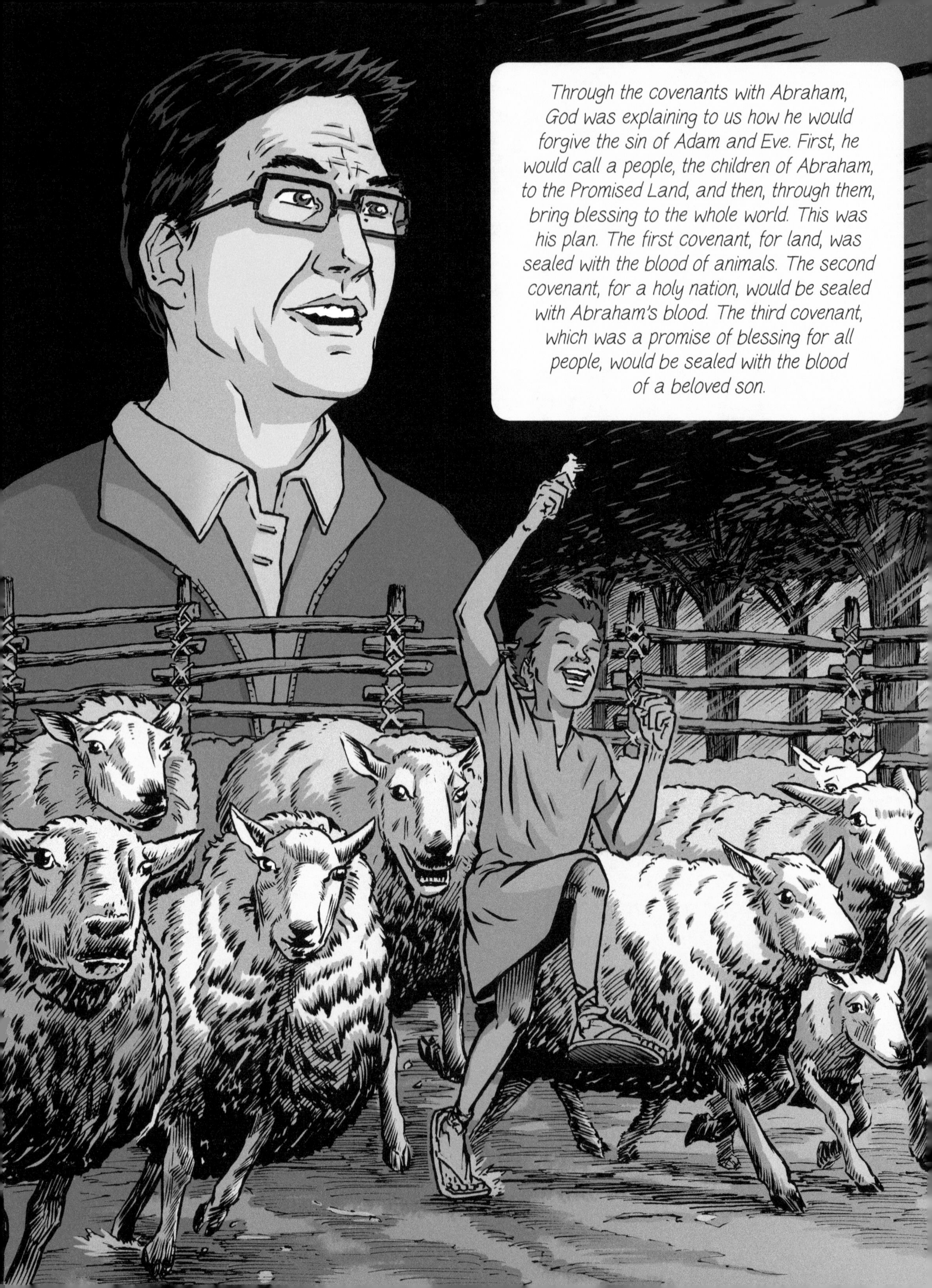
Through the covenants with Abraham, God was explaining to us how he would forgive the sin of Adam and Eve. First, he would call a people, the children of Abraham, to the Promised Land, and then, through them, bring blessing to the whole world. This was his plan. The first covenant, for land, was sealed with the blood of animals. The second covenant, for a holy nation, would be sealed with Abraham's blood. The third covenant, which was a promise of blessing for all people, would be sealed with the blood of a beloved son.

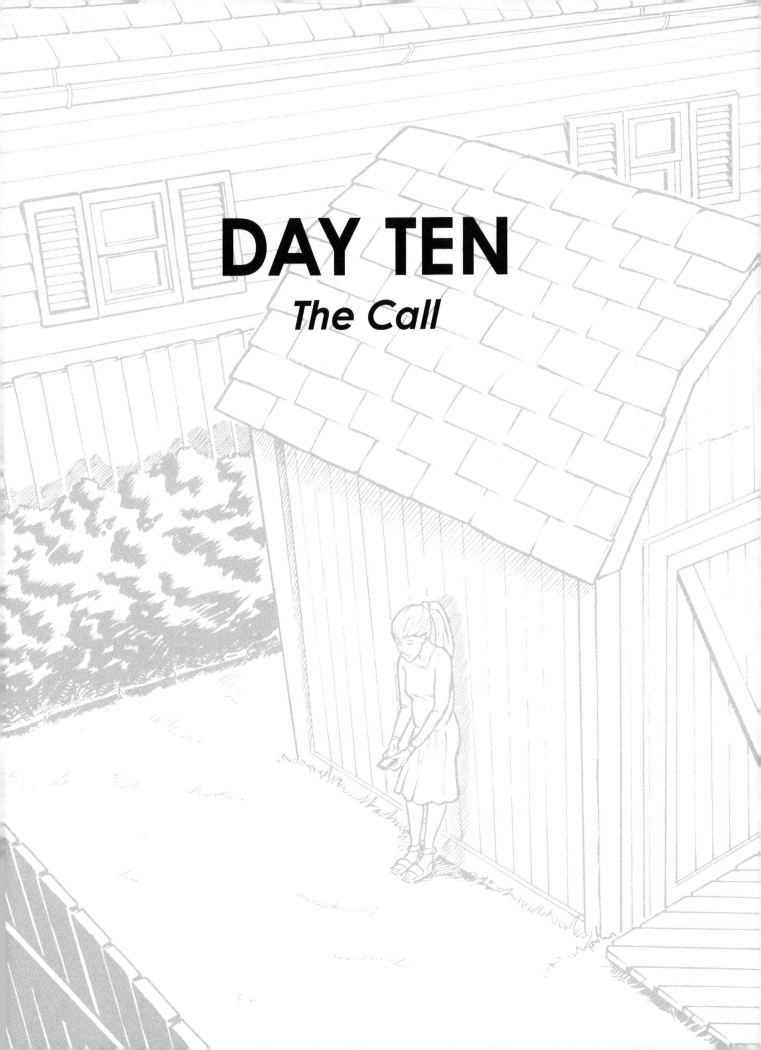

DAY TEN

The Call

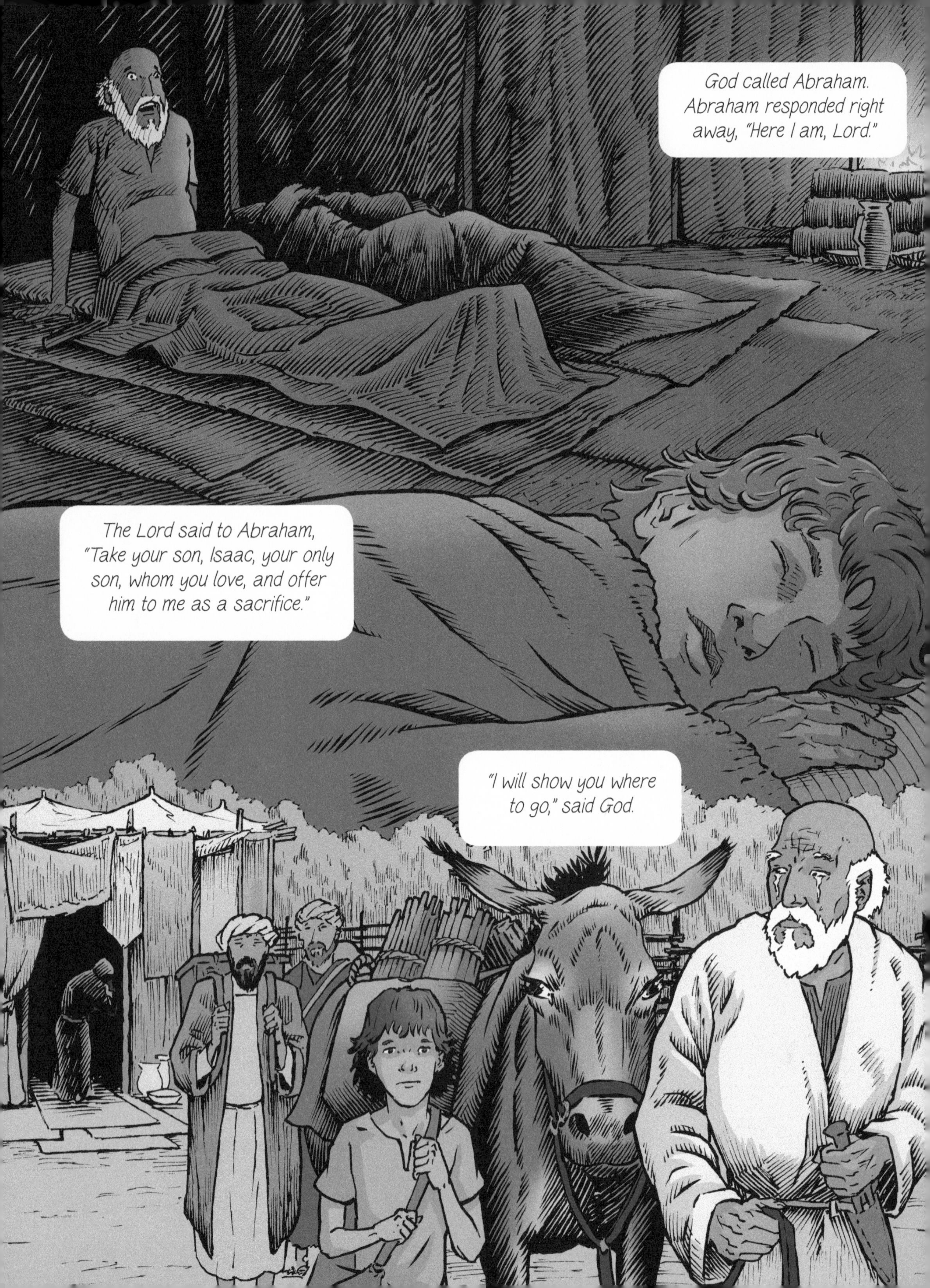
God called Abraham. Abraham responded right away, "Here I am, Lord."
The Lord said to Abraham, "Take your son, Isaac, your only son, whom you love, and offer him to me as a sacrifice."
"I will show you where to go," said God.

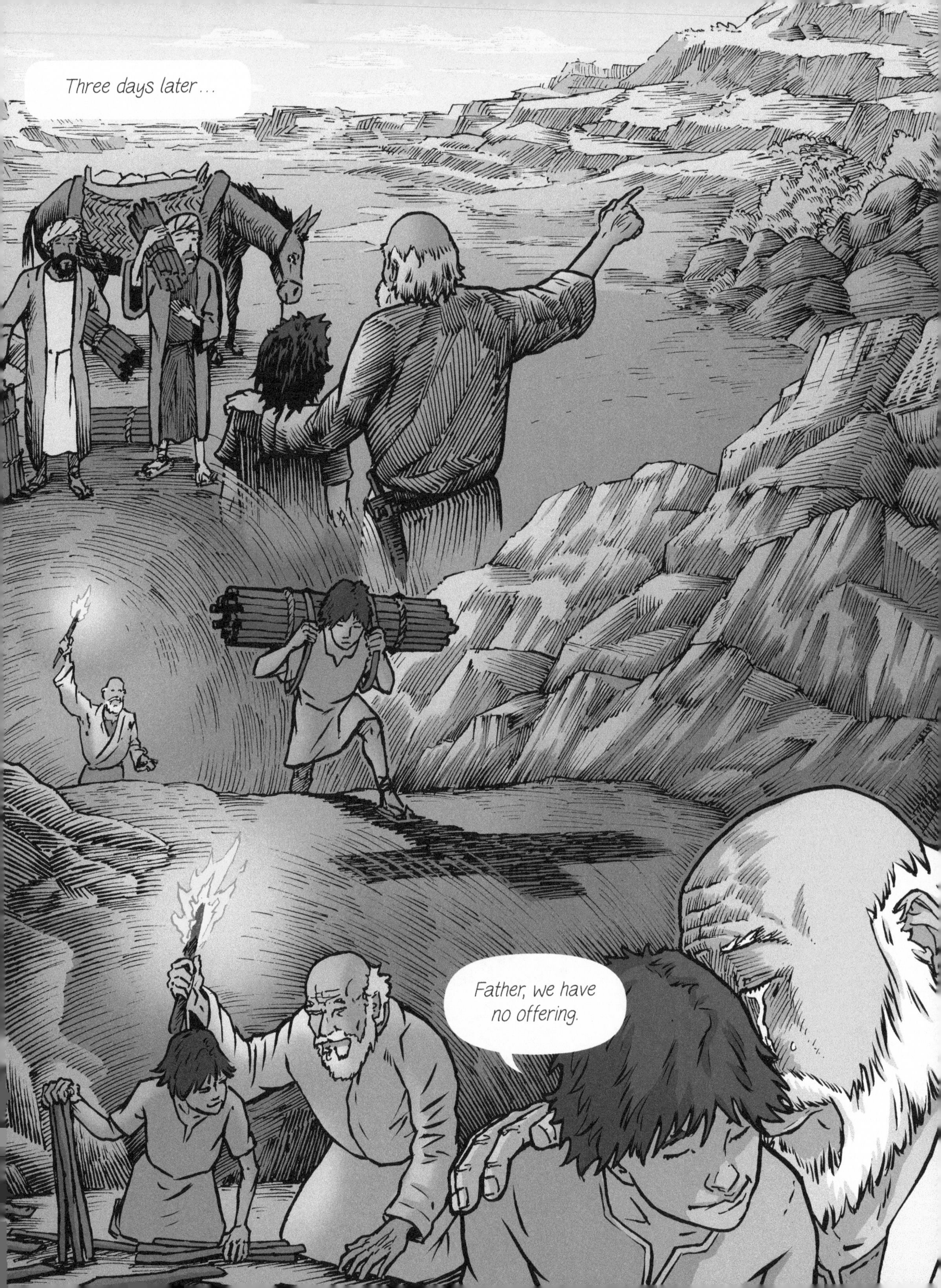
Three days later...
Father, we have no offering.

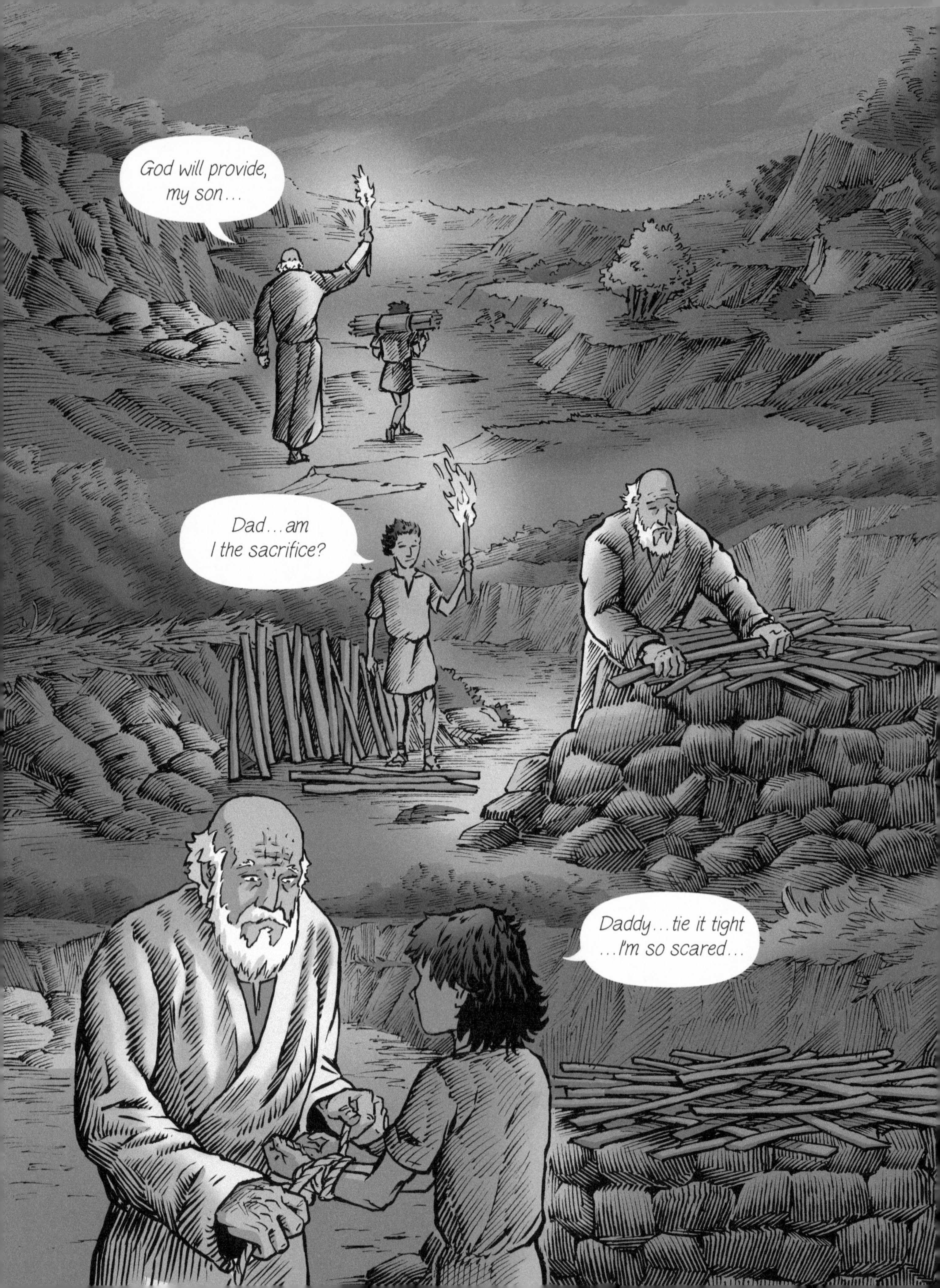
God will provide, my son…
Dad…am I the sacrifice?
Daddy…tie it tight …I'm so scared…

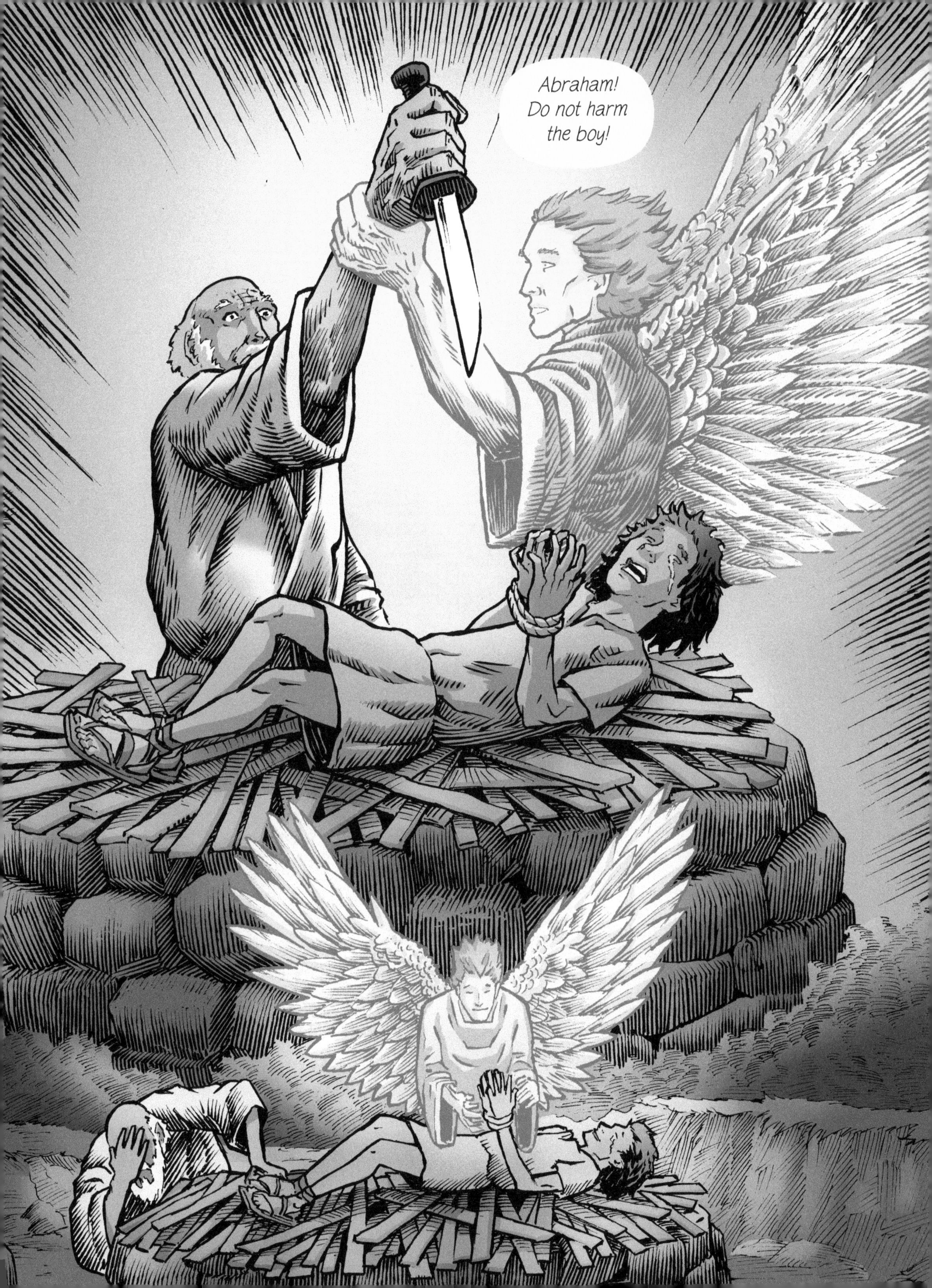
Abraham! Do not harm the boy!

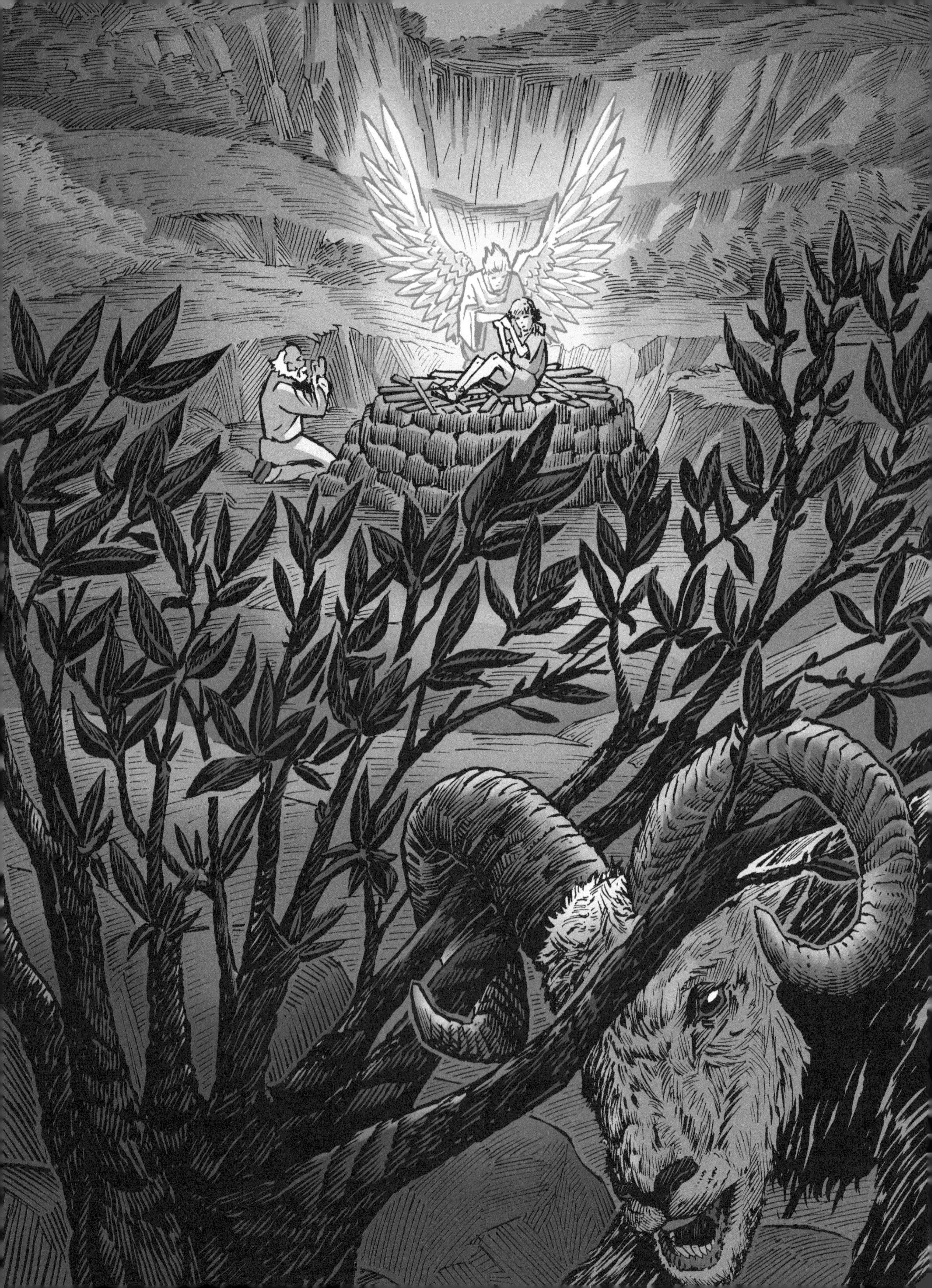

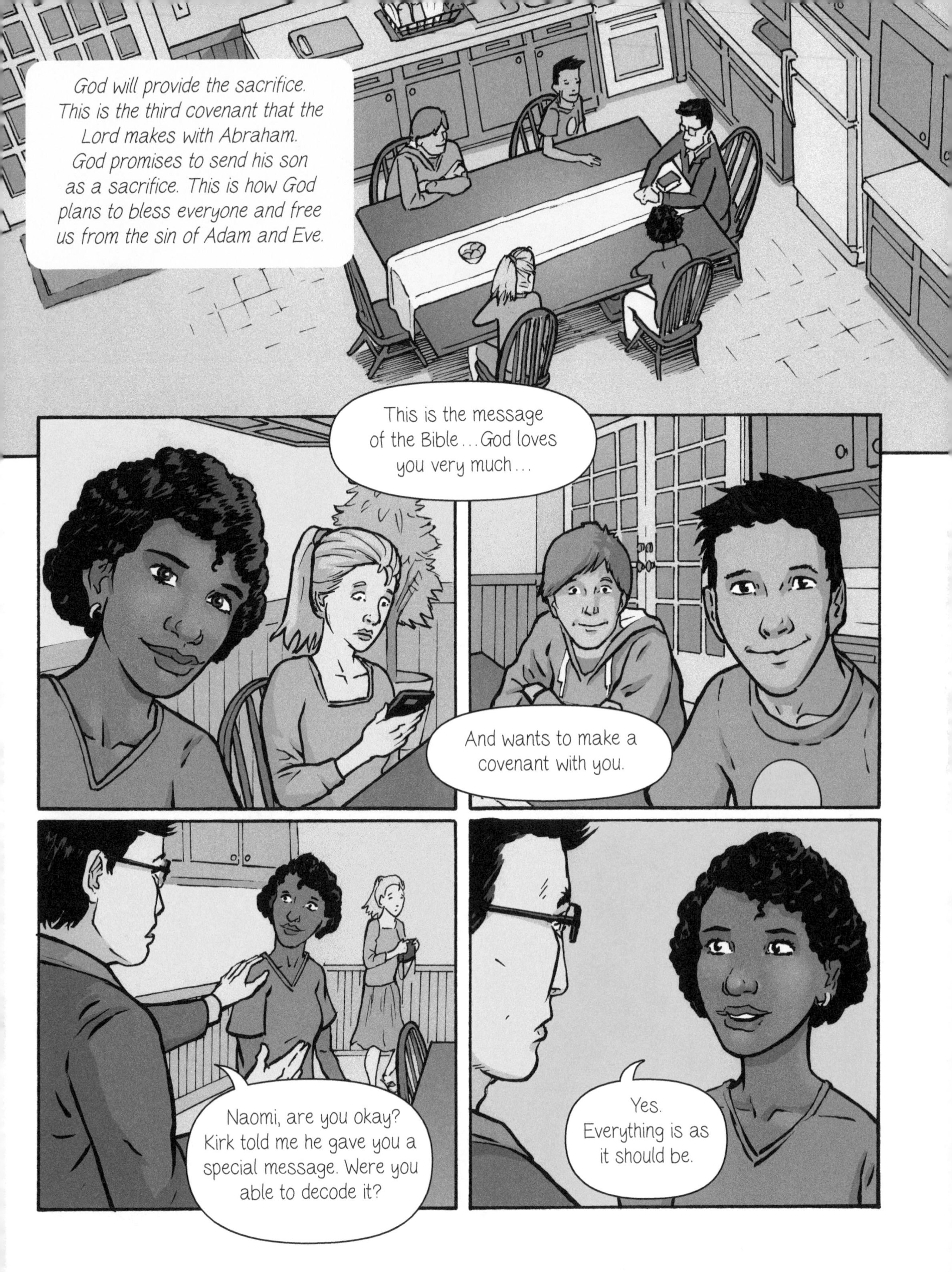
God will provide the sacrifice. This is the third covenant that the Lord makes with Abraham. God promises to send his son as a sacrifice. This is how God plans to bless everyone and free us from the sin of Adam and Eve.
This is the message of the Bible...God loves you very much...
And wants to make a covenant with you.
Naomi, are you okay? Kirk told me he gave you a special message. Were you able to decode it?
Yes. Everything is as it should be.

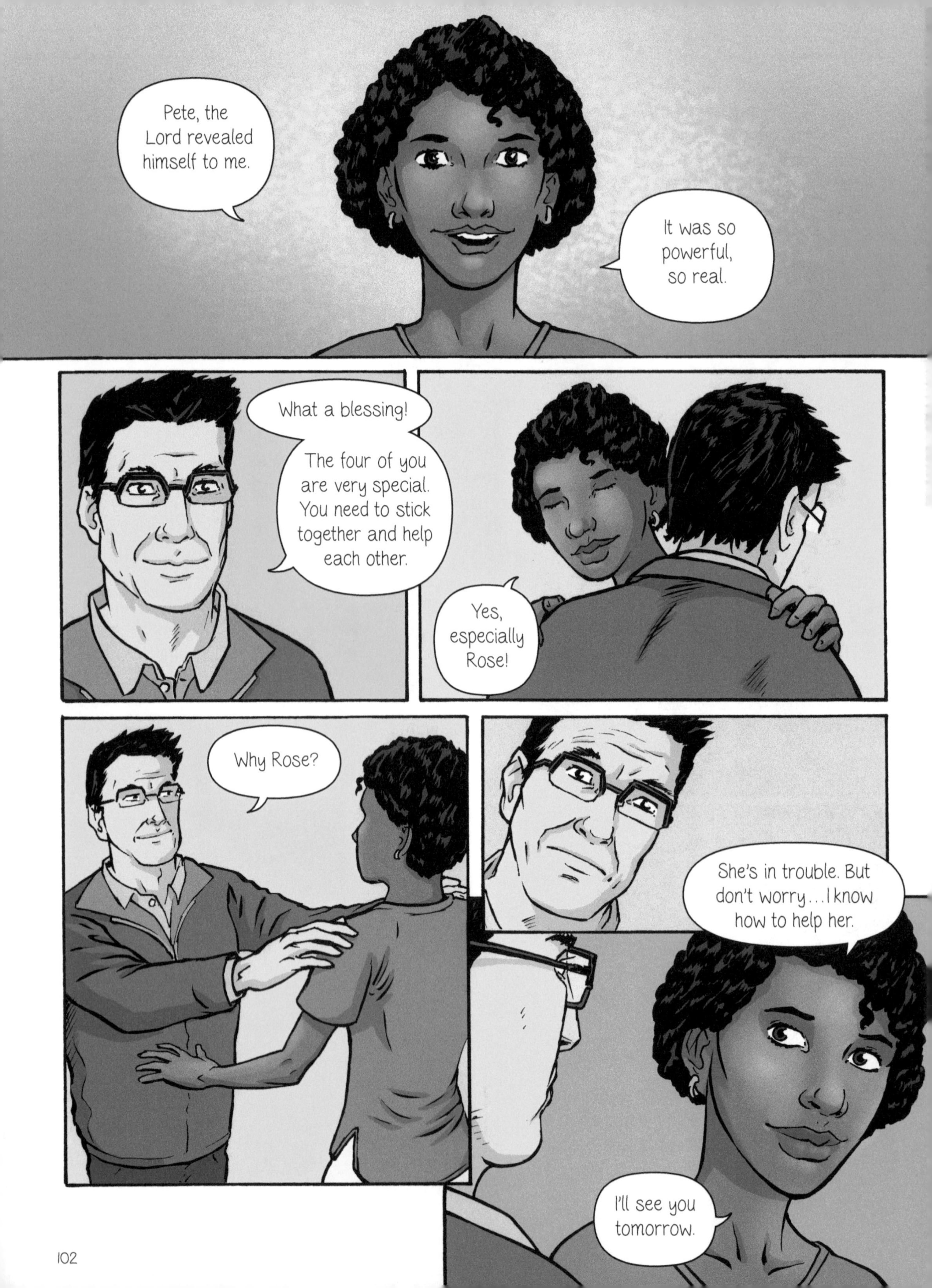

Pete, the Lord revealed himself to me.
It was so powerful, so real.
What a blessing!
The four of you are very special. You need to stick together and help each other.
Yes, especially Rose!
Why Rose?
She's in trouble. But don't worry…I know how to help her.
I'll see you tomorrow.

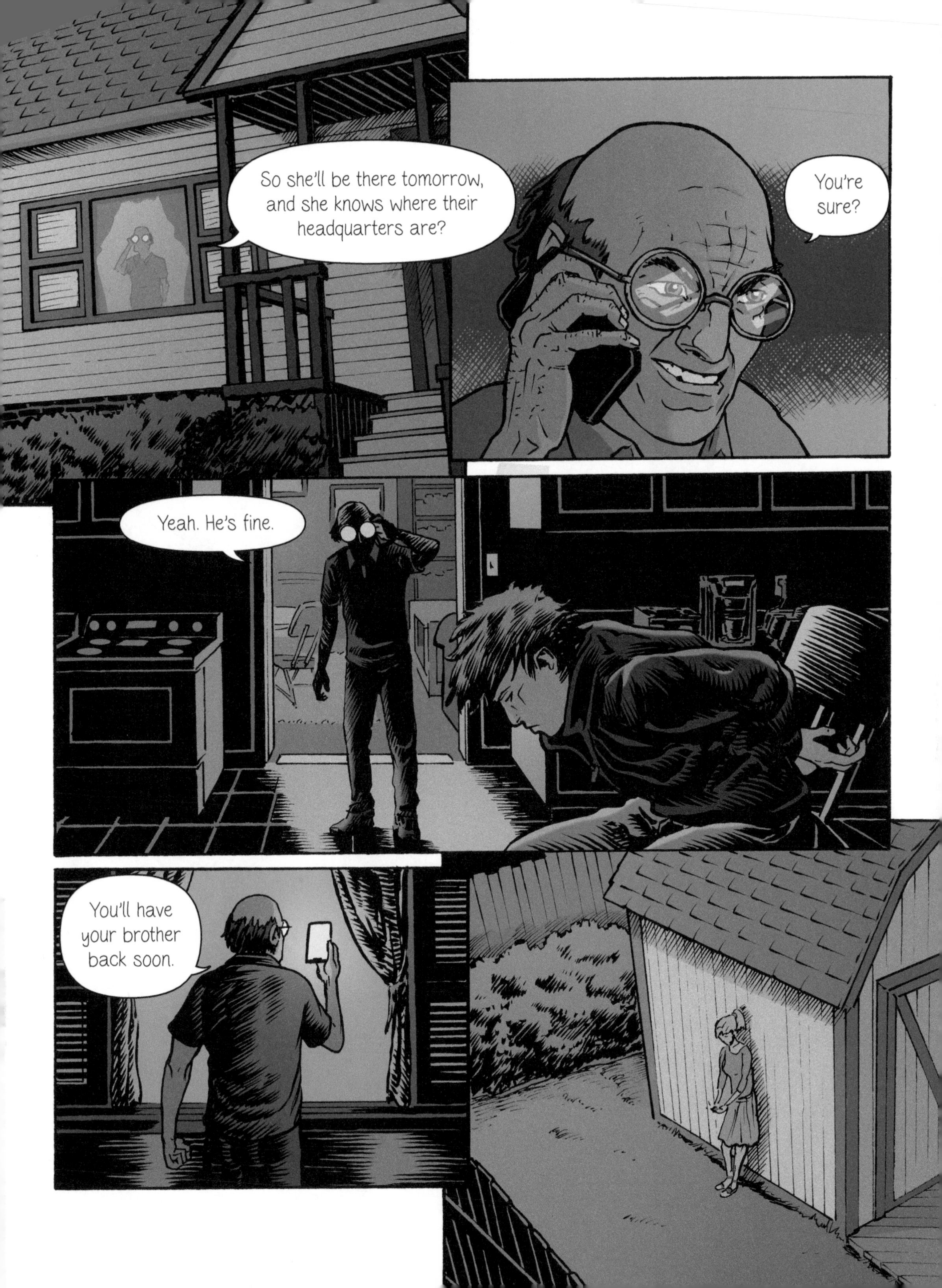
So she'll be there tomorrow, and she knows where their headquarters are?
You're sure?
Yeah. He's fine.
You'll have your brother back soon.

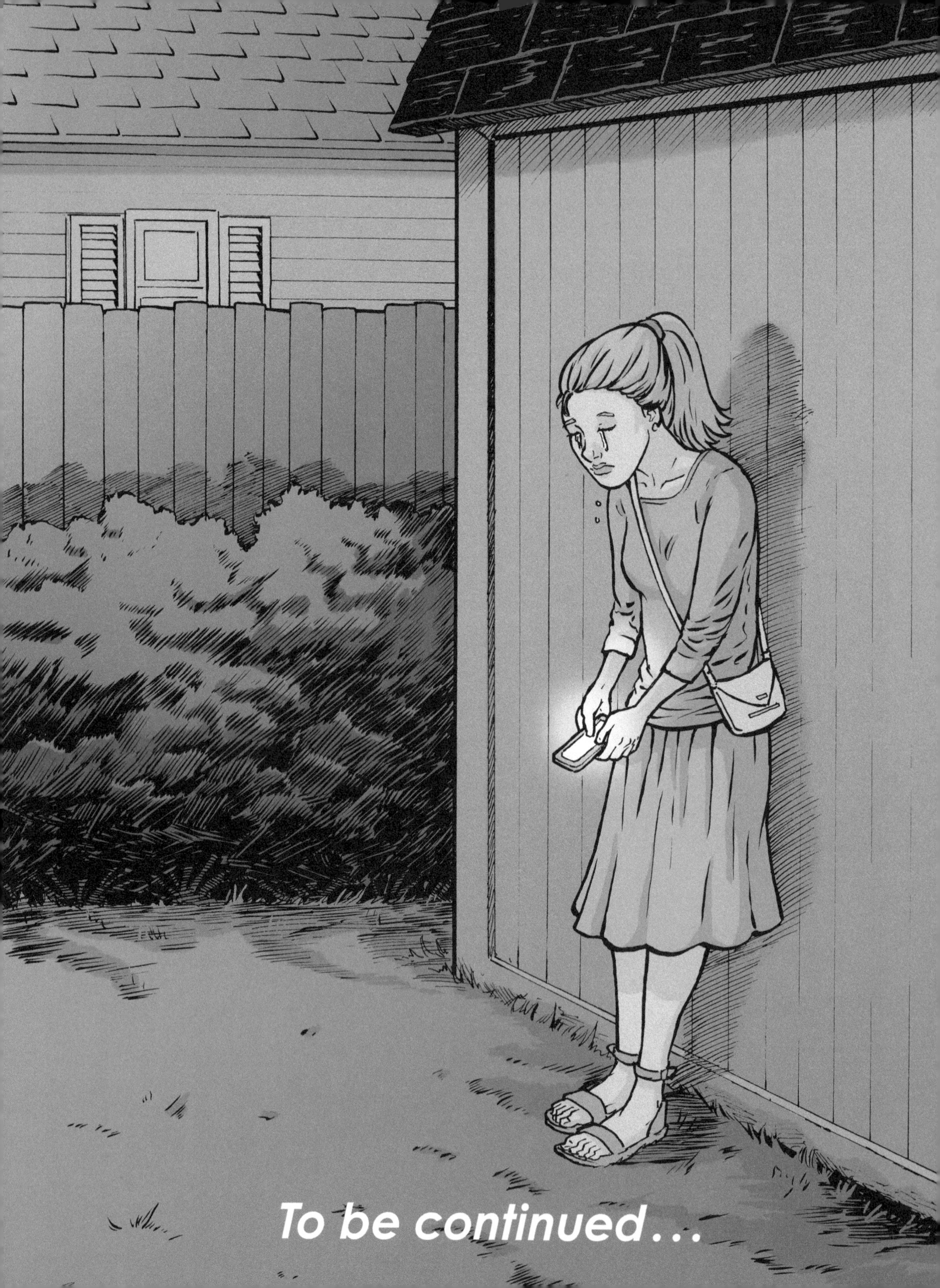
To be continued...

■□☾ ∝●✶ X▼ Ξ●✶∝◥ Δ∝▼Ξ✶●

●□@✶ O∝♥♥✶Δ ∝Δ♥✶● ♥∝@◥ ▼XΞ#◥ #X@ Ξ☾■@

♦XΔ▼∝ππ✶Δ ●□@✶'@ 8●□◥#✶● μ∝■8✶ #✶ X@

8♥∝O♦μ∝X♥X▼Ξ #✶●

∝♥♥ ♦✶✶π✶●@ @#□☾♥Δ O□μ✶ ◥□ #✶∝Δ⊗☾∝●◥✶●@

Xμμ✶ΔX∝◥✶♥■

#✶♥π ●□@✶ Xℋ ■□☾ O∝▼

M✶ Δ□ ▼□◥ ♦▼□M M#∝◥ ∝Δ♥✶● X@ π♥∝▼▼X▼Ξ

8✶ ▽✶●■ O∝●✶ℋ☾♥

♦X●♦

About the Author

Andrew Youngblood has always been passionate about Scripture. He loved reading the stories in the Old Testament as a child. The first thing he bought with his own money was a Bible. When he went to college, he was excited to learn how all the stories fit together. He took several classes, but they were all boring and confusing. He searched for several years until he was finally able to understand how the Bible worked as one story. Once he understood, he was so excited to tell others that he became a teacher!

Andrew has been teaching Scripture to students of all ages for over twenty years. It was the inspiration of his own children that recently led him to write a graphic novel. This is ironic though, considering how awful he is at drawing. His kids say that even his stick figures are bad! Thankfully, Alex Campbell and the fantastic team at Sky Blue Ink are amazing artists and have turned Andrew's Bible adventure story into a beautiful work of art!

Acknowledgements

One day out of the blue, Hilary received a call from me. Knowing I was looking for an artist, my wife showed me an article that mentioned Hilary and the team at Sky Blue Ink. Besides the moment when I first conceived of the series, that call was the most important moment in the creation of *Covenant Kids, Book One: The Law*. Throughout the process of realizing my vision, bringing it to life through art and story, she has been a driving force. I cannot thank her enough. Along with her honesty, professionalism, and sense of humor, one of the best parts of working with Hilary is her amazing team, especially Alex, who did all the artwork, and Joyana, who joined us at the end to do the layout. They are incredible.

Thanks also to my family, the communities of Cor Jesu Academy and Regina Chesterton Academy, and all those who have supported and encouraged me throughout this process. Thank you!

Covenant Kids
Book One: The Law

v1.0

Outskirts Press, Inc.
http://www.outskirtspress.com

Paperback ISBN: 978-1-9772-1354-9
Hardback ISBN: 978-1-9772-1356-3

Cover and Interior Art by Alex Campbell.
Edited by Hilary Sycamore of Sky Blue Ink
Book design by Hilary Sycamore and Joyana McDiarmid
Author photo by Chad Brown. Used with permission.

PRINTED IN THE UNITED STATES OF AMERICA

outskirts press™

CPSIA information can be obtained
at www.ICGtesting.com
Printed in the USA
BVHW021808251119
564774BV00016B/334/P

9 781977 213549